Praise for the novels of

DINAH MCCALL

(who also writes as SHARON SALA)

"Dinah McCall, who also writes as Sharon Sala, is one of the best in the genre...her stories have earned a place of honor on many a keeper shelf."
—*The Romance Reader*

"In a town that feels frighteningly real... Dinah McCall masterfully weaves a tale that is emotional and heart-wrenching...a great read."
—*Romantic Times BOOKreviews* on *The Return*

"McCall skillfully keeps the reader guessing."
—*Publishers Weekly* on *White Mountain*

"With excitement, adventure and mystery, this remarkable read will keep fans speeding through the pages."
—*Romantic Times BOOKreviews* on *White Mountain*

"Intense, fast-paced, and cleverly crafted, this engrossing tale will appeal to those who like their contemporary romances on the chilling side."
—*Library Journal* on *Storm Warning*

"A frighteningly real story of suspense and true romance, creating characters who will grab your heart."
—*Romantic Times BOOKreviews* on *The Perfect Lie*

Also by DINAH McCALL

**BLOODLINES
MIMOSA GROVE
THE PERFECT LIE
WHITE MOUNTAIN
STORM WARNING
THE RETURN**

DINAH MCCALL

THE SURVIVORS

MIRA®

ISBN-13: 978-0-7783-2435-5
ISBN-10:   0-7783-2435-4

THE SURVIVORS

www.MIRABooks.com

Printed in U.S.A.

On June 26, 2005, while I was writing this book, I lost my fiancé, Bobby, who was the love of my life, and whom I had known since we were kids. He died of liver cancer, in our home, and in my arms, and my life is never going to be the same.

But that's not all bad.

When I can think of him without weeping, I remember the energy that was always with him and how alive the house was when he was in it. He made me laugh more in the eight years we were together than I'd ever done before. He had a heart that was so big and encompassing, and to watch him with his beloved animals, especially the horses, was something I will never forget.

They loved him unconditionally, and the hour before he died, the horses penned up on our property began to nicker—calling back and forth to each other as if they knew. The others that were pastured across the road—approximately eighty of them—stood silently at the gate, clustered together without moving and all looking toward the house. It was eerie to see so many vibrant animals standing sentinel, as if waiting for their master to come.

And then he died.

When I looked out again, they were no longer there. They knew, as I did, that someone special was gone from their lives. The man who had lived with one foot in the world of the Indian and the other foot in the world of the white man was no more.

When the people from the funeral home took Bobby out to the hearse, the big black stud horse, whose name is Lvmhe—which means eagle in the Muscogee language, and which was Bobby's Indian name, as well—reared up on his hind legs in a most majestic salute to his master, then literally screamed, as if in pain.

I knew how he felt.

I'm not sorry to be sharing this sad tale, because truthfully, I could do nothing less. Like the horses he so loved, this is my salute to the man who helped my heart.

Fall is coming. Winter won't be far behind. It is a time for harvesting memories.

In the cold days to come, those images I have in my head and my heart will be what keeps me warm.

To Bobby

Prologue

Destry Poindexter was beating the hell out of his wife, Lucy. It wasn't something he thought about. It was simply a reaction to the fact that he'd been fired today. It was the third job he'd lost this year. That it was December, and only a couple of weeks or so until Christmas, made it worse.

Carlisle, Kentucky, was a nice town, but with little industry. If you didn't know how to be a mechanic or work a computer, you were shit out of luck, which was exactly where Destry found himself now. Lucy hadn't berated him. She'd just been there when he'd walked in the door and was suffering the consequences of his bad fortune.

"Stop, Destry! Stop! Please, God, you have to stop."

Destry doubled up his fist and hit her again—this time so hard that he lifted her off her feet. His voice was calm, his demeanor that of a parent punishing a child.

"Shut up. Just shut up," he said. "You're whining again. You know how I hate it when you whine."

Slap.

Lucy hit the floor, falling first on her hip, then hitting her head.

"It's your own fault this is happening. I'm sorry, but you give me no choice," he said.

Lucy rolled over, curling herself into as small a target as possible.

It didn't deter Destry. He just drew back his booted foot and kicked.

The blow was so vicious that Lucy heard her bones breaking.

"Oh God, help me," she moaned.

Deborah Sanborn was coming up from the root cellar between the barn and her house when she felt the first blow. The pain in her head was so sudden and excruciating that she dropped the quart of peaches she'd been carrying. She didn't even have time to be grateful that the glass jar didn't break as she grabbed her head and rolled on the ground.

Within seconds of the pain came the pictures, flashing through her head like a slide show with no sound.

Lord have mercy—Destry Poindexter was beating Lucy again.

As she lay there, she saw blood coming out of Lucy's ear and witnessed Destry deliver another blow to his wife's belly with his boot.

From out of nowhere, her dog, Puppy, appeared and began licking at Deborah's ear and whining as she nosed at Deborah's chin, urging her to get up.

"I know, I know," she said, as she pushed the dog back.

Gritting her teeth and closing her mind to any further visions, she picked up the peaches and staggered into her house.

Once inside, the warmth of her home against the bitter cold of an Appalachian winter was welcome. She set the peaches on the counter and shrugged out of her coat, dropping it on the back of a chair as she ran to the phone.

She knew the number to the sheriff's office by heart and dialed it quickly.

Frances Littlejohn was the day dispatcher for Wally Hacker, the sheriff who served Carlisle, Kentucky, as well as all the other unincorporated land in the county. Frances answered absently, trying to ignore a sore throat and the sniffles.

"Sheriff's office."

"Frances…this is Deborah Sanborn. Is Wally in?"

"He's outside in the parking lot changing a flat on the cruiser."

"Lord," Deborah muttered. "Tell him that Destry Poindexter is beating Lucy to a pulp. Tell him he's got her down on the floor and is kicking her. Dispatch an ambulance to their house, as well."

"Oh my," Frances muttered. "I don't know how you stand it…seeing all this awful stuff all the time."

"Me neither," Deborah said. "Just tell Wally to hurry."

"Will do," Frances said, and disconnected.

Deborah hung up the phone, then sank slowly downward until she was sitting on the floor. For a few minutes she just stared out the window blindly, unaware of the tears pouring down her cheeks or the fists she'd made of her hands.

She would have fought back, but Lucy Poindexter wouldn't. All Deborah could do was tell the sheriff what she'd seen and pray that Lucy survived this beating, just as she'd survived the countless others she'd endured.

Finally she remembered the peaches and that she'd been going to make a cobbler, and she pushed herself up from the floor and went to the sink to wash her hands.

A short while later she was cutting slits in the top crust to let out the steam as the cobbler baked. She put it in the oven, set the timer and went to the laundry room to change loads.

Even though Lucy Poindexter was enduring a life-threatening trauma, it was just another day for Deborah Sanborn.

Phoenix, Arizona

Forty-something Mike O'Ryan eyed the placement of the balls left on the pool table, lined up what would be the last shot, then popped the cue stick against the ball so quickly that his neighbor Howie never saw what happened. However, as soon as the ball dropped into the pocket, Mike looked up at Howie and grinned.

Howie Louglin looked back at him and frowned. "Wipe that grin off your sorry-ass face before I wipe it for you."

As usual, Mike's go-to-hell attitude shifted a gear higher.

"You know what, Howie? We do this at least once a month, and every time, I beat you. You know it's going to happen before we start, yet you persist in repeating this. You're a grown man…or at least you're supposed to be. Suck it up or go home."

"Yeah. Whatever," Howie muttered.

Still, he put the cue stick in the rack, then brushed the chalk off his fingers and onto the seat of his pants.

"Have a beer, Howie," Mike said.

"Don't mind if I do," Howie said, and circled the pool table in Mike's garage to get to the fridge. "Want one?"

"Sure, why not," Mike said, and took the long-neck that Howie handed him as he, too, hung up his stick.

They took a couple of drinks, then glanced out the garage door to the street beyond. The pretty widow who lived across the street was outside watering her shrubs—barefoot and in a pair of shorts and a sports bra.

It was ten minutes after eleven at night.

Howie eyed her shapely form as she bent and posed while dragging the hose around the yard.

"Reckon them plants have had enough water?"

Mike grinned. "Walk over and find out."

Howie sighed.

"Sure I won't be steppin' on your toes? I don't wanna step on your toes or anythin'."

Mike eyed the woman, then shook his head.

"You won't be stepping on anything of mine," he said. "Feel free."

Howie downed what was left of his beer, handed the

empty bottle to Mike, sucked in his belly and started across the street.

Mike dropped the empty bottle into the trash, punched the button to shut the garage door and went into the house without waiting to see if Howie was going to get lucky.

Knowing his pretty neighbor, he figured the chances were good that he would. And also knowing his neighbor, he was never going to be one of the losers standing in line at her door.

He locked up as he went through the house, absently checking doors and windows to make sure they were locked. He finished his beer in short shrift, set the empty bottle on the sideboard in his dining room and headed for his bedroom.

It was late. He was tired.

But even after he'd showered and was stretched out in bed with the television blaring and the remote in his hand, he was unaware of what was showing. He kept thinking about his son, Evan, wondering how he was faring, worrying about his state of mind.

Like every other O'Ryan, Evan was ex-military, but in his instance, he was ex only because of the life-threatening wounds he'd suffered in Iraq. He'd been stateside less than two weeks and had refused visits from his dad or any of the other men in the family ever since his return.

Mike had seen him once, more than two months ago, in Germany, where they'd flown Evan to heal after he'd been wounded and evacuated, but he hadn't seen him since.

He would have been pissed at Evan, but he couldn't bring himself to go there, because if the situation had been reversed, he suspected he would have acted the same way.

So he lay there in bed, thinking of the rut his life was in and how truly lonely he'd become.

And while he was soaking in a stew of his own making, he fell asleep.

1

"Senator, you need to hurry or you're going to miss your flight."

Patrick Finn waved at his assistant to indicate he understood, then moved his cell phone from his right ear to his left.

"Look, Wilson, I just can't do that and keep my constituents happy come next election. I'm in this for the long haul. If I vote for your bill, I'll be selling out over half the population of my state. We make our living in cotton and tobacco, you know. I can't in good conscience cast my vote to keep your people happy and destroy the tobacco industry at the same time. I know you understand."

The knot in Senator Darren Wilson's gut pulled a little bit tighter. He stacked notepads in stacks of threes as he listened, unaware that his OCD had kicked in again. This couldn't be happening. If he didn't get this bill through Congress as he'd promised, his life wouldn't be worth a nickel. He was in this mess because of gambling. Passing this bill had been his way out of a quarter-million-dollar gambling note, and welshing on the people he owed was not an option. Neither was backing out of his word.

He stared down at the handful of photos he'd received in the mail yesterday. One of his ex-wife, one of his daughter, who hadn't spoken to him in three years, and two of his grandchildren playing outside on the playground of their Dallas grade school. The pictures were numbered from one to four. He got the message. If he failed to come through for the people he owed, they were going to go after his family in the order in which the photos were numbered.

And God help him, his ex-wife was number one. At this point in his life, she pretty much hated his guts, but he didn't have it in him to sacrifice her or any of them to get himself out of debt. Besides, he knew that wouldn't be the end of it. They would still do him in. He would just have the privilege of knowing that he'd wiped every single member of his family off the face of the earth before he died, too.

He closed his eyes, cleared his throat, then gave Patrick Finn one more push.

"Finn, you don't understand. I *need* your vote to keep my family alive."

Finn frowned. He knew that Wilson gambled. Everyone on the Hill knew it. It came as no surprise that he was probably in trouble with a casino owner somewhere, or even some loan shark, but none of that was Finn's fault or business.

"I'm sorry, Darren, truly I am. But I can't sell out my

state because you can't stay away from the poker tables."

"No! Wait! You—"

"No, and that's my final answer," Finn said. "Now, I've got to go, or I'm going to miss my flight."

When the phone line went dead, Darren Wilson felt as if he wasn't far behind. He stared at the framed photos of his daughters and grandchildren on his desk, then shifted through the ones he'd gotten in the mail. Every aspect of his body mirrored his dejection as he took a small bag from the bottom drawer of his desk, then walked toward a large painting hanging on the opposite wall.

He pulled it back, revealing the wall safe behind it. A few quick turns of the dial and the safe came open. Inside was his contingency plan: a fake passport and fifty thousand dollars in cash.

He put the money in the bag and the passport in his pocket, closed the safe and checked it three times before putting the painting back in place. That it had come to this was at best depressing, but he had no option. Damn Patrick Finn all to hell. Leaving wasn't what Darren wanted to do, but if he wanted to stay alive, it was his only way out.

He draped his overcoat over the small bag, grabbed his hat from a hook on the wall and headed out of the door, pausing at his secretary's desk long enough to issue one last order.

"Connie, please cancel all my appointments for this afternoon. Something has come up."

"Yes, sir. Do you want me to reschedule?"

"Not today. I'll let you know later."

"Yes, sir," the secretary said again, and picked up the phone to do what she'd been told as Darren Wilson walked out the door.

A short while later, Patrick Finn was rushing through the D.C. airport, trying to catch his flight to Atlanta, where he lived. He had to swing by his home to pick up some clothes before heading out to Albuquerque, where he would rent a car and drive to Santa Fe, where he would spend Christmas. His wife and kids were already there with his parents, and he was looking forward to getting away for the holidays. He kept glancing at his watch as he ran, and knew it was going to be close. An accident on the freeway had left traffic at a standstill for more than thirty-five minutes. By the time the cab driver had pulled up at the airport, Finn was late.

He sprinted past stores that smelled of hot coffee and cinnamon buns, as well as pubs serving beer and sandwiches to passengers with time to spare.

When he finally reached Gate 36, he was just in time to watch the plane pulling away from the ramp.

"Wait!" he yelled. "That's my plane. I have to be on that plane!"

"I'm sorry, sir, but you're too late," the attendant said.

"I can't be too late! I'm Senator Patrick Finn."

It was nothing the attendant hadn't heard before, and as the plane taxied toward the runway, she was already calmly booking Patrick Finn on the next plane to Atlanta. Considering it was the Christmas holidays, it was the best she could do for him.

Finn knew it, too, but it didn't make him any happier as he waited the two and a half hours for the flight on which he'd now been rebooked.

It was late evening when the plane landed in Atlanta, and by the time he got off, he'd already decided just to buy some clothes in Santa Fe rather than go home to pack, then try to make it back through evening traffic to catch his next flight. He called his wife, told her what was happening, then settled down to wait at the gate for boarding to begin.

An hour later, the process began.

"Welcome aboard, sir," the attendant said, as he stepped off the ramp and onto the plane.

"Thank you," he said, nodding briefly as he scanned the aisles for his seat.

That it was not in first class was something he was going to have to live with. Holiday travel was hectic at best, and considering it was his fault he'd missed his first flight, he wasn't about to get picky about this one.

He thumped and bumped his one carry-on down the aisle until he got to his seat, smiling to himself as he realized it was on the aisle. He nodded to the pretty young woman in the seat behind him as he put his carry-on in the overhead compartment, then folded his coat and laid it on top of the bag.

"Good evening, miss," he said cordially, as he closed the door to the compartment.

"Good evening," she answered, then returned her attention to the magazine she was reading.

Patrick winked at the little boy sitting across the aisle, then dug in his pocket for one of the silver dollars for which he was famous for giving out during his campaigns. He pretended to pull it out of the little boy's ear, then handed it to him as a treat.

"Wow! Granddad, did you see that? He pulled that money out of my ear."

"I sure did, Johnny boy. Better put that in your pocket before you lose it."

The little boy was so thrilled, he reached into his other ear, checking to see if there might be one in there, as well, before dropping the oversize coin into the pocket of his pants.

The older couple who were with the boy laughed along with the senator, and the moment passed.

Finn sat down, straightening his clothes, and was reaching for his seat belt when he heard a familiar voice. He looked up, stunned by the coincidence and silently cursing the hands of fate that had done this to him.

"Wow. What are the odds of this happening?" Darren Wilson said. "I'm in the seat next to you." He waved his boarding pass to prove his point.

Patrick stood up without comment to let Darren be seated, then sat back down.

"This was meant to be," Darren said.

Patrick refused to be baited. "Going home for the holidays?" he asked.

"Yes."

In fact Darren Wilson was on his way out of the country, hopscotching on whatever flights were available on such short notice, but he wasn't going to tell Patrick Finn that.

"Have a good flight," Patrick said. "I don't mean to be rude, but I'm joining the family in Santa Fe, so I'm planning on catching up on my sleep on the way."

Darren just smiled as he thought about what this could mean. Maybe this was one of those meant-to-be moments that would let him get out of trouble after all. He locked and unlocked his seat belt three times and then took a deep breath, before the urge to repeat finally ceased.

Patrick could pretend to sleep all he wanted, because whether Finn liked it or not, he was going to be Darren's captive audience for the next three hours. He went from a feeling of hopelessness to an adrenaline high. God was with him after all.

Thorn!

John Thornton O'Ryan huddled under his covers as a cold wind rattled his bedroom windows. It was one of those rare December cold spells that had Florida fruit farmers in a panic. Subconsciously, he shifted restlessly in his sleep as he tried to ignore whoever was calling his name.

Thorn!

The muscles in the calves of his legs began to twitch. Nothing he hadn't endured before due to the arthritis in his eighty-five-year-old knees, but enough to rouse him from sleep.

Wake up!

Thorn flinched as his subconscious responded immediately to the demand in his wife Marcella's voice. He opened his eyes abruptly and was halfway out of bed when he stilled and remembered that Marcella had been dead for more than fifteen years.

Wearily, he rubbed his hands over his face and glanced at the clock. It was just past three in the morning and only days until Christmas.

"I must have been dreaming," he muttered, and combed his fingers through the thatch of his thick gray hair.

The boy! Help the boy!

He stilled, this time in shock. His eyes were open. He was wide awake, and yet he still heard her.

"Marcella?"

When she didn't answer, he stood abruptly and reached for the lamp. Light flooded the room, revealing a thin film of frost on the outsides of the windows. He shuddered as his gaze raked the shadows.

"Marcy?"

Help the boy!

"The boy?"

Yes. Help the boy!

The only child in the O'Ryan family was five-year-old John Paul O'Ryan, Thorn's great-great-grandson, Johnny to the family. He glanced at the clock again. It was past 3:00 a.m. here in Miami, which meant it was after 2:00 a.m., Dallas time. But it wasn't the time that was causing Thorn's hesitation. It was the fact that Johnny's father, Evan, had only recently been released from an army hospital after serious injuries incurred during a tour of duty in Iraq. Thorn's great-grandson had yet to deal with the fact that his military career was over. He'd lost an eye, suffered serious head injuries, and had left with some very noticeable scars on one side of his face and neck.

Thorn had to consider Evan's emotional and physical condition if he called this time of night, yet he couldn't bring himself to ignore what had just happened. He might be getting old, but he wasn't senile. Marcella's entire world had revolved around the men in her life. From her husband, Thorn, to their son, James, and his son, Michael, to their great-grandson, Evan. Even though Johnny had been born ten years after Marcella's passing, it didn't mean she was unaware of his existence. Not to Thorn's mind.

His shoulders slumped as he reached for the phone. He didn't know how Evan was faring, but he was about to find out.

Dallas, Texas, 2:30 a.m.

After three years as a widower and then being called back to active duty over eighteen months ago, Evan O'Ryan had almost forgotten what it was like to share a bed. And since the day an Iraqi land mine had taken out his truck, leaving him in pieces, he'd just about forgotten what a good night's sleep was all about.

He'd been back in Dallas less than two weeks, trying to come to terms with what the war had done to him. The physical scars were obvious. From time to time he still startled himself by catching a glimpse of his own reflection, but that was getting easier to accept. The real difficulties he faced were mental.

He hadn't seen his son in almost a year. He'd missed Johnny's fifth birthday, and a year and a half of his life. It was a high price to pay for a war he wasn't sure he believed in. And thanks to that war, he could no longer work the job he'd had before he'd been deployed.

He'd come home only to lose his pilot's license because of the handicaps he now bore, and was looking at at least a half dozen more surgeries to minimize the scarring on his face and neck. If that wasn't enough, he didn't know what the hell he was going to say to his son to explain why Daddy looked like a bad dream.

Still, he'd managed to stay alive, refusing to orphan his only child, the fear that had been uppermost in his mind from the day he'd received his orders. The baggage that had come with making that happen would have to work itself out. He didn't have time to feel sorry for himself. He wanted his life back. He wanted his son home. And, after the sacrifices he'd made, he didn't think that was too much to ask.

So he'd gone to bed, knowing that in two days his wife's parents, Frank and Shirley Pollard, who'd been taking care of Johnny since he'd been deployed, would be on his doorstep with his son. That didn't leave him much time to buy a Christmas tree, get out the decorations and do what he could to put his house in order. A year and a half to a five-year-old was a lifetime. He needed to be sure that the house looked as it always did during the holidays, because *he* damn sure didn't look the same.

It was with these troublesome thoughts that he'd gone to bed, but as always, his sleep was restless. He'd been in bed for almost four hours and was trapped in the web of another round of bad dreams when the phone began to ring.

The sound was loud and startling, and he caught himself reaching for his rifle before he realized the rifle wasn't on the cot in his tent and neither was he.

"Christ," he muttered as he grabbed at the phone with a shaking hand. Misjudging the distance, he managed to knock it off the table before he could answer it, and cursed the loss of his eye and the mess it had made of his depth perception.

Finally he had the receiver in hand and stifled another curse as he managed to answer.

"Hello?"

Thorn sighed. Judging from the sounds he'd just heard, maybe he should have waited until morning, although it was too late now for second thoughts. He gripped the receiver a little tighter and cleared his throat.

"Evan...it's me, Grandpop. Sorry I woke you."

Evan struggled through the chaos in his mind to a corner of sanity. Grandpop? At this time of night?

"What's wrong? Are you sick? Has something happened to Granddad? Or to Dad?"

Thorn cleared his throat again.

"I'm fine, and as far as I know, so are they."

Pain shot from the place where Evan's eye had been to the back of his jaw. He groaned softly, then gritted his teeth until the spasm had passed. A couple of seconds came and went before he could form words, and when he did, he regretted that they sounded so sharp.

"Glad everyone's okay, but this is a hell of a time for a chat."

"You're right," Thorn said. "So I'll get right to the point. I had a visit tonight from your grandmother, and I need to know if Johnny is all right."

Evan shook his head, like a dog shedding water.

"Grandpop, are you sure you're all right? I mean… Grandmother is—"

"Hell, boy, I know she's gone. There hasn't been an hour of my life for the past fifteen years that I haven't been reminded of that in some way or another. So quit worrying about my sanity and answer the question. Is Johnny all right?"

"Yes, sure," Evan said.

Thorn frowned. "You're sure?"

Now Evan was frowning. "Yes, I'm sure."

"When was the last time you talked to him?"

"Monday," Evan said.

"Well, boy, today is Wednesday. Anything could have happened in the past two days."

A muscle twitched near the corner of Evan's mouth.

"I know that, but don't you think Frank and Shirley would have called to let me know if it had?"

Thorn thought about the couple who'd given their daughter to this man and then lost her for good when she died. The only connection to her they had left was

Johnny, and they doted on him. Still, he couldn't bring himself to ignore Marcella's warning.

"Look, Evan, you're not going to like this. Hell, most likely you won't even believe it, but trust me when I say I do. Your grandmother woke me up out of a real good sleep and told me to 'help the boy.' Your son is the only boy in the family, so I figured she was talking about Johnny. Now, do your grandpop a big favor and call the Pollards. Insist that one of them go into Johnny's room and make sure he's okay."

Evan sighed.

"Grandpop! It's a quarter to three. I can't call them at this time of night...uh, I mean, morning, and ask something like that."

"Yes, you can. You have to!"

Evan shoved a hand through his hair in frustration, wincing when his fingers hit a tender spot beneath the new growth coming in.

"Okay... I can, but I'm not going to. There's no need scaring the—"

"Then give me their number," Thorn said. "I'll call them."

"Come on, Grandpop, they'll think you're—"

"I don't give a flying you-know-what about anyone's opinion of me. I'm telling you that something is wrong."

Evan glanced at the clock, debating with himself as to what he should do to calm his great-grandfather down. He didn't believe for a minute that his great grandmother's ghost had delivered some ominous message, but obviously Thorn did.

"Okay, Grandpop. I'll make a call, but it's on your head when they start having a fit over me waking everyone up."

"Call me back," Thorn demanded.

"Yes, sir," Evan said.

"I won't go back to bed until you call," Thorn added.

Evan smiled to himself.

"I know, Grandpop, and I'll call, I promise."

With that, Evan hung up and then sat on the side of the bed with his hands on his knees, debating the wisdom of waiting a few minutes and then calling Thorn back and pretending he'd called. But the moment he thought it, he discarded the notion. O'Ryans didn't lie, especially to one another.

With a muffled curse and then a reluctant sigh, he picked up the phone and punched in the number of his father-in-law's house, well aware that Frank Pollard was going to give him hell for the call.

He didn't think anything of the first four rings that went unanswered, but when the fifth, then the sixth, came and went and an answering machine picked up, he frowned.

"Okay, so maybe the ringer is off," he muttered, and waited for the answering machine to beep. "Frank, it's Evan…are you there?"

The fact that still no one answered was somewhat upsetting. Granted, it was now four in the morning, Michigan time, and Frank was a little hard of hearing. Yet the moment he thought it, he knew that excuse didn't wash. Shirley's hearing was just fine.

"Frank? Shirley? It's me. Evan. Are you there? If you are, I need you to pick up."

The machine beeped, ending the timed sequence for messages, and the line went dead.

Evan inhaled on a shaky breath. He was overreacting, and it was all Grandpop's fault. He needed to think rationally. Frank and Shirley knew that when they brought Johnny home for Christmas, he would be staying. As of yesterday, Johnny's school was out for Christmas vacation. They'd probably taken Johnny somewhere special to commemorate his time with them. Yeah, that had to be it. But even now that he had it figured out, he still needed confirmation. He would call Frank's cell phone. No matter where they were, Frank always had his cell.

He got up, turning on lights through the house as he went. He grabbed his address book out of the desk, flipped through the pages until he found the number to Frank's cell phone, then grabbed the phone and made the call. Satisfied that his concerns would soon be put to rest, he leaned against the wall, waiting for Frank to pick up.

It rang.

And then it rang again and again until it rolled over into voice mail. He left a message, but when he finally disconnected, his hands were shaking. This was crazy. Nothing was wrong. He was making a big deal out of nothing. So Frank wasn't answering his cell. Maybe he was out of range. Maybe the battery had run down. Maybe…

Harold! He would call Frank's brother, Harold. Frank and Shirley always asked Harold to feed their cat when they traveled. Harold would know if they were on a trip.

He flipped through the address book again, found Harold Pollard's number and dialed. By now he couldn't have cared less what time it was. He had to know all was well.

Harold answered on the third ring. Evan heard the sleep and confusion in his voice, and apologized only as an afterthought.

"Harold…it's me, Evan O'Ryan, Johnny's dad. I'm sorry for calling so late, but I've been trying to reach Frank and Shirley and having no luck."

Evan could hear Harold clearing his throat and fumbling, probably for the lamp.

"Evan?"

"Yes, Harold, it's me."

"Frank and Shirley aren't home," Harold said.

Evan breathed a quick sigh of relief. He knew it! He had jumped to a dire conclusion, and all because of Grandpop's crazy dream. But his relief soon faded when Harold continued.

"They wanted to surprise you and show up a couple days early, so they took a 6:00 p.m. flight out of Lansing. They should have been in Dallas by now."

Evan gripped the receiver a little tighter, as if holding on to it would help him hold on to his senses.

"But they're not," Evan said. "Do you know the flight plan or what airline they took?"

"Yes, yes, of course. I have it written down in the kitchen. Hold on and I'll get you the info."

He could hear Harold fumbling some more, then nothing, as Harold left the room. A few moments later, Evan heard him pick up an extension.

"Here we are," Harold said. "Um…let's see. Okay, it was Majestic Airlines, Flight 522. They left Lansing at 6:00 p.m. They were switching flights in Atlanta, going to Albuquerque, and then straight into DFW just before midnight. The flights are all out of the way, but it was all they could get this near Christmas. I can't imagine why—"

"Probably a delay in Atlanta," Evan said as he wrote down the information. "Thanks, Harold. I'll call the airline and check it out."

"Yes, well, all right," Harold said. "But if there's a problem, be sure and let me know."

Evan hung up the phone, then grabbed the phonebook. Although he was still a little disconcerted, he figured that Johnny and the Pollards must have arrived in Dallas so late that they'd taken a hotel for the night and were planning on surprising him in the morning. He hated to ruin their surprise, but he needed to know they were all right.

He found the number and dialed. It rang a couple of times, and then a recording came on. By the time Evan got through the automated menu to a living, breathing person, he was frustrated all over again.

"Majestic Airlines, how can I help you?"

"My name is Evan O'Ryan. I'm trying to get some information on Flight 522. My son and his grandparents are on that flight. Could you tell me what time it landed in Dallas?"

"I'm sorry, could you repeat that flight number for me?" the woman asked.

"Flight 522."

The woman's voice shook slightly when she spoke again, but Even didn't notice.

"Sir, if you could hold for a moment while I check the status…"

"Sure," Evan said.

He heard one full chorus of "Yellow Submarine" by the Beatles before someone picked up the line, only this time it was a man.

"This is Robert Farmer. I understand you want information on Flight 522?"

"Yes," Evan said. "I want to know what time it landed in Dallas."

"And you're inquiring about whom?"

Evan frowned. "My son and my in-laws."

"What are their names?" the man asked.

"Johnny O'Ryan is my son. Frank and Shirley Pollard are my in-laws."

There was a brief moment of silence, and then the man cleared his throat. "Yes, yes, they're on the passenger list."

Evan sighed.

"Look. I know they're on the list. What I need to know is what time their flight landed."

A long pause followed Evan's question. It was enough to tie a hard knot in his gut.

"Mr. O'Ryan, we've been trying to locate you for some time. Our information was that you were in the military."

"The operative word is 'was.' My injuries got me sent stateside."

"I see."

There was a long pause. Evan thought he heard the man sigh before he continued.

"I'm sorry, Mr. O'Ryan, but Flight 522 is missing. It went down in the mountains outside Carlisle, Kentucky, just after dark."

The shock, followed by a pain worse than any of those that had caused his wounds, sent Evan into a downward spiral as he slid to the floor, his voice breaking as he clutched the phone to his ear.

"No, no, please God, no."

"Yes, sir. I'm terribly sorry."

"This can't be happening. There must be some mistake."

"No, sir. I'm truly sorry. There's no mistake."

"Survivors…there must be survivors?"

The man sighed again. "At this point, we know nothing."

"You have to know something," Evan said, and felt sick. He ducked his head between his knees to keep from losing consciousness, then took a deep breath. "You've already organized a search party?"

"Yes, of course," the man said.

"Where?" Evan asked, and then choked on a sob.

"In the mountains above Carlisle. If you'll give me

the number where you can be contacted, we will keep you informed of ongoing—"

Bile rose to the back of Evan's throat. "I'm not waiting for a phone call. I'm going to the crash site, myself. I've got to find my son."

"Sir, please! You'll help us most by giving me your phone number. Once we have a headquarters established for the search site, we will—"

"I'm not waiting," Evan insisted, and rattled off his cell number, then hung up.

The silence in the room was frightening.

"Jesus," he mumbled, as his vision blurred.

The knot in his belly was so tight he thought he would throw up. The last time he'd been this scared was the day he'd come home from his wife's funeral and realized he was going to have to raise their son all alone.

Now this? He wouldn't let himself even consider the possibility that Johnny might be dead. God couldn't be that cruel.

Then he thought of the phone call from Thorn. God in heaven, Grandpop had been right!

Suddenly panic set in. He crawled to his knees, then got to his feet and stumbled through the house to his bedroom. He was shoving underclothes into a suitcase when he remembered he needed to book a flight.

He stopped packing long enough to call the airline. Within minutes, he had a seat on a flight leaving at seven and went back to the chaos he'd made of the clothing on his bed.

As he circled the bed to get his wristwatch, he glanced down at the picture on the table beside his bed. He sat down with a thump, picked up the photo, then began to cry.

The picture was of Johnny sitting on Santa's lap at the Galleria mall during their first Christmas alone. He stared at it until his vision blurred and his hands began to shake, then he put it back on the table, dashed into the bathroom and threw up.

He was washing his face with cold water when he remembered he'd promised to call Thorn. It was nearly 5:00 a.m. where his grandpop lived. As he dialed the number, he wondered if the old man had gone back to bed. When the call was answered on the first ring, he knew better.

Thorn's voice was hesitant, as if he didn't want to hear what Evan had to say.

"Hello? Evan?"

Evan took a deep breath, trying to settle the quaver in his voice, but it was no use.

"Yeah, Grandpop, it's me."

"What did you find out?" Thorn asked.

"Johnny was on a plane with the Pollards. It went down in the mountains in Kentucky."

Even though Thorn had believed Marcella's words, he was still shocked to hear them confirmed.

"Oh, Lord," he mumbled. "Tell me he's one of the survivors."

"They don't know anything yet," Evan said. "I'm on a flight that's leaving at seven. I'll let you know more when I get to the crash site."

"They won't let you anywhere near the site and you know it," Thorn said. "Besides, you're not in any physical shape to take off on a trip like that by yourself."

"I'm not waiting for answers, Grandpop. I can't. I have to find him. I have to find my son."

Thorn felt sick.

"I know, boy. I know. Where is the crash site located?"

Evan swallowed past the knot in his throat.

"In the mountains near a place called Carlisle, in Kentucky. I've got to go, Grandpop. I don't have much time to pack, and I need to ask a favor."

"Anything," Thorn said.

"Call Dad and Granddad for me, will you? Tell them what's happened, and that I'll be in touch when I know something more. Oh, and call Harold Pollard, too, will you?"

Thorn felt torn about what his call had unleashed. Even though he couldn't ignore Marcella's warning, he was unable to ignore Evan's condition, as well.

"Evan, son, you need to wait for—"

"Grandpop, it's my son we're talking about. I'm supposed to take care of him, and instead, I've been in a damned desert a half a world away, trying to help take care of a mess that will never be resolved. If you were me, would you be willing to wait?"

Thorn sighed.

"No."

"Okay, then," Evan said, then added, "I'll be in Carlisle before noon."

"I'll pray," Thorn said.

The muscles in Evan's throat tightened as Thorn disconnected. He stood for a moment, then walked across the hall into his son's bedroom and turned on the light.

A bright red stuffed Elmo sat propped up on the pillows lying on top of Johnny's Sesame Street bedspread. A Big Bird lamp was on the table beside the bed, and a Cookie Monster rug lay on the floor. Evan was shaking as he walked across the room and picked up Elmo.

He turned out the lights, then walked back across the hall, tucked Elmo into a corner of his suitcase and finished packing his clothes. He glanced at the clock. It was time to leave for the airport. Then he looked at the photo of his son in Santa's lap. The fear that had been threatening to undo him was turning into anger and a sense of purpose. Life had kicked him in the balls, but it wasn't over. It was time to kick back.

"Hang on, Johnny. Daddy's coming," he muttered, then grabbed his suitcase and headed for the door.

2

Seven hours earlier: Flight 522

Molly Cifelli had been trying to sleep ever since she'd boarded the plane in Atlanta. She was flying home for Christmas break, with a brand new master's degree in child psychology and a job with child welfare to begin after the first of the year. Since her parents' deaths five years ago, home was no longer home but only a place to be away from school. Now that she'd graduated and was starting a job, she had to decide if she wanted to sell the family home or rent it out. She was leaning toward selling but still hadn't made up her mind.

The week of finals had been exhausting, but the satisfaction of knowing that she'd done well was worth all the sleep she'd sacrificed to get where she was today.

Normally she was able to sleep anywhere, even on a plane. But this time she had the misfortune to be sitting behind two men who'd done nothing but argue since she'd boarded. She'd heard them address each other as Darren and Patrick, and she wondered why they were traveling together, since they obviously didn't get along. Rarely could she hear what they were actually saying, and then only in bits and pieces. It was the angry tone of their lowered voices that told her their trip together was anything but pleasant. So, since sleep was out of the question, she turned her attention to the family group sitting directly across the aisle from her.

The little boy called the elderly couple Grandad and Gran, and they called him Johnny. When he wasn't looking, she stole glances, wondering if his father was the reason for his black hair and blue eyes, and if it was his mother who'd given him the dimple in his right cheek.

Earlier she'd overheard the grandparents telling a flight attendant that the boy's father was a soldier, and that their daughter, who was Johnny's mother, had died when he was little more than a baby. When she heard them say that their son-in-law had been in Iraq and that they were taking Johnny home for Christmas, she could only imagine the joy of the father-son reunion.

Finally she began to tune out the chatter around her as exhaustion claimed her. She sat with her eyes closed, only now and then catching snippets of the conversation across the aisle. She did hear the little boy brag to the attendant about how brave his daddy was, and that his daddy had been hurt but was getting all better. The innocence in his voice brought tears to her eyes. She wondered about the soldier who was also a single father and could only imagine how tough it must have been for him to go to war and leave his son behind.

Eventually the flight attendant left, and for a few minutes, the area was quiet. Molly had just drifted off when, once again, the men sitting in front of her began to quarrel. She woke with a frown and caught herself holding her breath as the drama, all too audible in the otherwise silent plane, played out in grunts and whispers.

"Damn it, Darren, I've already given you my final word. I'm not doing it, and that's that."

"This is my life we're talking about," Darren said. "It's just one vote for you. One simple 'nay' and the bill will die."

"And when word gets out that Senator Patrick Finn voted against a bill supporting the tobacco industry, it will be the vote that ends my career. I'm not responsible for your problems, and I'd appreciate it if you'd quit trying to make all this my fault. I'm not the one who gambles. I'm not the one who owes the mob. How much is it, anyway?"

"How much is what?" Darren asked.

"Your debt. What do you owe them? I'm curious, because I've always wondered what the true cost of betrayal might be."

"I'm not betraying anyone," Darren said angrily.

"Just the people who voted for you," Patrick said. "Now, if you don't stop this harassment, I'll ask the attendant for another seat."

Molly held her breath. What on earth? It sounded as if the two men were politicians, but she couldn't figure out what they were arguing about.

Then the man called Patrick fired a last warning shot.

"I'm sorry, Darren, but you're mixed up with organized crime and I cannot stand aside and let you sell out our nation in the interests of the mob."

"What are you talking about?" Darren asked.

"I'm talking about turning you in when the House goes back into session."

"You can't!" Darren begged.

"I can and I will," Patrick said. "You've left me no choice."

"If you do that, they'll kill me for sure."

Molly heard Patrick sigh, then heard the seat squeak in front of her. She was afraid to look up for fear they would be looking at her—that they'd realized she'd heard everything.

Still, it shouldn't have mattered. It wasn't as if they could do anything to her right here on the plane, but she felt uneasy.

"You should have thought of that before you sold your soul to the devil," Patrick said at last. "Now, shut up and leave me alone. This discussion is over."

There was a long moment of silence. Molly thought the discussion was over, and then she heard Darren fire back a chilling response.

"Don't count on it, Patrick. Santa Fe is a long way from the airport. Anything can happen."

Patrick cursed. "Don't threaten me, Darren. You don't have the balls to do anything about it."

Now the silence between them was long and angry. Molly kept quiet and was glad she did, because Darren suddenly stood up and walked back toward the bathrooms. She imagined his gaze on her face, judging to make sure she was asleep. She felt threatened by what she'd overheard and prayed for a swift flight.

A few minutes later she heard the man return to his seat, followed by a second series of short, angry whispers that she tried to ignore.

Across the aisle, the little boy and his grandparents were blissfully unaware of the drama. She could hear them talking to one another, the grandparents laughing at the child's comments and assuring him that Daddy's wounds would soon heal.

A short while later the attendants began serving beverages in the cabin, and the ongoing drama between the two men went silent. She pretended to awaken as the flight attendant offered her a cold drink. She busied herself with opening her package of salted pretzels and was chewing her first bite when it sounded as if something exploded beneath her feet. She felt the floor vibrating, immediately followed by a loud roar. When the oxygen masks suddenly dropped out of their overhead compartments and began dangling and swaying like airborne jellyfish, there was a collective gasp. As the plane dipped nose down and began to plunge toward earth, the screaming began. One by one the overhead storage compartments popped open, shopping bags, coats and carry-ons spilling out into the aisles and the passengers' laps.

The flight attendants valiantly pulled themselves up the aisle, fighting against gravity, shouting for the passengers to put their heads down and assume crash position. The scent of burning rubber and electrical wiring quickly filled the cabin, along with the first faint wisps of smoke.

Molly's screams froze in the back of her throat as she looked straight into the panicked gaze of a flight attendant. Her expression seemed to mirror what Molly felt. At the same time, Molly was saddened as a sense of inevitability swept over her. She thought of her parents. It seemed that she would be joining them far sooner than she would have imagined. She thought of the five long years she'd spent at college to become competent in a profession she would never get to practice.

Then, just as suddenly as the plane had nosed down, it began to level off. There was a communal cry of thanksgiving from the passengers that ended when the windows began popping out of their openings. A wild rush of air flowed through the cabin, sucking the breath from Molly's lungs so fast that screaming became impossible. In the fraction of a second before the plane hit solid ground, she thought she saw a winter forest of dead trees and green pines. Then an exit door flew off the hinges and everything went black.

She never knew when her seat belt snapped, or when she was thrown out into the aisle on top of the carry-on luggage. Pain shattered her briefly into awareness as she landed facedown on the corner of someone's briefcase. Before she could give voice to the pain, she lost consciousness again.

* * *

Molly woke up to an intense blast of cold air in her face and an absolute silence. The quiet was surreal after the screams and the unending sounds of buckling metal and shattering timber. Her head was pounding, and as she lifted shaky hands to her forehead, she felt something wet running down the side of her face. She touched the spot, winced, and then shivered as her fingers came away covered in blood.

When she tried to focus on something other than her injuries, she became disoriented all over again. It took a few moments for her to realize that the plane had come to rest on its side, then a few more seconds to see that no one else was moving.

Her heartbeat skipped, then slammed against her rib cage with a panicked thud. Without moving, she could see the flight attendant who'd served her drink and pretzels, now wedged beneath some seats with her head lying at an awkward angle to the rest of her body. Her eyes were open, her mouth frozen in a scream of horror.

An Asian businessman was still clutching the briefcase he'd had in his lap, although the entire right side of his head appeared to have been mashed inward.

Molly stared until tears blurred her vision and her heart felt as if it would fly out of her chest. She had a moment of overwhelming sorrow for what had happened, for what she was seeing, as well as guilty joy that she was still alive.

She took a slow, unsteady breath and started to call out for help, hoping—praying—that someone besides herself had survived the wreck, and then she heard a man groan.

"Darren…help me…I can't feel my legs."

"My head…it's killing me," Darren said.

She stifled a gasp. It was the two men who'd been arguing.

At that point something fell; then the hull of the plane seemed to groan as it settled. The air was full of smoke, but the plane had yet to burst into flames.

"Help me," Patrick said again.

"I'll help you," Darren said as he pulled himself up off the floor and loomed over Patrick, who was still strapped in his seat. "I'll help you straight to hell."

Molly stifled a gasp. From where she was lying, she could see Darren as he got up. His head and nose were bloody, and he seemed to be dragging one leg, but he was mobile enough to put his hands around Patrick's throat and end his life.

Patrick's struggles were weak. It took less than a minute for him to die.

At that point Molly closed her eyes and began to pray. There was no one to come to their aid—no one to hear—and the cold, passionless expression she'd seen on the killer's face was horrifying. When she heard footsteps moving toward her, her heart skipped a beat. Breathing as shallowly as she possibly could, she lay still—as still as the dead around her. When she heard the footsteps stop, her heart followed suit. When they finally moved away, she went weak with relief.

Only when she could no longer hear anything but the

wind, did she chance a peek. No one was moving inside the demolished cabin. Darren was gone.

Before she could think what to do next, she heard someone crying, then the faint voice of a child.

"Gramps…Gran…wake up. Please wake up."

The child! Dear God, the child was alive.

Ignoring the pain that shot suddenly up her back, she crawled to her feet. Within seconds, a wave of nausea sent her reeling. It was all she could do to stagger through the bodies and debris to get to the little boy.

When she finally reached him, she stifled a cry of dismay. He'd crawled up into his grandfather's lap and wrapped his arms around the old man's neck. One quick glance told Molly that the child was in shock. His body was shaking, and his cheeks were streaked with tears. Stifling another wave of nausea, she reached for him and gently touched the side of his face.

"Johnny…your name is Johnny, isn't it?"

His expression was blank. Glancing around to make sure they were still alone, she began looking for his coat and backpack.

"My name is Molly," she said. "We need to grab our coats and get out before the plane catches on fire."

Johnny O'Ryan had been taught never to speak to strangers, but he couldn't help himself; he clutched desperately at the pretty woman with the soft voice.

"Granddad won't talk to me," he whispered.

Molly's vision blurred, but she blinked away tears. This was no time to cry.

"I know, honey. I'm sorry."

Johnny looked up at her then, searching her face for the truth.

Molly glanced nervously around, then looked back at the child. His expression was nothing short of desperate. A fresh set of tears welled and rolled down his face.

"Did the bad man kill them, too?" he asked.

Molly gasped. Dear God, had the child also been a witness to Patrick's death?

"What man, honey?"

He pointed to the man Darren had just killed.

"The man who choked him. I saw him do it. Did he choke my granddad and gran, too?"

"Oh, Lord," Molly muttered.

That settled it. There was no turning back. They had to leave, and leave now. She couldn't trust the boy not to let slip what he'd seen once Darren came back—and he *would* come back, she was sure of it—any more than she could hide what she knew.

The way she looked at it, their only chance for survival was if the killer didn't know they were alive. She didn't know where he'd gone, but the timing of their escape was urgent.

Ignoring the pain in her head and back, while suppressing the urge to vomit, she lifted Johnny out of his grandfather's lap. As she picked him up, he cried out in pain. Her heart dropped. She hadn't considered that he might be injured, too.

"I'm sorry," she said. "Where do you hurt?"

"My side," Johnny said.

"Do you think you can walk?" she asked.

He nodded.

"I'm really cold. Are you?" Her gaze fell on a small fur-lined khaki parka. "Is this your coat?"

He nodded, then looked back at his grandfather again.

"Granddad's head is bleeding."

His voice was so faint, she had to lean forward to hear.

"I know, honey. I'm so sorry."

The little boy's chin quivered.

"Is he dead? My cat French Fry died. We buried him down by the creek."

Molly put her arms around him and pulled him close.

"Yes, I think he is," she said. "Hold out your arms, honey. You need to put on your coat."

Johnny thrust his arms into the fur-lined sleeves, standing silently as Molly zipped up the coat, while he tried to understand why his grandparents could no longer see or speak. The blood on their faces was scary. He knew blood meant pain. He was sad that they were hurting.

"If we put Band-Aids on their ouchies, would they be okay?" he asked softly.

Molly stifled tears. She felt as helpless as he looked.

"No, darling, I'm afraid not. The plane crash hurt them too much to get better, just like it hurt all these other people. But your grandparents would want you to get home safely, wouldn't they?"

Tears rolled silently down Johnny's face as he nodded.

She patted him on the back and glanced over her shoulder, afraid that they would be found out before they escaped.

Just then she saw the SpongeBob SquarePants backpack Johnny had carried on the plane and remembered noticing that he had snacks and juice boxes in the bag. She picked it up.

"Here, honey, maybe we should take this."

Johnny allowed her to put the backpack on him as his gaze slid to his grandmother.

"Is Gran dead, too?"

Molly glanced at the elderly woman as she pulled her own coat out from beneath a laptop computer and quickly put it on.

"Yes, I think she is," Molly said.

Johnny leaned against Molly, as if his legs had suddenly gone weak.

"I'm so sorry, honey," she said softly.

His voice was shaking. "Can't you make them wake up?"

Her heart ached for the little boy. His world had been shattered, and there was nothing she could do to make it better.

"No, I can't," she said. "No one can. But they would want you to be okay. They would want you to stay well so you could go see your daddy, remember?"

Tears rolled down his cheeks, but he didn't let out a sound.

"We need to leave, Johnny. We need to leave now. Will you let me help you?"

This was against everything he'd been taught, but his world had just been destroyed, so he decided it would be all right to go with her.

Finally he nodded.

Molly breathed a sigh of relief as she pulled herself upright. Thankful for her heavy coat and the fact that she was wearing wool pants and a sweater, she led him toward the opening where the plane had broken literally in two.

Ignoring the fact that her whole body was one big ache, she glanced around quickly, making sure the killer was nowhere in sight, then felt in her coat pockets, assuring herself that her gloves were still there. She took a wool scarf from a carry-all that had been ripped apart and wrapped it around her neck. The weight of the clothing felt comforting, but there was no time to waste.

She didn't know where the killer had gone, but every now and then she thought she could hear bumping and thumping below where she was standing. It was only a matter of time before he reappeared, and when he did, they had to be gone.

A handful of the airline's lightweight blankets were bunched beneath a dead man's leg. She paused in the aisle long enough to grab a couple of them, which she tied around her waist. Then she took Johnny's hand, and together they made their way through the debris and bodies until they reached the jagged opening. Along the way, she grabbed all the snacks and drinks the backpack would hold, then zipped it back up.

"God be with us," she muttered, and stepped out into the snow, then turned and helped Johnny down.

Debris was scattered as far as the eye could see. She didn't know where they were. All she could see was that the plane had landed on an incline and there were trees everywhere. It appeared that they'd gone down in the mountains—her best guess was the Appalachians.

She looked up at the sky. It would be dark soon, but it was still light enough for her to see the setting sun. Assuming that the man would eventually come back into the cabin to spend the night, she prayed that the darkness would give them time to get away undetected.

With a quick glance down at the boy, she tugged the hood a little closer around his face and softly whispered, "Come on, Johnny. Let's go see if we can find some help, okay?"

He didn't answer, but he also didn't argue. For now, it was enough.

Darren Wilson's knee was throbbing, as was his head, and every time he bent over, there was added pain in his chest. He wasn't sure, but he might have broken some ribs. He wanted nothing more than to crawl back into the plane, cover himself with some blankets and wait to be rescued. The inevitability of rescue was without question, but he needed to find the bag with his money first. It had been in the overhead compartment, but now it was nowhere in sight.

He had no choice but to backtrack along the trail of scattered debris and hope he could find it before dark.

It didn't take long for him to discover that the job wasn't going to be as simple as he'd hoped. To his dismay, most of the bags looked alike.

"Son of a bitch," Darren muttered, then glanced up at the sky, judging the amount of light he would have before night fell and wondering if they would be found before morning. He couldn't know for sure, but either way, time would be short. It didn't give him much leeway to find his money. With a muttered curse for the pain in his body and the mess he was in, he began his search.

He started out with confidence, but by the time an hour had passed, he had still come up empty. Frustrated and miserable from the pain and the cold, he suddenly looked up and realized he was quite a distance from the crash, and it was getting dark. Added to that, it was starting to snow.

A light dusting of flakes was drifting across the surface of the wreckage, sugar-coating the carnage. Somewhere off to the south, he thought he heard a howl. His pulse spiked. Was that a wolf…or just a lonely dog? In either case, it gave him the creeps enough to abandon his search in favor of the relative safety of the plane. The fact that it had never caught fire was good—the fact that the bodies inside were being kept in cold storage was also good. He began telling himself that everything was going to be all right. Surely he'd been blessed, or else why would he have been the only survivor?

A spurt of conscience reminded him that there had

been another survivor after all, but he'd taken care of that. He started toward the plane, lengthening his stride. He was almost there when he stumbled on something buried beneath the snow and fell flat on his face. The pain in his leg shot all the way up his back, and he was blinking and cursing and rubbing snow out of his eyes when he saw them.

Tracks.

Two sets—leading from the plane and out into the forest, and not yet filled in by the new snow.

Ignoring his pain, he scrambled to his feet, staring down at the tracks in disbelief.

Other survivors?

Where had they been when he had been in the cabin choking the life out of Senator Patrick Finn?

Had they been unconscious—or witnesses to what he'd done?

Why would they leave the relative safety of the plane for the dangers of unknown snowbound territory unless…

"Oh, shit…no! Tell me this isn't happening."

He ran toward the plane as fast as he could and began searching the interior, trying to remember who'd been on board compared to the bodies scattered about. He paused beside Patrick's body and as he did, automatically looked back to the seats behind him. There had been a young woman there. And she was nowhere in sight! He thought back to the ongoing argument he and Patrick had been having. What if she'd overheard?

He pivoted sharply, counting bodies on the other side of the aisle and trying to remember how many seats had been occupied and how many had been empty.

His gaze fell on the elderly couple. A kid. There had been a kid with them. Where the hell was he now?

"Hey! Where are you?" he yelled, then said it again, and again, only louder and louder, until he was screaming.

Panic set in as he began tearing through the compartment in the gathering darkness. He had to know! He had to find them and look into their eyes. If there was fear there, he would do what he had to do, just as he'd done with Patrick.

But how? It was almost dark.

Light. He needed to find light.

Grateful to have a plan, he began searching for a flashlight to help him follow the tracks. Finally he found one inside the cabin near the co-pilot's body, and with no thought for the possibility of getting lost in the dark, he grabbed a heavy coat from the debris beneath his feet. The sleeves were a bit too long, but fashion savvy was the least of his worries.

He jumped out of the plane just as the sun disappeared behind the trees. Within minutes, night would be official. He didn't know how long the woman and kid had been gone, but it was too risky to assume they hadn't seen anything.

"Damn, damn, damn," he muttered, then aimed the flashlight down at the tracks and began running, dragging his injured leg as he went. If he was lucky, he could catch up with them before the falling snow covered their tracks.

It never occurred to him that the snow would cover his tracks, too, or that he might have survived the crash only to risk perishing on the mountain in the dark.

3

The snow wasn't as deep beneath the heavy cover of trees as it was out in the clearing. This made it easier for Molly and Johnny to move at a swifter pace, but at the same time, it was easier to get lost, because there was less light. Full darkness was only minutes away when she realized that they'd come upon what appeared to be a small cave. Since they were going to have to sleep somewhere, this appeared to be a better place than out in the open.

She had hoped against hope that they would stumble on a house, or a ranger station, but it hadn't happened. She wondered if the airline was aware of the crash yet, if they'd begun notifying next of kin. She didn't have anyone, but Johnny did. She could only imagine his father's grief and fear when he learned of the crash.

There had been plenty of cell phones scattered around the plane, though she'd never bothered to get one of her own, but she'd never thought about grabbing one. She'd been too focused on getting them out alive. Now she had no idea where they were and no way to contact anyone, but she was more concerned about Johnny than about being lost.

She suspected he was still in shock. He hadn't cried out once—not even when a low-hanging branch slapped him in the face, not even when he stumbled and fell. Not even when they came close to walking off into a ravine. Despite her degree in child psychology and the new job waiting for her with child protective services, her experience with children in general was somewhat limited. She would have expected him to cry or complain, anything but maintain this eerie silence and blank, empty gaze.

She stopped, eyeing their footsteps in the snow leading up to the cave and gave silent thanks for the continuing snowfall. Their tracks would be covered soon, so if the killer *had* noticed they were gone and tried to follow them, he would be unsuccessful. Still, she stood outside the cave for a few moments more until she was satisfied that their location should be relatively safe. Now all she had to do was deal with Johnny.

"Johnny?"

He didn't look up.

Molly knelt, winced as the pain in her back rippled down the length of her leg, then ignored it and took him by the shoulders.

"Johnny...please talk to me. Are you all right?"

"I'm cold," he said.

Relief shifted within her. At least he was talking.

"Me, too," she said, then hugged him gently. "Are you hungry?"

He nodded.

"So let's see what we have in that backpack," she said with forced cheer.

She took it off his shoulders and led him into the cave.

The entrance was small, as was the cave itself. Johnny could stand up in it, but Molly had to crawl on her hands and knees to get around. There were some old animal bones near the back, as well as a large pile of leaves. The leaves would make good bedding, but the bones would have to go.

As soon as she got rid of the unsavory bits and pieces, she settled Johnny onto one of the blankets she'd laid over the leaves. One of the best things about spending the night in here was that it was dry. She had no way to build a fire, but at least they wouldn't be lying in the snow.

As Johnny sat down, he gazed nervously around.

"What about lions and tigers?" he asked.

Molly started to smile, then suddenly shivered. He did have a point. What about the wild animals?

"Oh, I think we'll be fine," she said. "But just in case, I'll find us a great big stick, okay?"

Johnny hesitated, then shrugged.

"Yes… I guess it will be okay."

"Good boy," she said, and hugged him again, then dug through the backpack, found a granola bar and a juice box, and handed them to him. "Eat this, honey. I'm going to find that big stick."

Johnny grabbed her arm.

"No! Don't go! Don't leave me!" he cried.

The panic on his face hurt her heart. Poor little boy—grandparents dead, and a man murdered before his eyes. She couldn't imagine what he must be thinking.

"Oh, honey, I'm sorry. I didn't think. Of course I won't leave you. We'll find the stick together. We'll eat together, then we'll sleep together. Okay?"

She felt him shiver and suspected it wasn't from the cold.

"Okay," he said.

She put the food back in the backpack, then set it against the wall of the cave before taking him by the hand.

"There's a big dead tree out there beside those pines. See all those limbs poking up out of the brush?"

His little voice trembled as he fought back tears. "Yes."

She gave him a quick hug. "I bet we can find a really big stick there. What do *you* think?"

Johnny clung to her all the way across the clearing, turning loose only when she began to sort through the limbs. Finally she found one she thought would work and managed to break it off from the main trunk.

"How about this one?" she asked as she hefted it up to her shoulder.

"All right," Johnny said.

The remark was a little odd, but Molly figured Johnny didn't care what it looked like, he just wanted to get back inside the cave. By the time they returned, it was completely dark. Once again, Molly dug the food out of the backpack, and they ate more by feel than sight. When they were done, she laid the makeshift weapon near her feet; then, using a large pile of leaves as a pillow, she rolled them both up in the blankets and pulled the child close.

There were a few awkward moments. Molly could feel his body stiffen, but rejection didn't last long. When he started to cry, she pulled him as close against her as she could and rocked him where they lay.

"It's okay to cry, honey," she said. "I'm cold and scared, too. But I'll keep us safe. I promise."

"Okay," he whispered, and with the innocence only a child could give, relaxed in her arms.

"I'm sorry about your grandparents," she said softly.

"Are they in heaven?" he asked.

"Yes, I'm sure they are," she answered.

There was a moment of hesitation; then he spoke again. "Do you think they can see me?"

Molly sighed. "What do you think?" she asked.

"I think…yes."

Molly wanted to cry for him, but her tears would do neither of them any good.

"Me, too," she said, then gave him a gentle squeeze. "Go to sleep now."

Within moments, she heard the rhythm of his breathing change, but her rest didn't come as easily. Every crack of snow-laden branches outside the cave made her jump. Every howl of the wind led her to imagine they were about to be eaten. And when she closed her eyes, all she could see was that man killing his friend.

"Please, God," she finally whispered. "Keep us safe."

* * *

Darren ran out of daylight quickly, even though the beam from the flashlight kept him on the right trail. He didn't know how long he walked, or how far he'd come from the crash site, when he almost fell into a ravine. One minute he'd been on solid ground, and the next thing he knew, the land had disappeared and the light was shining down into a black, bottomless void.

Reeling from the shock, he grabbed onto a nearby sapling, pulled himself back to safety, then sat down with a thud, sending snow flying.

"Oh God, oh God, oh God," he muttered and pulled his knees up beneath his chin, then lowered his head onto his hands and cried. "Why?" he cried. "Why me?"

He bawled and cursed as snot froze on his cheek. He'd spent years as a senator. The reality of his situation didn't seem possible. Important people like him didn't just die like this—did they? Then he thought of John F. Kennedy Jr. and his plane crash, and got sick to his stomach. No one was more important politically than a Kennedy, and that hadn't kept him alive.

The deal was, it wasn't enough that he'd survived the crash. If that woman and kid were running because they'd witnessed what he'd done, he was still dead meat. He couldn't afford to take the chance that they would perish in this weather. He had to find them and make sure they didn't get a chance to talk. As badly as he wanted to go back to the plane and take his chances, he couldn't afford the risk.

After a few desperate moments, he found what

passed for shelter beneath some low overhanging limbs and settled in for the night, telling himself that morning was bound to make searching for the woman and kid easier. Once he dealt with them, he could come up with some kind of explanation for wandering away from the crash site. As for them, they would be written off as having wandered away to perish in the mountains.

Now that he'd set that plan in his mind, he rolled up in a ball and tried to sleep, but he couldn't stop thinking about Patrick. The look in his eyes when he'd realized he was going to die. The way his tongue had pushed against the back of his front teeth, then all but exploded out of his mouth when Darren kept squeezing his throat.

Darren wiped a gloved hand over his eyes, trying to wipe away the image. He'd never killed anyone before. Then he thought of his family and the threats that had been made against them, and told himself that he'd done what he had to do.

Once he'd accepted that excuse for himself, he finally relaxed, and even though he was in pain and danger of freezing to death, exhaustion pulled him under.

Deborah Sanborn had lived her entire life in the Appalachian Mountains, thirty minutes above the little town of Carlisle, Kentucky. Her father, Gus Sanborn, had worked in the mines since the age of seventeen. He'd married her mother a year later, and less than a year after that, their only child, Deborah Jean, had been born. When she was six years old she'd been sitting at

her school desk, doing a page of penmanship, when her
world made a one-eighty turn and never went back.

She'd just finished writing an entire line of lower-
case *w*'s when the lead on her pencil suddenly broke.
She stared down at the hole it had put in her paper, and
when it began to morph into the dark opening of the
mine her daddy worked in, she started to cry.

The teacher, thinking she was crying because she'd
torn her page, began to reassure her that it would be all
right.

At that point Deborah Jean stood up, announced that
her daddy was dead—that they were all dead—and then
fainted. Before the teacher could run for help, the shriek
of the whistle down at the mine cut through the air. The
shrill staccato rhythm was the sound that signaled a
cave-in at Lawton Mining number 4.

That day, twelve of Lawton Mining's finest perished
in a cave-in seven hundred feet below the surface. It
took more than two weeks before they were found and
removed. By that time, everyone in Carlisle knew that
Gus Sanborn's baby girl, Deborah, had been born with
what they called "the sight."

Half the population was suddenly afraid of her, and
the other half wanted her mother to let little Deborah
"see" the future for them. It didn't take Deborah's
mother long to realize that her baby girl's gift was what
was going to keep food on their table. She set Deborah
up in her father's easy chair in the corner of the living
room, and from noon to dark on Saturday, Deborah
Jean held court.

That she put food on their table was secondary to the fact that her "gift" had forever set her apart from her friends. Their parents no longer welcomed her into their homes for fear she would jinx their futures. Gus's death left her lonely and ostracized, and the ensuing years had not changed her fate. At forty, she was still unmarried and still lonely, living in the old family home high on the mountain above Carlisle, still having visions that broke her heart.

It had been snowing off and on for a couple of days now, enough so that it made doing outside chores difficult. Still, after the vision she'd had a few days ago of Destry Poindexter beating up on his wife again, her days were ordinary and for that she was grateful.

She had milked the cow, and fed the dog and barn cats, a good hour before dark. Once she'd strained the milk and poured it into a crock, she left it on the screened-in back porch to separate overnight. In the morning the layer of thick, ivory-colored cream would be crusted with frost, but it wouldn't be enough to hamper her from skimming the cream into a pitcher, then pouring the milk into jugs.

Her neighbor Farley Comstock would come over to get most of the milk and some of the cream. Farley had nine kids to feed, with another on the way, and there was no way Deborah could use everything the cow produced. In return for milk, Farley kept her in firewood, saving her from having to cut and split what she needed to stay warm.

After her supper, she'd tried to watch some television but had given it up for a good book in bed, and had fallen asleep in the middle of chapter seven.

She had been asleep for hours, dreaming of the days when her Granny had still been alive—of bread-baking day and eating the crust off of the first loaf out of the oven, slathered in home-churned butter. In her mind, she was watching Granny spread grape jelly onto the bread and butter, and could almost taste the results. Then everything changed.

The part of herself that remained cognizant knew when her mind went from dream to something else— something far more sinister than a sweet childhood memory.

She saw the boy child first. Tears were frozen on his face, and for a moment she thought he was dead. Then she saw the gentle flare of his nostrils as he breathed, and a part of her rejoiced, for she knew that he still lived. The woman who held him was young and pretty, but there was frost on her dark hair, as well as on the blankets beneath which they slept. Deborah felt a quick sense of panic. Time would not be kind to them.

Suddenly her vision jumped backward like a movie on rewind as she watched them trudging through the woods. She saw broken trees and the debris that only man could produce, and realized she was looking at the site of a plane crash. She heard screams, smelled smoke, then saw the plane coming down.

Her mind jumped forward again from impact to the near silence that ensued. When she followed the vision into the smoke-filled cabin, she sensed danger. Oddly enough, it seemed disconnected from the crash itself. When she witnessed the young woman rise from the rubble and go to the child, the vision ended.

The moment it stopped, she woke.

It was just after five in the morning—too late to go back to sleep, too early to begin the day's work. There was only one thing left for her to do.

Make coffee.

She would begin the day with a cup of coffee the sweet consistency of syrup and hope the weather report announced that the snow was moving out of the region.

Deborah washed her face and brushed her teeth quickly before climbing into a pair of her oldest, softest blue jeans. She chose one of her daddy's old flannel shirts, pulled on a new pair of wool socks, then stepped back into her house shoes and headed for the kitchen, tying her long ash-blond hair into a ponytail at the nape of her neck as she went.

She turned on the light in the kitchen and headed straight for the coffeepot. Only after the coffee was brewing did she think back to her vision. She would have to call the sheriff. Her conscience wouldn't let her ignore what she saw, even though she often wished she could. Rarely did the visions ever come to any good, but she couldn't let that matter. Somewhere a woman and a child were in need of rescuing. It was up to her to let the authorities know they were alive.

As soon as the coffeepot dinged, signaling the cycle was complete, she poured herself a cup, added sugar, then more sugar, stirring with each heaping teaspoon until it was the desired consistency, then lifted the cup to her lips. It was thick and sweet, just as she liked it.

As soon as the first sip had gone down and her nerves had settled, she took the portable phone to the kitchen table and dialed the number of Wally Hacker's office.

"County Sheriff's office."

"Frances, it's Deborah. Is the sheriff in?"

"Lord, woman, don't you ever sleep?" the dispatcher asked.

Deborah sighed. "I try. Is he in?"

"He's in the back, asleep. I'll holler at him."

"Thanks," Deborah said, well aware that Sheriff Wally Hacker would not thank her for waking him up, or for giving him another wild goose to chase down.

She waited, listening as Frances's footsteps faded away, then waited some more as she heard her coming back.

"He said give him a minute and he'll be right here."

"All right. Thanks," Deborah said.

Curious, Frances couldn't wait to hear the news secondhand.

"What did you see, girl?"

"I'll tell Wally. He can tell you, that way I won't have to repeat myself so many times."

"All right," Frances said, obviously disappointed, then couldn't help but add, "How do you do it?" she asked.

Deborah sighed. "You ask me that every time."

Frances laughed. "Sorry, I guess I do, don't I? Oh,

well, it never hurts to ask. Maybe one of these days you'll give me an answer."

"Only if someone explains it to me first," Deborah said.

"Really?" Frances said, surprised. "You mean you...wait! Here comes the sheriff."

Deborah braced herself for Wally Hacker's gravel-tinged drawl of disdain.

"What the hell's wrong now?" he asked.

"Good morning to you, too," Deborah countered.

Hacker sighed. "Sorry. I didn't get to sleep until after midnight. What's up?"

"Was there a plane crash in the area?"

Hacker's heart skipped a beat. As long as he'd known Deborah, it still floored him that she could do this.

"Is it already on the news?" he asked.

Deborah felt the air sliding out of her lungs as surely as if she'd been punched in the stomach.

"Nothing is on television but an old Audie Murphy movie and a rerun of the Food Network's 2001 dessert battle. So there *was* a crash?"

"Yeah, but it hasn't been located yet. They know it went off the radar. They keep picking up an intermittent beep from the locator, but the snowfall is screwing up a pinpoint on the location. They're having to wait until daylight to start the search. That's what I know. What's your story?"

"A young woman and a small boy were on that plane. They lived through the crash and are somewhere in the mountains."

Hacker cursed. "Why the hell would they leave the plane?"

"I don't know, Wally. I just know that they did."

"You're sure?"

She sighed.

"Yeah, yeah, I know," Wally muttered. "You wouldn't have called unless you were."

"Do you need some help?"

"No."

"I'm here if you do," she added.

"I know that, too," Hacker said. "Thanks for the call. I'll pass on the message to the searchers."

"All right," Deborah said, hating to break the connection between herself and the man she knew would be in charge. He wasn't taking this seriously enough, but she didn't know any other way to impress upon him the intensity of the survivors' need.

The sheriff saved her the decision of whether or not to hang up and did it for her, leaving her with the buzz of a dial tone in her ear. She hung up reluctantly, took another sip of her coffee, then set it down and went out onto the back porch, where she lifted the cotton cloth from a large crock and peeked inside. The cream from last night's milking had come to the top. It was time to skim it off and pour up the milk for Farley.

She carried the large crock into the kitchen, skimmed off the cream and poured a pitcher of milk for herself, then set it aside. Then she poured the remaining milk into a couple of jugs, knowing Farley would be by later to pick them up.

With that chore finished, she glanced out toward the barn. It wasn't light enough to see to start other chores, so she went back into the kitchen, welcoming the warmth. At the same time, she was struck by a sense of urgency. She frowned. This wasn't normal. Usually, once she'd given up her vision, it no longer bothered her, but this time something didn't feel right.

She carried the cream to the refrigerator and set it on a shelf. As she closed the door, the ever-familiar sensation of losing focus came over her. Even though she knew she was still standing in her kitchen with her hand on the refrigerator door, she saw something entirely different.

She saw footsteps in the snow, leading away from the plane. That would be the woman and child. She didn't understand why she was seeing this again. Then she realized she was looking at a third set of tracks. She saw a man's feet, then his legs, but she couldn't see his face. Someone was following them! Her heart rate accelerated when she realized she felt danger. Something was wrong. The man intended harm, but that didn't make sense. Why would someone want to kill the survivors of a plane crash?

Suddenly the vision was gone as quickly as it had come. Deborah gasped, then tightened her grip on the refrigerator door until the room had quit spinning. The old house was silent, except for the usual squeaks and creaks it sometimes made in protest of the winter winds. She glanced down at her house shoes and sighed. The last thing she wanted to do was be outside in this weather, but fate gave her no choice. She didn't, as yet, know why, but she had to go to the crash site. Someone still needed her help.

She wrote a note for Farley, asking him to milk the cow and feed the animals until she got home, and, as always, telling him to take the cream and the milk, and tell Karen hello.

She glanced around the kitchen, making sure that she'd turned off all the appliances, turned down, but not off, the propane heating stoves throughout the house, and went to get dressed. Whether she liked it or not, she had to find the crash site. Sheriff Hacker had to be made to understand that not only did the two missing passengers need to be found, but they also needed to be protected. Someone wanted them dead.

Evan got to Carlisle by noon. It was the most exhausting thing he'd done since coming home. He'd tossed his bag into the motel room he'd rented without looking at the beds. He would like nothing better than to lie down and sleep the day through, but he couldn't afford to be weak. His little boy needed him in the most desperate way. He'd already sorted out the things he needed to pack for the search. Food and water, dry socks and gloves, a change of clothes, matches, a small hatchet and a large knife, a lightweight sleeping bag designed for extreme cold, some basic first aid, some packets of trail mix—and Elmo, Johnny's favorite character.

The stuffed toy had little to do with survival, but Evan had to take his own physical appearance into consideration. His son might need a reminder as to what home and Daddy were all about.

He was in the act of zipping up his backpack when there was a knock on the door of the motel. Frowning, he turned toward the door as a second knock sounded.

"Yeah? Who is it?" he called out.

"It's us, Evan. Open up!"

Evan's heart skipped a beat. That sounded like his dad, which was impossible. Mike O'Ryan lived in Arizona.

He crossed the room and opened the door.

"Dad!" Then he looked past his father's shoulder to the men coming up behind him. "Granddad? Grandpop? Where…? How?"

Once the patriarch of the O'Ryan family had called, the other men had not been able to pack fast enough.

Thorn had known that, at eighty-five, he wouldn't be a lot of help, but he couldn't bear to stay behind.

His son, James, Evan's grandfather, was almost as fit at sixty-four as he'd been when he'd come home from Vietnam.

Mike, Evan's dad, was relieved to be looking at his son face-to-face—even under these conditions. A veteran of the Gulf War, he'd been a young father, and now, at the age of forty-five, he was a young grandfather, as well. Knowing that Evan was still recuperating from his injuries and that his only grandson was in danger, his impatience was the greatest. The moment he saw his son's face with the scars and the black leather eye patch, he wrapped his arms around him, thumped him on the back a couple of times and then just held him.

All the fear and frustration that Evan had been feeling seemed to lessen. He knew the old saying about safety in numbers, and in this case, there was a lot of truth in it. Four generations of soldiers were joined in a common purpose. That they were all men of the same family just made it better, because they all had the same thing at stake.

Find Johnny, before it was too late.

4

Darren woke up with his belly growling hungrily and the need to pee. When he started to get up, he winced and then stopped. His injuries weren't life-threatening, but they were enough to make him suffer. He needed some antibiotics and a warm, dry place to rest. He wasn't going to get either one here.

Cursing his luck, he finally crawled out from under the tree where he'd slept and got to his feet. He stood for a few minutes, trying to realign himself with the direction in which he'd been going last night. Once he'd figured it out, he clapped his hands together three times in succession then started moving. He guessed that the crash site had been located by now, but it would take the searchers a while to realize they were missing three passengers from the manifest. His plan was to get back to the crash site before noon and spend the night in a nice warm bed. He could have amnesia, which would keep him from having to explain himself in any way, and that would be that.

He thought and planned as he continued to walk, and when he finally relocated two different sets of prints, one of an adult with small feet and one of a child, paralleling the ravine, he knew his luck had changed. He didn't know how far ahead of him they were, but he still had a trail to follow, and that was all that counted.

Molly Cifelli woke suddenly. The rapid movement sent pain shooting through her side and back. She moaned, which roused the little boy beside her.

He woke up screaming. Molly put her arms around him and held him until he stopped.

"It's okay, Johnny, it's okay," she kept saying. "It's me, Molly. I'm right here."

Finally his cries diminished to the occasional whimper. She held him close and rocked him in her lap until there was, once again, silence inside the cave where they'd slept.

As he quieted, she glanced outside. It was daylight. She wanted to believe that the killer hadn't followed them, but she couldn't take that chance. They were as helpless out here as babies, and it was a feeling she didn't like. She cupped Johnny's face with her hands, making him focus on her and her questions.

"Do you hurt anywhere?"

He shrugged.

"I don't know about you, but I need to go to the bathroom. I'll go first, then you can go, okay?"

This time he looked up.

"Okay."

"Wait right here," she said. "I'm going to be right outside the mouth of the cave. You can talk to me all the time if you want."

"I won't cry," he said.

Molly hugged him.

"It's all right if you do," she said. "I feel like crying sometimes, too."

Johnny sighed, but he relaxed and said nothing more as she disappeared outside.

"I'm still here," she called out.

"Okay," he said.

She hurried, then told him to come outside.

"Your turn," she said when he came out quickly.

She pointed toward some bushes, and he went behind them. When he came out, Molly was digging through his backpack. She found snacks and boxes of fruit juice.

"Would you like to pick out what we eat?"

Johnny looked interested. Being back in control, if only choosing food, was apparently a good thing for him. He eyed her silently, then glanced at the food she'd laid out, chose two boxes of tropical fruit juice and two packages of cheese crackers.

"Just what I wanted," Molly said, and gave him a quick hug as he laid the food in her lap.

They ate quickly and in silence. Molly kept looking nervously about until Johnny caught on to what was happening.

"Is the bad man going to catch us?" he asked.

"No, darling, no," she said, but the moment she said it, she knew she was telling a lie. She didn't know what was going to happen to them, but she feared for their future.

"Are you finished eating?" she asked.

He nodded.

"So am I. I think we should start walking again. We need to find some help today."

"What if we don't?" Johnny asked.

Tears blurred Molly's vision, but she wouldn't let herself cry.

"We will—we have to. You're going to help by remembering that we need to be quiet. Just in case that man *is* following us."

"The man who killed his friend?"

Molly sighed. God, this was an awful thing for this little boy to be going through, but it was what it was, and the truth might be what kept him alive.

"Yes, that man."

"Is he going to kill us, too?" he asked.

She hesitated, then frowned.

"I won't let him, okay?"

Johnny looked at her for a long moment, then threw his arms around her neck and hugged her.

She hugged him back, feeling his cold little body and the fierce grip with which he held her. It was called trust. He'd given it blindly and in desperation. She would protect it—and him—with her life.

A short while later they left the cave. Molly was a realist. Even though they were on the move again, she knew she was hurt in some way that was eventually going to stop them. She had to get them to safety before that happened.

The O'Ryans heard an ambulance as it raced past the motel. It was their first sign that the crash site had been located, and an investigation and search were in progress. It ended the reunion.

"Let's get out of here," Evan said, and grabbed his backpack.

"I'll drive," Mike offered.

Evan gladly handed the keys to his dad. He wouldn't admit it, but he was drained, both emotionally and physically. Ever since the phone call from his grandpop, he'd been sick to his stomach, thinking of the horror his little boy was going through—imagining him afraid and injured. He wouldn't let himself think that Johnny had not survived. His grandmother had warned them to "help the boy." That had to mean Johnny was still alive, didn't it?

The drive toward the crash site took them north down the main street and then straight up the mountain. Rescue trucks, cars with government logos, investigators from the FAA and all the medical personnel from the surrounding areas had been called into service. Their presence was already evident as the O'Ryans passed through Carlisle. When they started up the mountain, the unusual amount of traffic on the old road was marked by deep ruts in the still-falling snow.

The family reunion at the motel had been warm and exuberant—like a shared relief in seeing a familiar face. But after warm hugs and unshed tears, they were oddly silent during the ride to the site. They each had their own memories of the little boy who was the youngest link in their chain, but no one voiced the fear they all shared. Thinking it was difficult enough—giving voice to the possibility that Johnny O'Ryan had perished was impossible.

Today Mike felt used up and worthless. The Gulf War had been the last straw in his first marriage. The failure had been hard to bear, but the marriage had given him his only son. That he'd been given sole custody had been his saving grace. It had gotten him through a second failed marriage a few years later and kept him from a succession of empty flings after that. In the back of his mind, he'd always had Evan to think of first. Even after Evan had married right out of high school, Mike had stayed close. When his daughter-in-law died, he'd moved into Evan's house temporarily and helped take care of both his son and grandson until Evan had been able to cope.

Once again Evan needed him, only now there was nothing he could do, and he hated the helplessness of it all. Evan was hurting. He was hurting. They were all sick to their stomachs over what they might learn at the crash site, but it was out of their control.

James O'Ryan sat in the backseat beside his father, Thorn. His mother, Marcella, had been dead for years. Six months ago he'd finally given up and had his own wife, Trudy, admitted to a place where Alzheimer patients went to die. His son hadn't been married for years, and Evan was a widower. He frowned at the thought. What was it with the O'Ryan men that was so deadly for their women? They survived wars and grew old alone. Their women left or died young, whether in spirit or in body.

James made himself quit thinking of Trudy and shoved a shaky hand through his hair, absently disrupting the silver-gray spikes and wishing he could scrub away the thoughts of what might be happening to Johnny.

As they kept driving up the mountain, there was a sheriff's car at the side of the road, obviously stuck in the ditch, but no sign of any officers. James could only imagine the frustration the officer must have felt, having to thumb a ride the rest of the way up. He eyed the stuck cruiser as they passed, then focused his attention on the road ahead.

"Hey, Mike…this may be as far as they let us go," he said, pointing to the welter of parked official vehicles and the webbing of yellow crime scene tape that had been strung through the trees to the left of the road up ahead, and the two uniformed officers who were standing in the road.

"Like hell," Mike muttered, and kept driving without any sign of slowing down.

They all knew Mike's penchant for butting heads with authority, so no one argued when he accelerated and sped past the angry officers, quickly covering the legs of their pants with flying mud and snow.

"They aren't going to like that," Evan said.

Mike glanced up once in the rearview mirror, squinting slightly as he watched the officers grabbing handheld radios as they ran toward their car.

"I'd say they already don't," he drawled, and returned his attention to driving.

"They're going to make us go back," Thorn said.

"Gonna have to catch us first," Mike said, pulling to a skidding halt beside the road. They quickly grabbed their gear and headed into the woods, angling back down in the direction of the site, based on where all the emerging vehicles and the crime scene tape were set up.

Silence reigned as they hiked, saving their breath to make better speed, until Evan drew a deep, shaky breath.

"I'm scared," he said softly.

James patted his grandson on the shoulder.

"We're all scared, Evan, but we'll get through this together."

Evan nodded, although he wasn't sure he agreed, and turned to stare blindly ahead. He didn't know when it first registered that he was seeing debris from the crash, but when it did, shock washed over him. He pulled at the black eye patch over his left eye in frustration, as if that would somehow expand the scope of his vision.

"Dad," Evan said.

"I see," Mike muttered.

Evan was shaking and didn't even know it. All he could think was that his little boy could be in pieces, just like this. "Oh God, oh God," he whispered.

The rest of them remained silent. What could they say in the face of this much destruction?

Suddenly Mike stopped, almost slipping on the treacherous slope.

Evan's focus shifted, then he exhaled in frustration.

Two armed guards were standing in the trees, blocking their path. Without waiting for them to approach, he started striding toward them.

The patch on his eye, his pale skin and the slight drag of his left leg seemed to slightly ease the tension the two guards were feeling. All they'd known was that a rental car with four men had run a roadblock down the hill, then been located by the roadside, abandoned. But this man didn't appear to be threatening. However, when the other three men approached in his wake, the guards raised their weapons at the ready.

"Sir!" the first guard said. "You need to turn around and go back the way you came."

"My son was on that plane," Evan said.

Both guards relaxed. Family. Sometimes they did things like this, although coming to the actual site of the crash was unusual.

"I'm sorry, sir," the guard said. "I understand your concern, but I'm afraid I'll have to ask you to leave."

"Are you married?" Evan asked.

A bit startled, the guard nodded. "Yes."

"Children?" Evan asked.

"Two boys," the guard answered.

"Were they on that plane?" Evan asked.

The guard's gaze wavered, then dropped. "No."

Evan drew a deep, shaky breath. "Then you *don't* understand my concern. My wife is dead, and what you see of me is all the Iraqis left intact. I haven't seen my son in more than a year. He was coming home for

Christmas. I am not leaving this mountain without him. Do you understand what I'm saying?"

The guard sighed. Damn. Not only a grieving father, but a soldier, as well. He reached for his radio and pressed the button.

"Sir? This is Grady. Can you send someone up here?"

"Not in this fucking lifetime," a voice with a distinct Cajun accent answered.

Mike O'Ryan, who'd been silent until now, suddenly grinned like a wolf. "You tell that Cajun Popsicle to get his frozen butt up here, ASAP."

The guard looked startled, and from the cursing that came back over the radio, the man on the other end of the line had heard everything Mike O'Ryan said. The guard yanked the radio back up to his ear as he glared at Mike.

Mike stuck his hands in the pockets of his coat and rocked on his heels while the rest of the men stared in disbelief. Mike was a rebel, but it wasn't like him to be rude.

"Uh…sir…yes, sir," the guard said, and then signed off before pointing at Evan. "You and your mouthy friend, stay right where you are."

"Glad we understand each other," Evan said, and shoved his hands in his pockets, too.

Snow continued to feather down around them, drifting weightlessly through the still, cold air.

James glanced at his father. Thorn was the eldest, but by no means in need of coddling. Mike was standing with his gaze fixed on the trees below. James couldn't imagine what had gotten into him, but it wasn't the first time he'd gotten them all into a tight spot with his volatile temper.

Suddenly Mike's posture changed. James followed Mike's gaze to the bright yellow snowmobiles that were zigzagging through the trees toward them.

"Mike…"

Mike glanced at his father. "What?"

"Don't lose your cool."

"In this weather? Impossible," Mike said.

Evan tensed, then moved toward his dad. Whatever happened, they were in this together.

"It's all right, son," Mike said. "I've got this covered."

"I've got your back," Evan said softly.

Mike's smile slipped sideways as his eyes filled with tears. "I know that, son, and I've got yours. Now, rest easy. It's not what you think."

At that moment the snowmobiles came to a sliding halt. The man who got out of the lead vehicle was huge, both in height and girth. His hair was black, as was his beard, and it crossed Evan's mind that the man resembled the caricature of the giant in Johnny's *Jack and the Beanstalk* storybook.

The big man paused, scanning the crowd. When his gaze fell on Mike O'Ryan, he started walking toward him, cursing with every step.

Mike headed toward him, grinning.

"Is that the best you can do, you hairy ox? Damn it,

man, don't they have any soap and razors back in Natchez?"

Then they both started laughing, and thumping each other on the back. Finally it was the Cajun who pulled back.

"What the fucking hell are you doing on my mountain?" he asked.

Mike pointed to Evan.

"Evan…this is Antoine Devereaux. We were in the Gulf together. Tony…this is my son, Evan." Then he pointed to the men behind him. "The big man with the white hair and rock star hairdo is my dad, James, and the good-looking one is my granddad, Thorn." His smile slipped. "My grandson…Evan's boy, Johnny…was a passenger on that plane."

Tony Devereaux sighed. "You know you can't be here."

"But we *are* here," Mike said. "You know our backgrounds. You know our training. We're not going to get in your way. We're not going to disturb the investigation. We just came to get our boy."

Tony lifted his eyes to the heavens, then closed them briefly against the pain of what he was going to say. Then he looked back at Mike.

"My friend…and you know that you are…there are no survivors."

Evan felt the ground go out from under him. He would have fallen had it not been for the quick thinking of Mike and Tony. Almost instantly, he began fighting against their grip, trying to get free.

"Don't," he said. "I'm fine. I just need to get Johnny."

Mike's eyes were swimming in tears, but he couldn't let go of his grief for worrying about Evan.

"Evan…you heard what Tony—"

Evan turned on his father, his face contorted in anger.

"Stop!" he cried. "You know what Grandpop said. Why would Marcella tell us to 'help the boy' if he was already gone?"

Thorn's shock at the news began to lessen. Evan was right.

"He's right," Thorn said. "Marcella told me to 'help the boy,' not bury him. We need to see the body. Could we see the body?"

Tony sighed.

"Look, we just started pulling victims out of the wreckage about an hour ago, and we're still not through."

"Just let us look," Mike begged.

Tony tugged at his beard as he watched the play of emotions on their faces. But it was the look of anger on the young father's that helped him make up his mind. If the situation were reversed, he would be just like Evan—furious that God had dared let this happen, and in disbelief until he'd seen with his own eyes.

"I can't have all of you traipsing around up there."

"Dad and I will stay here," James offered.

Thorn nodded in agreement.

"Fine," Tony said, then pointed at Mike and Evan. "Pretend you belong there. Don't freak out at the blood and—"

"I don't freak," Evan snapped.

"He's been in Iraq," Mike explained.

Tony looked at the scars on the young man's face and the patch over his eye, and then sighed. Evan had probably seen far worse than what was up on the mountain. He pointed to the snowmobiles. Each one held two people, and he pointed to the men in them and told everyone but the second driver to get out. Then he turned to Mike and Evan and said, "Get in."

Mike and Evan did as they were told and rode, without speaking, to the site of impact.

The rows of blanket-covered bodies were growing as the rescuers carried additional bodies out of the fuselage and laid them out beside the others. Evan's frantic gaze swept the rows as he looked for one much smaller than the rest.

"Come with me," Tony said as they got out.

They followed silently.

"Do you know where he was sitting?" Tony asked.

"With his grandparents. Their names are…were… Pollard. Frank and Shirley Pollard. His name is Johnny O'Ryan."

Tony moved to a nearby table underneath an open tent and picked up a clipboard.

"Passenger manifest," he explained as he scanned the list.

"Yeah…here are the names," he said, then looked up at Evan and frowned. "I'm sorry to have to tell you, but they've already been located."

Evan's heart sank. "Can I see them?" he asked.

Tony glanced at Mike, who nodded.

"Yeah, sure. This way," Tony said, and then reminded him, "Keep it quiet, man. You're not supposed to be here."

Evan didn't answer, but the tightness in his jaw and the glitter in his eye were answer enough.

Tony checked the list again, making a mental note of the numbers that had been assigned to the deceased in question, and then walked between the rows of victims until he came to the right place. He looked up at Evan.

"You still okay?"

"Just let me see," Evan muttered.

Tony lifted the blankets from both faces.

Evan flinched, but that was all.

"That's them."

Tony dropped the blankets back in place.

"Now, where's Johnny?" Evan asked.

"He hasn't been found yet," Tony said. "When he is, we'll let you know."

"He would have been with them. If that plane was going down, they would have had him in their arms."

Tony frowned. "Look, son…I hear your frustration, but in a crash like this, bodies can be anywhere, and children rarely have identification on them."

"Then let me look at the children you *have* found," Evan said.

"So far, just two girls," Tony said.

The knot in Evan's belly eased just the slightest bit. "Are you searching for survivors in the outlying areas?" he asked.

"We'll search until everyone has been accounted for. It's still early days," Tony said.

"He's alive," Evan said. "I know it."

Mike wanted to believe him, but the devastation of this crash was hard to get past. The debris seemed to be scattered over a quarter of a mile, which meant a body could have fallen out of the plane at any time.

"Why didn't it burn?" Mike asked.

"Part of it did," Tony said. "The wings came off on impact a ways back in the trees and burned. There's not much left of those. You can see from the skid marks how far the belly slid before it stopped. The tail section came off about a hundred yards from the wings. All of that burned, as well."

Mike blanched, thinking of Johnny being ripped from his grandparents' arms—screaming in pain and fear as fire engulfed him. "Jesus," he muttered, then looked away.

But Evan didn't waver. "He's not here. He's not dead." Tony sighed.

Evan shook his head. "He's not dead, I tell you."

Before anyone could argue the point further, Evan felt a touch on his arm. He turned around to find himself eye to eye with a tall, slender woman who stood steadfast and shivering from the cold.

"He's right, you know. The child isn't dead...and neither is the young woman with him," she said.

"What are you talking about?" Mike asked.

Tony had a different question altogether. "God Almighty, lady, where did you come from?"

She pointed north up the mountain.

"What the fuck are you doing down here?" Tony asked, making no apologies for his language.

"I came to help," she said. "A young woman and a child are lost up there."

Tony threw up his hands. "And how do you know that?"

"I saw them. They're in the woods, and they're in danger."

Evan grabbed her by the arm. "You saw them?"

Deborah flinched. Normally she didn't like being touched, but he'd taken her by surprise. She pulled away without making a fuss, though she really wanted to scream. There was so much pain associated with this young man that she could hardly breathe. All she could do was nod.

"Where? Why didn't you bring them with you?" Evan asked.

Deborah braced herself. This was where it always got tricky.

"I don't know exactly where they are, but I can lead you to them," she said.

Mike didn't know what she was up to, but this crap she was dishing out was making him nuts. He grabbed her by the arm and all but shook her in frustration.

"Lady! You saw them, but you went off and left them? Are you crazy?"

From the moment of contact, Deborah couldn't take her eyes off this man's face. She didn't know who he was, or his name, or if she would ever see him again.

But she knew that within the next few days, they would make love. The knowledge was startling for a woman who had only been with two men in her entire life, the last one almost twelve years ago.

"Answer me!" Mike said. "What the hell is the matter with you?"

"I haven't physically found them yet. But I can," she added.

"I don't understand," Evan muttered.

Deborah Sanborn sighed. Few ever did.

"My name is Deborah. Deborah Sanborn," she added. "And I saw them last night—in a vision."

Tony threw up his hands. "Oh, for the love of Christ! A fucking psychic. Get off my mountain, lady, and get off fast, before I have you arrested."

Deborah flashed the big man an angry look.

"Look, mister, I don't know who you are, but I can guarantee that this mountain is more mine than yours. I've lived up here all my life, and I don't know you from Adam. However, if you're referring to the crash site, I have no intention of interfering with your investigation. I came to help a man find his little boy, and I'm not going home until I do."

As Tony stood toe to toe with the woman, there was a piece of Mike that actually admired her guts. Antoine Deveraux would have given a grizzly pause for thought, yet she hadn't moved an inch. Before any more words could fly, another man appeared, and he was sporting a badge and wearing a gun.

"Hey, Deb…what are you doin' to my investigator,

here?" Then, without waiting for an answer, he turned to the O'Ryans and introduced himself. "Hello, people. Name's Wally Hacker. I'm the county sheriff, and I'm pretty sure you aren't supposed to be here."

"I brought them up—but not *her*. You know this crazy woman?" Tony asked.

"Yeah, I know Deb. Everyone around here knows Deb." Then he looked at her and winked.

She glared.

Evan didn't care who knew who. This was the first person who'd given him any hope since the phone call from his grandpop last night. He wasn't about to ignore it.

"Skip the social amenities," Evan said as he watched Deborah's face. "You swear Johnny is still alive?"

"Yes."

The knot in Evan's belly tightened. "And you really can help me find him?"

"Yes."

"When do we leave?"

"Damn it, Evan, wait!" Mike said.

Evan turned, staring at his dad in disbelief. "For what?"

Mike bit the inside of his lip to keep from throttling this woman. Who the hell did she think she was, giving people false hope? He glared at her.

She stared back unflinchingly.

His nostrils flared. Damn. Okay, so the crazy woman believed herself. That didn't mean he had to. He turned back to the sheriff.

"You said you know her?"

Wally Hacker grinned at Deborah as he answered Mike.

"Yeah. Went to school with her."

"So what do you think about her claiming to have visions?"

Hacker shrugged. "Well…let's see. I reckon she's had dozens during the time I been sheriff, and they've all been on the money. She was right a few days back when a local decided to kick the living hell out of his wife. Deborah 'saw' it and called me. The man's in jail, and his wife's in the hospital, as we speak. As for the crash, she called me before daylight this morning to tell me it had happened. Looks like she was right again."

Mike frowned. It wasn't what he'd expected to hear.

"You mean she claimed to have 'seen' this plane crash? That's hardly surprising, considering her claim to live nearby."

"It's not nearby," Deborah said, and pointed. "It's almost eleven miles that way, and I didn't 'see' the crash. I saw a boy and a young woman lost on the mountain. I saw them in danger. It wasn't until I started backtracking the vision that I saw the crash."

Mike still wasn't buying it.

"How come they let you on the site when they didn't want to let us?" he asked.

"No one let me in. I walked down…from up there."

Mike's mouth dropped as he stared up the mountain.

"You *walked* here? Eleven miles?"

"It's easier walking downhill. Besides, I started before daylight."

Mike's opinion of her changed. She'd made a monumental physical effort to get here. There had to be something in this for her. Then he keyed in on what she'd just said.

"What do you mean…'backtracking the vision'?"

"I see the immediate, then I see what got them there. Sort of like watching a movie in rewind."

"Bull," Mike muttered. "Okay, so that's your story. It still doesn't mean you're a psychic."

"Look," Deborah said, "I don't care whether you believe me or not, but what do you have to lose?"

Mike's eyes narrowed. "And what do you charge for this…service?"

"Nothing," she said. "But for you, I could be persuaded to make an exception."

The sheriff laughed. "Deb, quit pullin' their legs, now."

Evan threw up his hands in defeat. "Will all of you just shut the hell up? I want to find my son. Will you help me?"

"Of course," she said. "By any chance…do you have anything with you that belongs to your son?"

Evan started to say no, then remembered. Elmo. He'd brought Johnny's Elmo.

"Yeah, I do."

Mike rolled his eyes.

"Oh, hell, son. If you're bound and determined to do this, you know I'm coming with you, but Dad's gonna

want to come, too. You sit tight. I'll go get him and send
Grandpop back to the motel in the process."

"Can I take one of those snowmobiles?" Mike asked
Tony, and when the big man nodded, he started back to
the vehicle at a jog.

As Mike was leaving, Sheriff Hacker's radio
squawked. He answered.

"Hacker here. What's up? Over."

"Sheriff, they're sayin' there ain't no more bodies,
but the count is off. Over."

The rhythm of Evan's heartbeat skipped.

"Off by how many? Over." Hacker asked.

"Three. They've got a woman and a child unac-
counted for, and a senator. Over."

"What are the names? Over," Hacker asked.

"Molly Cifelli. Johnny O'Ryan. And the senator's
name is Darren Wilson. Over."

Hacker's eyebrows arched as he wrote down the names.

Evan looked at Deborah. He didn't understand how
this was going to work, but he was grateful that she was
there. He eyed the big Cajun, who was still glowering.

"So, Mr. Devereaux, when are you going to start a
search?"

Tony gestured at the sky.

"We can't search by air until the snow lets up, and it
will take some time to organize a ground search."

Evan cursed. "By that time, my son could have
frozen to death."

"I can find them," Deborah said.

"As soon as Dad gets back, you're on," Evan said.

5

Deborah was nursing a hot cup of coffee, compliments of Sheriff Hacker, when she saw Mike O'Ryan returning, accompanied by another man. Deborah's eyes widened briefly. She could tell without introduction that he, too, was an O'Ryan, just older and taller than the two she'd already met.

This one was wearing a navy-blue sock cap, a heavy winter coat and boots similar to Mike's and Evan's, but his backpack was a well-worn olive drab. She'd overheard Evan telling Sheriff Hacker that all the O'Ryan men had military backgrounds. The big Cajun from the FAA had corroborated the story by adding one of his own about how Mike O'Ryan had saved his life during the Gulf War.

Reluctantly, she got out of the cruiser, dumped what was left of her coffee on the ground and picked up her own pack. By the time the two men approached her, she had it settled comfortably on her back.

The one they called Mike was intriguing. She didn't hold his opinion of psychics against him. Nearly everyone she came in contact with had a similar reaction. Still, if he glared at her too many more times, a few well-chosen words about what she saw in his past would probably bring him up to speed.

However, Evan—who walked up at just that moment—was another matter. She eyed him carefully. It was obvious that he was still recovering from severe injuries, but he would stay the course. The glint in his eye and the set of his jaw were proof enough to her that he would do whatever it took to find his child.

Just then the sheriff reappeared from the other side of a pile of wreckage.

"Hey, Wally, thanks for the coffee," she said.

"Any time," Hacker said, then eyed her carefully. "While you're out there, remember we're missing three souls, not two."

"I know," she said, remembering the danger she'd sensed was following the woman and the child. It could mean anything from them being in danger from the freezing weather to some animal. She just wasn't sure. She could say something about it, but it was so vague that she decided against it for now.

"You got your cell phone?" Hacker asked.

"Yes, but it's not going to work in the mountains, and you know it."

"So what are you going to do if you need help?"

"I'll just look into my crystal ball and bypass future difficulties."

Hacker grinned, then turned to the three men who stood beside her. As he did, his grin vanished.

"I don't know you people, but I'm taking it on face value that you're all on the up-and-up. 'Cause if you're not, and you do one thing to hurt Deborah Sanborn, I'll make you sorry…all of you. Understand?"

"Yes, sir," Evan said.

Deborah was a bit surprised and oddly grateful to Wally for standing up for her. It didn't happen often and she was touched by his concern. She eyed the three men carefully. They looked at her without comment.

"Evan…isn't it?" she asked.

"Yes, ma'am," Evan said.

"You said you had something that belonged to your boy?"

"Yes, ma'am, that I do," he said, and shrugged off his backpack, then dug through it.

When he handed Deborah the red Elmo doll, she was immediately thrown into the past. She didn't know that her eyes gave away her lack of focus, but Mike saw it. Despite the fact that he didn't believe in psychics, he couldn't help wondering what was happening with her. Whatever she was looking at right now, it damn sure wasn't that stuffed toy.

Deborah's fingers curled into the soft belly of the toy, watching the laughter of a young mother at a little boy's first Christmas. Seeing a far different version of Evan O'Ryan holding his son and kissing his wife under a sprig of mistletoe. Watching a much younger Johnny sleeping with Elmo for a pillow.

She frowned. It wasn't the past that she wanted. She needed to tune in on Johnny now. Frustrated, she stuffed the doll down inside the front of her eiderdown coat, then pulled the zipper up as she turned to the men.

"Is this all of you?" she asked.

"I sent Grandpop back to the motel," Mike said.

She eyed Evan. "It will be rough going."

"I can do it," he said.

She nodded. "Then let's go."

"Wait!" Mike said.

She paused, waiting for him to speak.

"How will you know where to go?" he asked.

She thought of the silent, emotional pull of the lost souls. How do you explain that to non-believers? She couldn't. So she patted the bulge underneath her coat.

"Elmo will tell me."

"Jesus," Mike muttered.

"Yes, and Him, too," she added, then turned her back on the men and started walking. She didn't have to turn around to see if they were following. She could hear Mike O'Ryan muttering every step of the way.

Molly woke up with a gasp and for a moment couldn't remember where she was, but when Johnny stirred and burrowed a little deeper into the warm nest she'd made for him in her arms, it hit her.

They'd been in a plane crash and were hiding from a killer.

It felt like a nightmare, but she was awake, and the truth still weighed heavily on her shoulders. She looked around, remembering as she did that Johnny had become hysterical, so they'd taken shelter beneath some tree limbs. She'd held him and talked to him until he'd fallen asleep in her lap. Even though she knew they needed to keep moving, he had been physically and emotionally unable to continue, and she wasn't strong enough to carry him.

Now, from the shift in the angle of the light and the shadows on the floor of the forest, she was guessing it was midafternoon. Most likely the crash site had been located earlier today. It was probably crawling with all sorts of people. If she knew which direction to go to get back there, she would take Johnny now. But she didn't, and she had no way of knowing if the killer was following them. If she started back and ran into him before she found the plane, there was every chance that they wouldn't live to see another day. While she was contemplating their options, Johnny O'Ryan opened his eyes and screamed.

Molly's heart gave a hard thump as she tightened her hold.

"Easy, honey. It's me. Molly. Remember?"

Johnny was shaking as he sat up, then tightened his arms around her.

"We fell out of the sky, didn't we?" he asked.

Molly tightened her own arms around him and hugged him close.

"Yes, but we're okay. It's past noon. Are you hungry? Do you need to go to the bathroom?"

He nodded yes to both, and the next few minutes were devoted to relieving themselves, then washing their hands in the snow. Under the circumstances, it was the best they could do.

Molly rummaged through the backpack for food while Johnny sat cross-legged on one of the blankets. She handed him a box of juice that she'd already opened, then a couple of packets of peanuts.

"It's not exactly McDonald's, but it's food, right?"

He took it without comment, tore into the peanuts, then began to eat. Every now and then he would take a sip of the juice, then look up at her, judging her expression against the overwhelming sadness in the pit of his stomach.

Molly saw the tears in his eyes, but to his credit, they never fell. He was a tough little kid. If the truth were known, he was probably holding it together better than she was. She was scared half out of her mind, and if she ever started crying, she wasn't sure she would be able to stop.

When they'd eaten their peanuts and finished the juice, Molly left the trash in a pile under the trees where they'd been lying, then folded up the blankets. There was a bead of juice at the corner of Johnny's mouth. She wiped it away with her thumb, then gently smoothed his hair from his forehead.

"So, Johnny…I think we'd better get moving, don't you?"

He looked at her for a moment, then leaned forward as his arms slid around her neck.

Molly felt him trembling. She knew exactly how he felt.

"Are you scared?" she asked.

"Will the man kill us, too?"

She wrapped her arms around his little body and pulled him close.

"No, baby, he's not going to kill us. I won't let him, okay?"

He was silent for a few moments, then finally nodded. "Okay."

"So let's get moving," Molly said.

They stood up, only to find that it was starting to snow again. Molly said a silent prayer as she took Johnny's hand, reoriented her inner compass and set off downhill in what she thought was a southwesterly direction.

But the clouds soon hid the sun, and the snow fell fast and thick. Hours passed, and she lost her sense of direction. She knew they were in trouble when she realized that they'd passed the same split tree twice. She stopped, staring in disbelief and wondering what the odds might be of two lightning-struck trees that looked the same.

Oh, no. Oh, Lord help us...we've been going in circles.

She looked down at Johnny. He looked so cold and so small, but thankfully didn't seem to realize what a predicament they were in.

"How about we rest for a while?" she asked.

He nodded wearily.

She could only imagine how tired his little legs were. He'd had to take two steps to her every one and yet had somehow managed to keep up. She leaned down and pulled the hood of his coat a little farther down on his head, although there was no way she could get them warmer.

She turned in a semicircle, scanning the area for a place to take shelter—at least until this latest snowstorm had passed. She thought of the cave they'd spent the night in, but had no idea where it was. The trees were thick, but the underbrush was sparse. Taking shelter there would be like standing in the open. Not enough limbs at their level to make a good windbreak. Still, she had to find something.

Johnny tugged at her hand, then pointed at the split tree.

"What, honey?" Molly asked.

"In there," Johnny said. "We can make a house in there."

Molly stared. At first she didn't see what he was talking about, and then she realized he was pointing to the bare branches of the fallen tree. Using a little imagination, Molly could see how the network of branches had formed the skeletal shape of a roof. If it was covered, the small space beneath would be a good place to wait out the storm.

Molly dropped her backpack and began grabbing at the lower branches of the evergreens, pulling in fierce, frantic jerks until they peeled away from their trunks.

"Like this, Johnny. Help me put them like this."

She began jabbing the pine branches through the framework of dead limbs, filling in spaces, then ran back to the trees, pulling off more small pliable limbs, which Johnny quickly poked through the holes until they had put a roof on their new shelter.

Molly's gloves were sticky with sap and pine needles as she thrust the last armful of branches through some thinner places. Johnny was already underneath, brushing away the snow from under the new roof. By the time Molly dragged a big armful of pine boughs and their backpacks in with her, Johnny had cleaned the entire floor area.

"Hey, Johnny! Good job!" she said as she spread the boughs out at the back of the shelter.

Johnny almost smiled, then ducked his head and pulled his knees up beneath his chin.

Molly purposefully ignored his withdrawal and pulled the blankets out of her backpack.

"Here, honey…help me," she said, then spread out the blankets over the boughs.

When they were finished, she pulled his backpack into her lap and dug through the contents, judging their meager food supply against how long it might take before they were found. There were several more packets of nuts, a couple of small bottles of water, four boxes of juice and a handful of granola bars.

"We need to eat. Think you could do that?"

Johnny nodded.

"How about a granola bar?" Molly asked, and then began peeling back the paper.

Johnny took the bar, then paused, looked at it, then up at Molly. She smiled, hoping he would be encouraged by her lack of panic, when in truth she had never been as afraid as she was right now. She was the adult here. She felt obligated to get them through this, but she didn't have the first idea of how to make that happen. While she was going out of her mind, Johnny quietly broke the snack bar in half and handed part of it back to her. Molly was taken aback by his generosity and his understanding of their situation.

"Thank you, honey," she said softly, and took a small bite. Johnny followed suit, then together they ate, sharing the juice box, as well.

When they were done, Molly laid the backpack aside. As she did, something fell out of a small side pocket.

"Hey, what's this?" she said, as she pulled a small whistle and chain out of the leaves and snow.

"It's my whistle," Johnny said. "Daddy gave it to me when I was a little kid. I think I was three."

Molly stifled a smile. Two years later and he no longer considered himself a little kid. She suspected he came from a long line of very macho men.

"It's a cool whistle. What's it for?"

"For if I get lost from him," he said. "Like in the grocery store or at the mall or something."

Molly's estimation of the absent father rose a notch. Smart dad.

"That's a really good idea," she said. "Maybe you could wear this around your neck."

Johnny put it over his head. "Yeah…'cause we're lost, aren't we?"

Molly tried not to cry. "Yes, I think we are."

"It will be okay," Johnny said. "I can blow my whistle until somebody finds us."

Molly eyes filled with tears. This just wasn't fair. They'd survived a plane crash, only to witness a murder. The worst thing they could have done was leave the scene of the crash, but they'd had no choice. Molly was convinced that they would have wound up like that man—what was his name? Patrick. His name had been Patrick. He'd survived, too, but not for long.

She glanced at Johnny. His little face was red and chapped from the cold, but he didn't complain. She couldn't bear to tell him that they might not be found at all, or that if they did take a chance and blow the whistle, it could lead the killer, not their rescuers, to them.

"Let's roll up in the blankets, okay?"

Johnny readily agreed.

Molly shuffled some of the pine boughs around until she'd made them a nest; then she pulled the two blankets up over them, tucked in the edges all the way around and pulled Johnny up as close to her as she could. His head was right beneath her chin and his little backside rested in the curve of her lap. Molly wrapped her arms around him and gave him a quick squeeze.

"You're a pretty good sleeping buddy. Did you know that?"

"That's what Daddy says."

Molly was surprised.

"He does?"

"Yeah. It's because I don't kick in my sleep."

Molly smiled to herself.

"Well, that's good to know. Now…are you okay? Not lying on any rocks?"

"No," Johnny said.

"Okay…well, we'll just rest for a while and then see how it goes."

"I'll blow my whistle a couple times first," he said, and matched the action to the words before she could stop him.

Molly bit the inside of her cheek to keep from bawling. She hoped their pursuer was too far away to hear, because there was no way they could keep going without a rest. So she said a quiet prayer for God to keep them safe and tried to keep her mind off her misery. As Johnny slowly relaxed and fell asleep in her arms, she kept watch, praying for rescue and listening for danger.

The snow continued to fall, slowly covering the pine boughs until, from outside, their shelter took on the appearance of a small snowdrift.

Darren Wilson was not just in trouble for gambling and murder, he was in serious pain. The best he could tell, he had a couple of cracked ribs and something wrong with his right knee—maybe a torn ligament. Whatever it was, it hurt like hell to walk.

But he couldn't stay still. If he did, he would freeze. Besides, he was out here in these damned woods because of that woman and kid. He needed to find them even worse than he needed money to pay off his gambling debts.

As he stood within the silence of the snowfall, he realized he could barely see out of his right eye and only a bit more out of his left. He'd been following the tracks he'd found in the forest just fine up until about an hour ago. That was when it had started to snow again, filling up the tracks and blanketing the surrounding area.

At any other time he might have appreciated the pristine beauty of it, but not now. Once again he was losing track of where the woman and kid had gone, and once again it was getting dark. This would be the second night he'd spent out in this god-awful weather—and without food or water.

What had angered him most was the pile of juice boxes and snack food wrappers he'd found beneath a tree. Obviously the woman had taken food from the plane. If only he'd had as much foresight, he might not be quite as miserable.

"I would give a year of my life for a bottle of Extra Strength Tylenol," he muttered as he resumed his trek while he could still see.

He didn't know how he was going to do the woman and kid in once he found them, but he did know it had to be done. There was no reason for them to have fled the scene of the crash unless they had witnessed him killing Patrick Finn.

He knew the crash site was most likely a beehive of activity today. He also knew that the FAA would soon figure out they were three bodies short compared to the names on the passenger list. The only positive thing about this whole mess was that an all-out search would be difficult to impossible in this snowstorm. That gave him extra time to find his quarry before the searchers did.

He pulled the collar of his heavy coat up over his
ears, hunched his shoulders, zipped and unzipped his
coat three times, then cursed himself for the need to do
so before resuming the hunt.

6

The snow was almost a foot deep now and impeding their speed of travel. Even though James was in his sixties, he wasn't having any problems with the depth, but Evan, still recovering from his wounds, was struggling, and it made Mike antsy. His son's physical health and stamina were obviously not up to par. He wished there was a way he could have talked Evan into waiting back at the motel with Thorn, but there was no way he would have insulted his son with the suggestion. It was Evan's son who was missing. He would never be able to stand back and let others look for the most important person in his life. Still, when Evan stumbled in the snow, it was all Mike could do to keep quiet. He started toward Evan, then stopped when he saw Deborah pause and speak to him.

Deborah sensed, rather than saw, Evan falter. She paused, then turned around, pretending she was winded.

"Evan?"

He nodded, too breathless to answer.

"Are you all right? We can slow down if you need to."

"No."

The fear in his eyes was obvious. There was no need to discuss the reason. He needed to find his child.

She glanced at Mike. He was glaring at her. Her first reaction was regret. She didn't know why he was angry at her, when she'd done nothing to cause the situation that they were in, but she hated it, and she knew from experience that only time would help what they were all feeling.

Mike thought he saw her eyes tear up, which surprised him. He hadn't expected that his reluctance to trust her might be painful. The way he looked at it, if she was so dead set in coming with them, then she should be able to put up with whatever was going on. Still, he had to admit that if she was conning them, she most likely would have spoken up in defense of herself before they set out.

Only she hadn't.

He glanced at her again, then looked away. Damn it, he didn't mean to hurt her feelings, but surely she understood. Finding Johnny was a matter of life and death, and they were following a complete stranger who claimed to have psychic powers. It was the craziest thing he'd ever done.

He gritted his teeth, then looked up, refusing to feel guilty. To his surprise, she was still watching him.

"How do you know you're going the right way?" Mike asked.

"Because I do," Deborah answered, then glanced at Evan again. "Are you okay to go?"

"Yes, ma'am, I'm fine," he said.

"Okay, then," Deborah said, and once again led the way.

Mike cursed beneath his breath. He was getting tired of following her orange backpack, as if it were some homing beacon. He would bet money she didn't know what the hell she was doing. Unable to stay silent, he began arguing.

"We've been walking for three hours, and there is no way they could have walked so far away from the plane. They're bound to have some injuries. No one can fall out of the sky and walk away without a scratch. Besides that, darkness would have caught them, and they would have had to stop."

Evan interrupted. "But that was last night, Dad. This is the second day, and it's almost dark again. They're about to spend their second night in this weather, and they could be anywhere."

Mike's eyes narrowed angrily. Without thinking, he surged past Evan and didn't slow down until he came even with Deborah.

"I'm talking to you," he barked.

"Really? I'm sorry," Deborah said.

"Oh, come on now," Mike muttered. "Don't tell me that you're hard of hearing?"

"No, of course not," Deborah said. "I heard you talking, all right. You've done nothing *but* talk since we walked away from the crash site. However, I didn't know you were talking to *me*. So what was the question again?"

Mike opened his mouth just as a limb full of snow

suddenly unloaded down the back of his neck. They all stopped to help brush him off.

"I'm fine, I'm fine," he said, all but pushing everyone away as he shook snow off his coat.

Deborah arched an eyebrow. "You're welcome."

Guilt hit Mike like a blow to the chin. He wouldn't look at his father or his son for fear he would see disgust on both their faces. Truth was, he was sort of disgusted with himself. He didn't know why he was being so combative toward this woman. She'd obviously walked a long way in really bad weather on a mission to help them. Even if he didn't believe her claim of being psychic was worth a damn, he had to give her credit for showing up.

"I'm sorry," he said abruptly. "I've been acting like an ass, and there's no excuse for it."

"It's okay," she said. "Everyone is under a lot of stress." Then her voice softened. "I can't imagine what you must be feeling, but I swear to God, I can help."

There was a long moment of silence, and then Mike took a slow, shaky breath. This time he was the one with tears in his eyes.

"I need a break," James suddenly said.

"Me, too," Evan said, and sat down on a snow-covered log while his grandfather took to the bushes.

Deborah slid the backpack from her shoulders, then sat down and leaned back, resting her head against the trunk of one of the trees. Wearily, she thought of how long it had been since she climbed out of bed, and closed her eyes.

Mike started to look away, then didn't. Instead, he found himself staring at her, noting the heart-shaped face and dark lashes that framed what he knew were a pair of very blue, very expressive, eyes. At first glance, the hair he could see peeking out from under the hood of her coat appeared to be gray or white, but the closer he looked, the more he thought it was a very light blond. His gaze slid to her mouth, eyeing the sensuous curve of her lips. As he watched, snowflakes fell on her skin and lashes. It took him a few moments to realize that they weren't melting. That was when he realized how cold she must be. If her claim was to be believed, then just to get to them, she'd begun her journey down the mountain in the dark to reach the crash site when she had. Then she'd turned around and started out on the search without any real rest or warm-up. Dismayed by her strength of character compared to his own bad behavior, he walked over to her and crouched down until they were eye level.

Deborah heard him coming but refused to look. It wasn't until she felt his hand on her face that her eyes flew open. He was so close that she could see her own reflection in his eyes. Distrusting him, she quickly pushed his hand away. "What are you doing?"

"You're cold."

She frowned. "And that would be a surprise because…?"

He sighed. "I think there's still some hot coffee in a thermos in my pack. Would you like some?"

Deborah stifled a shiver. She was dressed for the

weather, but the coffee sounded like manna from heaven.

"Yes, I would, and thank you."

Mike quickly dug through his backpack, found the small thermos and then poured the contents into the lid, which also served as a cup.

"It's probably not as hot as it should be," he said, and handed it over.

Deborah's gloved hands were shaking as she lifted the cup to her lips. She took a quick sip, then closed her eyes and moaned in quiet ecstasy as the warm liquid slid down her throat. Even though she sugared her own coffee at home until it was close to syrup, this tasted great.

"Mmm, wonderful," she said, and quickly drank the rest before it had a chance to get cold. As soon as the small cup was emptied, she handed it back. "I didn't save you any," she said.

"That's all right," Mike said. "I had plenty this morning."

Then he rocked back on his heels. "Are you for real, lady?"

Deborah smiled.

Mike felt like he'd been sucker punched. When she smiled, her face seemed to glow from within.

"Yes, I'm for real," she said, and then saw James coming out of the trees. She sat up straight and reached for her backpack. "We'd better get—"

The scene before her completely disappeared as she watched a small boy put a whistle to his lips and blow.

She heard two sharp blasts and then nothing. She jumped to her feet. Unaware that she had grabbed at the Elmo doll she'd stuffed down her coat, she began turning in a circle, as if trying to orient what she was seeing with their present location.

The moment she jumped up, Mike followed suit. Now all three men were standing around her, confused by her strange behavior.

"What? What is it?" Evan asked, but Deborah didn't even know they were there.

The vision disappeared as suddenly as it had come. She blinked, then staggered as her world stopped spinning.

"A whistle. He's blowing a whistle."

Evan's face turned as white as the snow. "Oh, God."

Mike grabbed his son by his arm.

"What is it?" he asked.

Evan stared at Deborah. "God in heaven, no one could have guessed at something so obscure. You *are* for real, aren't you?"

"Yes, of course I'm for real," Deborah said. "What does the whistle mean?"

"I gave it to him when he was three so that if we ever got separated when we were buying groceries or out shopping, he could blow it loud and long until I found him."

Mike was dumbfounded. He still didn't believe in psychics. This had to be a trick.

James put his arms around Evan. "So let's go get our boy."

The men looked at Deborah, but she was behaving strangely. She would take a few steps downhill, then stop and turn back, gazing up the slope. She did this a couple more times before Mike grabbed her arm. "What's going on?" he asked.

She looked down the mountain, then frowned. "Something's wrong."

Now Evan was worried again. "Like what?"

"They've been walking in circles," she muttered.

"Jesus," Evan whispered.

"They're going the wrong way," she breathed.

"What do you mean?" Mike asked.

"With the snow and no way to tell where the sun is in the sky, they must have gotten confused."

"Confused? What do you mean by confused?"

Deborah pointed. "Up. They're going up instead of down."

"No way," James said. "Anyone can tell uphill from downhill."

But Deborah wasn't paying any attention to what they were saying. The moment she'd turned around, she'd felt the pull. For whatever reason, the woman and the little boy were now going up instead of down. And there was more. She hadn't said anything to the family, but she sensed a change in their physical well-being. Whether it was because they were in danger of freezing to death or in danger from another source remained to be seen. What she did know was that they needed to be found quickly, or it would be too late.

"This way," she said suddenly, and started moving.

"Hey, wait!" Mike said, but no one was paying him any attention. "Oh, what the hell," he muttered, and followed the others.

Molly didn't know how long she'd been asleep, but when she woke up, the first things she noticed were the cold and the silence. Her shoulder was hurting, as were her legs and back. The more time that passed since the crash, the worse she felt.

Johnny was curled up in her arms, and she could feel the warmth of his breath against her cheek. The whistle he'd blown earlier was hanging outside his coat. She fingered it, then put it to her mouth. The metal was startlingly frigid against her already cold lips, but she blew it lightly just the same. To her surprise, the little boy didn't even flinch. She cupped the side of his face and then patted his cheek.

"Hey, Johnny, are you hungry? How about you wake up and we'll have something to eat?"

He murmured something beneath his breath but didn't open his eyes.

Molly's heart skipped a beat. Why didn't he wake up? He needed to wake up. She shook him lightly but persistently.

"Johnny? Johnny? Can you hear me?"

He nodded, but he still didn't open his eyes. "Cold," he said.

"Yes, I am, too," she said, and pulled him closer against her, then wrapped the blankets tighter around them both. "Is that better?"

He nodded again.

It occurred to her that maybe they should get up and move around, but she didn't follow through. She thought about looking out to see if it was still snowing, but she didn't move for fear of disturbing him. She didn't think of hypothermia, didn't realize that their makeshift shelter might turn into a crypt.

"Blow the whistle," Johnny said softly.

"Yes, all right," Molly said, and gave it a short blast. What the hell. Maybe the rescuers would hear and beat the killer to them.

The sound seemed muffled beneath the limbs and the snow, so she blew it once more, then let it drop.

"You have to blow," Johnny murmured. "It's so Daddy can find me if I'm lost."

Molly's heart twisted. They were more than lost. If only a whistle could fix the mess they were in.

"Molly?"

"Yes, honey?"

"Are we still lost?"

She blinked back tears. "Yes."

"If you blow the whistle, Daddy will find us."

Molly didn't know how to answer. What could she say? She certainly couldn't tell him that the likelihood of that happening was slim. She patted the top of his head, then pulled the hood of his jacket a little closer around his face.

"We'll rest for just a little bit longer, then we're going to have to start moving again, okay?"

"'Kay," he said softly.

She scooted him closer, then closed her eyes and started to pray. There were so many things she'd wanted to do with her life, but the possibility of dying on this mountain was becoming a reality she had to face. So she said her prayers for herself and for Johnny; then she put the whistle in her mouth and blew.

"In a few minutes we're going to get up and start moving again," she warned.

But Johnny didn't answer, and before long she'd forgotten her own vow and fallen asleep.

Darren Wilson was shivering with every step he took. He wanted to just sit down and quit. Either he would be found or he would freeze to death. One way or another, it would be over—and he wanted it over. If he died, he wouldn't have to answer to Alphonso Riberra, the man to whom he owed more than a quarter of a million dollars. He wouldn't have to worry about Riberra killing his family, and he wouldn't have to worry that the lost woman and kid would give him up.

He stepped on a large stick hidden beneath the snow, then jumped when the sound echoed like a gunshot. He glanced down. The tracks he'd been following were all but gone.

"Christ Almighty…don't let it all end this way," he begged, and then wondered why God would listen to a man who'd done what he'd done.

As he stood there, he thought he heard a sound. He frowned. It sounded like a referee's whistle, which made no sense. But he heard the sound again—coming from somewhere above where he was standing. Whatever he'd heard was not an animal. All he had to do was make a choice to press on, or lie down and die. As much as he wanted the horror of all this to go away, he was afraid to die. People who did what he'd done didn't go to heaven, and while he wasn't completely convinced there was such a thing as hell, he wasn't in a state of mind to take the chance.

He started walking uphill, toward where he thought the sound had come from.

It had just been made official. Three people who'd been on the plane were missing from the crash site. Whether their bodies had fallen out while the plane was still in the air and landed some distance away from the site or they'd survived only to wander away in the woods, no one knew. The only truth the authorities had so far was that they were gone.

The FAA, representatives from the airline, and local and state authorities had assembled, blocked off search areas and dispersed search parties sometime just after noon.

Anthony Devereaux knew the O'Ryans had been gone since early that morning, but he'd heard nothing back. He'd gotten info from some of the searchers that the farther up the mountain they went, the heavier the snowfall. He didn't know how to explain the missing passengers, but he knew if there was a snowball's chance in hell of their being found, the O'Ryan men would find their boy. He just hoped to God that when they found him, they found him alive.

However, they were not part of his actual search party, so whatever they were doing was out of his domain.

"Hey, Devereaux…where do you want them to set up?"

Tony looked up. A deputy sheriff was standing in front of a large contingent of people from Carlisle. They'd come with food for the searchers, as well as cots and blankets for beds. He waved to indicate he'd heard the question, then headed their way.

Hours later, he was still on site, keeping track of the searchers by handheld radios, relaying information back and forth, and marking off sections on a map once a given area had been covered. By late evening, a five-mile radius from the site had been thoroughly searched; then they were forced to stop because of the oncoming darkness.

Some of the search groups stopped right where they were and set up camp, ready to resume at first light. Others hadn't come as prepared and were forced to return to the on-site headquarters.

Tony still hadn't heard from the O'Ryans, although some of the searchers that had come in claimed to have seen their tracks. One report Tony had gotten was puzzling to him. The searchers claimed the O'Ryans had changed direction and were now traveling up the mountain, instead of down, but he didn't have time to dwell on it. They were big boys who'd gone out on their own. They would have to take care of themselves.

* * *

Even though Darren didn't hear the whistle again, he still ran, dragging his bum leg at an awkward angle until the tracks he'd been following were gone. Then he went a little farther until he ran into the low-hanging limbs of a pine tree and hit himself square across the face. His nose, which he already figured was broken, began to bleed again.

He screamed out in pain, grabbing his face with both hands as he fell backward into the snow. Blood was pouring out of his nose and staining the front of his coat. He scooped up a large handful of snow and pressed it on the bridge of his nose, hoping to stop the bleeding. When the snow melted, he did it again, then again and again, until the blood was gone.

"God damn it all to hell," he muttered as he began cleaning off his face and gloves with more snow.

He couldn't breathe out of his nose, and his lower lip, which he'd already busted, was swelling on the other side, as well. He was so hungry he felt faint, and he knew that if he didn't eat soon, he would pass out.

He made himself get up, then began walking aimlessly. He had to keep moving or die. As he was walking, he saw the corner of something bright red poking out of the snow a few feet downhill from his location. He stopped, stared at it for a moment, then guessed it was probably another snack-food wrapper that the woman and kid had discarded. He knew that confirming his theory would at least assure him that they'd passed this way, so he headed toward the spot of color.

He slipped as he began moving downward and grabbed hold of a small sapling to keep from falling farther. When he got to the bit of red color, he discovered to his disbelief that it wasn't discarded paper after all. It was a whole energy bar that had obviously fallen out of their pack. He was almost in tears when he tore into it. He sat down with his back against a tree, taking momentary shelter from the snow, and took his first bite. Tears came to his eyes as he chewed. Nuts, oatmeal and raisins had never tasted so good.

He chewed on one side of his mouth three times, then on the other side three times, before swallowing. It didn't bother him that his obsessive-compulsive disorder had kicked in again, although he'd been in therapy for it for years.

But there was a small problem he hadn't been aware of until he'd started to eat. Some of his back teeth felt loose. Chewing on the left side of his mouth was excruciatingly painful. Even though he could have chewed on the other side with far less misery, his OCD wouldn't let him do it. The pain forced him to slow down his eating to the point that when he'd finished one third of the bar, he was crying.

He washed his mouth out with snow he let melt on his tongue, repeating the practice three times until he could no longer feel anything stuck to his teeth. However, clean teeth weren't going to fix what was wrong with him.

He gambled excessively because he needed to repeat every bet three times before he felt he could move on to the next. He also tipped three times too much, and chewed everything he put in his mouth three times on each side before swallowing. When he drank, he always ordered three drinks, even when he didn't want them, and he drank them. To do otherwise would bring the world down around his ears.

In fact, that very thought had been stewing in his head for some hours now. He'd killed Finn. He needed to repeat the act two more times before it would be all right. All he had to do was find the woman and the kid, then even up the score. When he finally got up from where he'd been sitting and began to search again, he didn't remember that he'd been going uphill and not down. Instead, he fixed his gaze on a large evergreen about three hundred yards downhill. It had limbs hanging low to the ground, which would give shelter to whoever or whatever crawled beneath.

Renewed by the piece of energy bar he'd eaten, he began mentally preparing himself to rout whatever kind of animal might be sheltering beneath the pine, then began to walk, anxious to get there before dark.

When Deborah ran out of daylight, she pulled a flashlight out of her backpack and kept on moving. She was so focused on looking down for tracks or signs that she didn't see the limb in front of her before it smacked her in the face.

The blow was so unexpected that it knocked her flat on her back. Her flashlight went flying as she grabbed her face with both hands.

"Oh…that hurt," she mumbled as tears quickened.

Mike had been right behind her. He saw the limb almost at the same time she went down, and there was nothing he could do to save her. He heard the thump as she hit it and tried to grab her as she was falling, but he reacted too late. The moment she went down, he was on his knees beside her.

"Deborah? Deborah? Are you all right?"

She struggled to a sitting position, then covered her face again. Her eyes were watering, her cheeks stinging from being slapped by the pine needles. If she'd been an inch taller, it would have most likely broken her nose. As it was, she felt a small knot forming on her forehead, just above the level of her eyebrows.

"What happened?" Evan asked as he, too, dropped to his knees.

"Some psychic," Deborah muttered. "I should have seen that coming."

It was the fact that she'd just cracked a joke in the midst of her pain that made Mike look at her in a different way.

"Can you stand?" he asked.

"The branch hit my head, not my knees. Of course I can stand," she muttered.

Mike chuckled. It was so damned dark in the woods that he could barely see his hand in front of his face, but he felt her impatience and sarcasm just the same. "Dad…get her flashlight, will you?"

James fumbled in the snow for the light as Evan and Mike helped her up. James handed the light to Mike, who promptly aimed it in her face. To Mike's surprise, Deborah didn't look away, and he found himself locked into her gaze. At that point he was the one who began losing focus. If she hadn't blinked, he might never have come back from where he'd been going.

"You're not bleeding," Evan commented.

"Then I shall be thankful for small favors," Deborah said. She took the flashlight from Mike, readjusted her backpack and this time ducked as she went beneath the limb.

Mike shifted his backpack, moved his flashlight to his other hand and followed right behind her.

"It's too damned dark to be walking," James said.

Deborah didn't respond.

Mike glanced back at his dad, who shrugged. They walked for a few minutes more, then Mike felt the need to comment.

"I can't see where I'm going," he muttered.

Deborah stopped. There was anger in her movements as she swept the trio with the beam from her flashlight. They were quite a group. James, who was the oldest, had snow and ice frozen to the stubble on his face. Evan's eye patch, which had started out black, was frosted over so thickly that it was almost the same color as his pale face. Mike's cheeks were burned a deep, angry red—she supposed from the bite of the winter wind—but his eyes still burned with something close to a glare.

She sighed.

"Can the three of you see me?" she asked.

They nodded.

"Then that's all you need to worry about."

"What? You trying to tell us that you can see in the dark?" Mike fired at her.

"I'm not seeing…I'm feeling. It's like someone has a rope around my waist and is slowly pulling me upward. All I'm doing is following the pull. If you want to find your boy, then shut up and follow me, because I swear to God, he's what's at the other end of that rope."

Evan didn't need to be told twice. He knocked the snow from the treads of his boots and nodded. "Yes, ma'am. I'm right behind you."

Mike and James could do nothing less.

Deborah turned around and resumed her march.

There was a bit of muttering to one another from behind her, but she paid them no mind. She knew what she knew, and there wasn't time to waste on explaining the process.

They'd been walking for almost an hour when Deborah suddenly picked up the pace. There was an urgency in her steps that the men couldn't help but notice. Not a one of them could bring himself to ask why. So when she suddenly stopped, they stopped, too, holding their breath and waiting to see what came next.

The whistle. It had been echoing in her mind all along, but now she couldn't hear it anymore. She didn't want to think what that meant. She began to pace back and forth, and then suddenly stopped and closed her eyes, trying to concentrate.

"What's wrong?" Mike asked.

Deborah's shoulders slumped.

"The whistle…I don't hear it anymore."

"Oh, God," Evan said, then covered his face with his hands and dropped, as if his knees had just given way.

"What can we do?" Mike asked.

Deborah was slightly surprised by the calmness in his voice.

"We can't stop looking," she said.

"We can't see a damn thing in the dark. We could walk right past them and never know it," James muttered.

"I'd know it," Deborah said.

Mike hesitated, then offered, "If Deborah says she can do it, I'm game."

Deborah was surprised that he seemed to be taking her side, but she was concerned about Evan. She wasn't sure he could go on.

She knelt beside him. He was so thin and so drawn. She could feel his suffering.

He looked up. Deborah resisted the urge to put her arms around him. He wanted to cry. She couldn't afford to let him give way.

Instead, she dug through her backpack and handed him a piece of jerky, then stood up and handed each of the other men a piece, as well.

As they watched, she took one more piece from her pack and began eating it, biting, then chewing slowly, as if to get the most nutrition possible from the cured meat.

James took a bite; then his eyebrows arched approvingly. "This is good stuff. Did you make it?"

"Yes."

"You'll have to give me your recipe. Trudy and I always—"

The moment he mentioned his wife, his voice stopped short and died. The other men knew why. Deborah sensed a sadness in James O'Ryan but wisely didn't comment.

"It's simple enough. I'll be happy to share it," she said, then put a hand on Evan's shoulder.

"Can you do this?" she asked.

"Hell, yes," he said. "You're the one who stopped, not me."

She laid a hand on his knee, then gave it a brief pat.

"All right. Everyone up."

As soon as they were all upright, she turned to face them.

"Here's the deal. It's no longer safe to walk any way but single file. You need to walk directly behind me so that no one has a misstep and falls off the mountain."

Mike's first instinct was to argue. It wasn't in him to let a woman do the hard work while he stood back and watched.

"Okay," he said. "But while you're claiming to be psychic, remember you're also the one who ran into the tree."

Deborah stifled a smile as she wiggled her nose. "It was just a branch," she said. "And while we all know I can't see in the dark, this is still my mountain. I know where I am…more or less. It would be safer to wait until morning, but I don't think Molly and Johnny have the time to waste. I don't know exactly what's wrong, but it's difficult to stay connected with them."

A fierce frown darkened Mike's expression. "I don't know what the hell you're talking about, but I'm right behind you. Evan, we're trading places, and don't argue." Then he pointed at James. "Dad, keep an eye on him."

James put an arm around his grandson's shoulders and gave him a brief hug.

"I can do that," he said gruffly.

"I don't need a babysitter," Evan said.

"No. What you need is a doctor," Mike said sharply.

"That's enough talk," Deborah said. "Let's go, and don't forget to stay directly behind me."

7

The luminous dial on James O'Ryan's digital watch registered just after midnight. Twice he'd had to catch Evan as he staggered from exhaustion, and he was just at the point of telling that damned woman she was going to have to slow down when she suddenly stopped.

Ever since the quartet had started up the mountain, Deborah's sense of urgency had not let up. Her feet were so cold that she'd long since lost feeling in her toes, and her face felt like a block of ice. If she had to change expression, she was pretty sure her face would break.

Because of the urgency, she'd moved without care or thought for the three men behind her, reacting to the inner voice that was leading her through the dark.

Once she tripped on something buried under the snow and fell flat on her face. It didn't help the pain she was already suffering from being hit by the branch. However, within seconds, James and Mike yanked her up by the arms and set her back on her feet. She didn't know that her nose was bleeding again, or that she'd busted her lip, because she was too cold to feel the moisture.

Mike saw the blood and winced, but said nothing. Instead, he took out his handkerchief, took off his gloves and proceeded to wipe the blood off her upper lip. Then he handed her the handkerchief, put his gloves back on and kept moving.

Deborah was silent but thoughtful as they continued upward. This was twice now that he'd picked her up and put her back on her feet. And twice she'd felt the growing connection to this man. She didn't know how this was going to turn out, but she knew that when these men left, she was never going to be the same.

One hour, then another, passed, and she feared that no matter how fast they moved, they were going to be too late.

Then they walked into a clearing, and Deborah felt as if someone had punched her in the stomach. All the air was gone from her lungs. It was a feeling she'd had many times before—like hitting a wall, unable to go any farther.

And she knew what it meant.

They were here. Somewhere in the dark, probably buried beneath the snow, was the little boy who needed her.

She held up her hand to signal silence, then began turning in a slow, steady circle, aiming her flashlight around the clearing. Although the snow had stopped falling, the night was dark, without so much as a sliver of moonlight by which to see. Again she stopped, her head tilted, as if she were listening to something they couldn't hear.

"What's up now, lady?" James asked.

Evan swayed on his feet, then pushed past the men to get to Deborah. He grabbed her by the shoulders. His eye was bloodshot, and he had a two-day growth of iced whiskers on his face. There was a muscle twitching at the edge of his mouth, and his lips were so cold it was all he could do to form words.

"Where is my son?"

Deborah's eyes widened, as if she'd suddenly re-membered she wasn't alone; then she shrugged out of Evan's grasp.

"They're here, they're here," she mumbled. "I don't see them, but I know they're here."

"Here?" Evan asked, then aimed his flashlight around the small clearing as his voice broke. "There's nothing here but snow and trees."

"They're here, damn it! Help me look."

Mike joined in, shining his flashlight into the darkness, catching nothing but brief glimpses of the thick stand of pines as Evan began calling out to his son.

"Johnny! Johnny! It's Daddy! Where are you?"

"Johnny! Molly!" Deborah called. "I can't see you, but I know you're here. Johnny... I can't hear the whistle! Blow the whistle for me!"

Molly was dreaming. She was sure of it. It had to be a dream, because she could hear voices calling her name.

In her dream, she opened her eyes. To her dismay, she could see nothing. Either it was night or she'd gone blind.

The child was still in her arms. But he was so still and so cold. She started to call out, then realized there was something in her mouth. Something hard and cold and frozen to her lips.

The whistle.

It had to be the whistle.

She had a vague memory of blowing it for the boy, but he wasn't talking anymore, and she wanted to go back to sleep.

"Blow the whistle!"

She flinched.

"Johnny! Molly! Blow the whistle!"

Molly frowned. She hadn't imagined it. Someone was calling her name. She tried to answer back, to call "Help, please help," but that whistle was in the way.

So she blew.

Once.

Twice.

Then again and again. Every inhalation drew oxygen into her lungs, and every exhalation went out through the whistle frozen to her skin.

Deborah gasped. "Did you hear that?"

"Hell, yes, I heard that!" Mike cried as he flashed his light around the area.

Evan began running from one side of the clearing to the other, shouting Johnny's name.

The shrill sound of the whistle mingled with the searchers' shouts, echoing from one side of the clearing to the other and distorting the origin.

Suddenly Deborah's instincts focused on a large mound of snow beneath a pair of dead trees.

"There!" she cried, pointing toward a large snow-drift.

The men converged on the site, then dropped to their knees and began digging. Deborah circled the drift and began digging from the other side. Within seconds, they all realized that it wasn't a solid drift of snow after all, but a large, snow-covered limb with branches cupping the ground. Even stranger was the fact that the tree was an oak, but the branches on which the snow had collected were evergreen.

Mike's heart skipped a beat. This was a man-made shelter, and from the appearance of the limbs, a recent one. He dug through the snow in desperation, praying for a miracle but fearing the worst.

Evan was the first one to break through. He thrust both hands deep into what he thought was snow, lost his balance and went facedown. With snow up his nose and snow in his eyes, he pushed himself up.

"It's not a drift!" he yelled. "There's open space here. Shine a light. Shine a light! I can't see what I'm doing."

Deborah jumped up and circled the area, then aimed her flashlight directly into the dark opening. At that moment everyone went silent, afraid to see what was in there, yet unable to turn away.

The quiet was startling and unexpected, and

everyone's fears all went to the same place. Had they come this far only to be too late?

Evan's heart was pounding so loudly in his ears that he didn't know the whistling had stopped. The moment the light had shone down into the opening, he saw something he would never forget. The whistle that he'd given his son was frozen to a young woman's lips. But where was Johnny?

"Johnny! Johnny!" he cried, and began pulling at the snow-dusted blankets covering the woman's body.

Within seconds he saw the back of a child's parka. He grabbed at the coat and pulled. The woman moaned. To his horror he realized that the chain holding the whistle was still around Johnny's neck, so if he picked up his son, he would rip the whistle from her mouth, taking skin and flesh with it. To get to Johnny, he had to separate the whistle from Molly's lips. He tried to slip the chain over Johnny's head but didn't have enough space in which to work.

"Oh, God… Dad…somebody…help me move this branch."

"Let me," James said. He stepped in front of the drift, slid his arms beneath the limb and stood abruptly, breaking it free from the icy ground and tossing it aside.

Now they could see what the branches and the snow had hidden.

The woman and child were wrapped in each other's arms and covered with a couple of small blankets. Immediately Mike recognized them as the kind used on airlines for passenger comfort. The young woman was probably beautiful, but it was hard to see past the gashes and bruising on her face.

"God… Dad…" Evan muttered as he viewed her injuries. Johnny was similarly hurt, but he had no way of knowing whether either one of them had any broken bones or internal injuries. In fact, he didn't even know if Johnny was still breathing, because it was obviously the woman who'd been blowing the whistle.

"Johnny? Can you hear me, son?" Evan said. "It's me, Daddy. I found you, just like I promised, and I've come to take you home."

The little boy's eyelids fluttered, but he didn't speak. The silence was frightening.

"That whistle is frozen to her lips," Evan muttered.

James thrust his hand in his coat pocket and pulled out a small flask.

"Here," he said. "But be careful where you pour. Don't want to choke her on the stuff."

Mike looked up at his dad and arched an eyebrow as he took the flask.

"What?" James asked. "You never know when a good shot of Kentucky bourbon will be needed. Besides, it doesn't freeze, all right?"

"Let me have it," Evan said, and quickly unscrewed the lid. Carefully, he held the flask to Molly's lips and poured. Drop by drop the liquor fell onto her mouth, until there was enough moisture to unstick the whistle. He handed the flask back, then yanked off his gloves. Gently, he rubbed the liquor on her lips and around the whistle until it finally came loose.

"All right," he muttered, more to himself than to anyone else, and leaned down to lift Johnny up.

To his shock, the young woman suddenly grabbed his arm. Her grip was strong—far stronger than he would have imagined. When he looked at her face, his heartbeat stuttered to a momentary stop.

She was staring up with a fierce, protective glare. It never occurred to him that all she saw was the silhouette of a man backlit by a small halo of light, or that she might think he was a threat, not a rescuer.

"Don't touch him!" she cried.

Evan fought back tears at the depths to which a stranger would go to protect his child.

"It's all right," he said softly. "I'm Evan O'Ryan. I'm Johnny's dad."

Her eyes widened in disbelief as she ran a gloved hand across the place on her lips where the whistle had been. Then she reached up and touched his face.

"Is this a dream?"

"No, ma'am," he said. "We're real. All of us. Now, rest easy. We're going to help you. Is either one of you too injured to walk?"

"No," Molly said, then pointed to Johnny. "But something's wrong with Johnny. He isn't talking to me anymore."

Evan gazed down at his son, then quietly picked him up. For a moment he just held him close, cheek to cheek. It was difficult to believe that this long-legged child was the little toddler he'd left behind.

"Johnny, can you hear me? It's Daddy."

Johnny was so cold—and so still. Fear made Evan hold his son that much tighter. "We've got to get him warm," he said.

"My house isn't far," Deborah said.

"Are you serious?" Evan asked.

"Absolutely," Deborah said. "We can be there in less than an hour."

"Then let's do it," James said, and reached down and helped Molly up before shouldering their packs.

"Oh!" Molly cried, as she put weight on her leg.

"I'm Mike O'Ryan, Johnny's grandfather," Mike said as he steadied her on her feet. "I can carry you, if need be."

"No, I can walk. I'm just cold and stiff," Molly said.

Mike turned around and found himself staring straight into Deborah Sanborn's eyes.

"You did it," he said softly. "God bless you, woman. You saved my son's sanity and my grandson's life."

"They're not safe yet," she said. "We need to get them warm."

Mike's gaze softened as he brushed snow from the side of her face. "And we will, thanks to you."

"What about your friend Tony? We need to let him know we've found them," James said.

"Cell phones won't work in these woods," Deborah said. "Wait until we get to my house."

Mike nodded, then turned and gave Evan a close look.

"Son, let me carry Johnny for you."

But Evan wasn't budging. "Thanks, Dad, but I've got him."

Mike frowned. "Just let me know if you need help." Then he glanced at his dad. "Ready?"

James nodded. "As I'll ever be. Let's go find a fire."

Mike slid an arm beneath Molly's shoulders, so that when she walked, she would be braced against him.

"Hold on, girl," he said gently.

Molly started to cry.

Mike looked startled. "Am I hurting you? Do we need to—"

"No, no," Molly said. "These are tears of relief, not pain. I just can't believe you're all here."

Mike pointed at Deborah. "If it wasn't for her, we wouldn't be." His gaze focused on her wide blue eyes and the reddened patches on her cheeks where the cold had chapped all the way through to the next layer of skin.

"Lead the way, pretty lady. We're right behind you."

Deborah turned toward home without speaking, but her heart was full and her steps lighter as she went. She knew they were worried about the boy, but he would be all right. They needed shelter, dry clothes and warm food, and it was all waiting for them less than two miles above.

As she walked, Mike O'Ryan's words kept echoing in her head. *Pretty lady. Pretty lady.* By the time they reached the perimeter of her property, those words had gone all the way to her heart.

They all saw the lights through the trees at once, but Mike was the first to cry out.

"I see lights!"

"We're almost there," Deborah said. "About a hundred yards more and then across the yard to the back of the house."

"Thank God," Evan said. "I can feel Johnny's breath on my face, but he hasn't said a word since I picked him up."

Molly was so relieved to know that their journey was almost over that she shed a few more tears.

James was too concerned about Evan and Johnny to comment, and said nothing as he brought up the rear.

When they were about halfway across the clearing, a dog began to bark.

Deborah stifled a sob. Puppy. And they were almost home. Seconds later, a pretty sable-and-white collie nearly knocked her off her feet.

"Hey, Puppy…yes, I'm home, and we have company, so be good."

The dog bounced around Deborah's feet and then ran a little way ahead, only to turn around and repeat it all over again. By the time they reached the back porch, they were experiencing what amounted to adrenaline deprivation. They'd been so keyed-up to get here that once they'd seen the lights, the simple act of crossing the clearing to get to the back door left them exhausted and dragging their feet.

They went through a screened-in porch; then Deborah opened the back door to the house and stood back to let the others enter. The warmth of the house hit them square in the face. Groans of appreciation for the unexpected comfort sounded long and loud. Puppy disappeared to a favorite spot somewhere else in the house—somewhere far warmer than the outdoors where she'd awaited Deborah's return.

"What kind of heating do you have up here?" James asked as they began unloading backpacks, and shedding their coats and boots.

"It's propane. There are several wall heaters throughout the house and one floor furnace in the living room, plus a fireplace."

"It feels like heaven," Evan said, and then laid his son down on a daybed in the corner of the big kitchen.

"Dad? Help me," Evan said as he began tugging at Johnny's coat and hiking shoes.

Mike had already helped Molly into a chair, and had taken off her coat and shoes. He was taking off his own boots when Evan called. He dropped his own coat near the door and raced to Evan's side.

"Your floor. We're getting snow all over your floor," James said as he dumped the backpacks and then shut the door.

Deborah hung her coat on a wall hook, then sat down on the floor and took off her boots. James reached down and pulled her up, then wrapped his arms around her and gave her a hug that all but squeezed the breath from her lungs.

"You saved my family. Don't know how we'll ever be able to thank you, but thank you, just the same."

"You're welcome," Deborah said, then extricated herself from his arms and went to Molly, who seemed dazed by the warmth and confusion. Deborah knelt in front of her, eyeing her bruises and wounds. They seemed superficial, but one could never be sure.

"Molly… I'm Deborah. Welcome to my home."

Molly inhaled slowly as tears continued to roll silently down her cheeks. "I thought we would die."

Deborah took both of Molly's hands and began warming them with her own.

"I'm going to take you to my bedroom. We'll run a big tub of warm water for you to soak in. You need to get warm, okay? As soon I make coffee, I'll bring you a cup."

Molly nodded as Deborah turned to James.

"There are cans of soup in the pantry. It's through that door. Pans are in the cabinet to the right of the sink. Can opener is on the cabinet next to the bread box. The stove is gas. Will you heat up the soup for the others while I get Molly into the tub?"

"Will do," he said, and disappeared into the pantry.

Deborah could hear the big man thumping around inside the small space, and smiled. One thing about the O'Ryan men. They weren't bashful about taking charge. Still, it took all her energy to move to the cabinets. She ran water into the coffeepot, poured it into the coffee-maker, then quickly measured out coffee into the filter. One flip of a switch turned the pot on. Within seconds, the scent of freshly brewing coffee permeated the room.

She glanced back at Molly before hurrying to the daybed, where Mike and Evan were working on Johnny.

"Evan, there's a second bathroom down the hall on

the left. Run some lukewarm water into the tub, and then put Johnny in it. As he warms up, you can slowly add more hot water."

Evan was pulling Johnny's jeans off as she spoke. His voice shook as he gave life to his fears. "His skin is so cold," he said.

"That's why the lukewarm water," Mike said. "Remember your survival training, Evan. We have to warm him up gradually."

Evan nodded. "Right," he said as he pulled off the last of Johnny's clothes.

There was a brief moment of shock as they gazed at the little boy's still body.

"God Almighty…the bruises. Look at the bruises," Mike said.

"No telling what happened to him as the plane went down," Evan said. Unashamed of his tears, he picked up his son. The child was so limp and lifeless, he feared their troubles were far from over. "You said the bathroom was down the hall?"

"Yes," Deborah said. "There are plenty of towels in the corner cabinet. Help yourself."

"I'll run the water," Mike said, and ran ahead of them.

Deborah went back to Molly, then helped her up.

"Come along, sweetheart. We need to get you warm."

Relief at having been rescued was beginning to soak in. Molly leaned against Deborah as they started down the hall.

"The warmth feels wonderful, but I can't quit shaking," Molly said.

"You got too cold. Hypothermia. If we hadn't found you and Johnny when we did, it might have been too late."

Tears pooled in Molly's eyes again. "I nearly killed us, didn't I? Is Johnny all right?"

"I think he will be," Deborah said as she ushered her into her bedroom, then into the adjoining bath.

Molly undressed as Deborah turned her back and began filling the tub. Too much had happened to Molly to be concerned with modesty, but she was touched that Deborah was still considerate. When the tub was at the right depth and temperature, Deborah turned off the water.

"In you go," she said, and steadied Molly as she stepped into the warm water.

"Oh, Lord, this feels good," Molly said.

Deborah longed for a nice hot bath, herself, as Molly slowly sank into the depths.

"Here's a washcloth and some soap when you're ready for them, but I recommend a good long soak first. Is there anything else you need?"

Molly grasped Deborah's hand.

"I don't know how you knew where to find us, but thank God you did."

"You're welcome," Deborah said, then she stepped back and sat down on a nearby footstool. "Can I ask you something?"

"Anything," Molly said.

"Why did you leave the crash site?"

Molly's eyes widened. "Oh, my God… I can't believe I almost forgot."

"Forgot what?" Deborah asked.

"Johnny and I...witnessed a murder."

Deborah gasped. The other set of footsteps! That explained the danger she'd believed them to be in.

"What did you see?" she asked.

"We saw one of the survivors kill another man. We were afraid if he knew we were alive and had seen him that he'd kill us, too."

Deborah was stunned. "How awful," she said. "And you say Johnny saw it, too?"

"Yes. That's why we left. I might have been able to deceive him into believing I hadn't seen anything, but Johnny was another story. Not only did he see what happened, but when he realized his grandparents were dead, he asked me if the bad man had killed them, too."

Deborah was horrified at what they'd gone through, but very impressed with Molly's presence of mind. For such a young woman, she'd reacted admirably.

"So what did you do then?" Deborah asked.

"As soon as the man left the cabin, I grabbed Johnny, some airline snacks and a couple of blankets, and we ran as fast as we could. It had begun to snow. There was a chance he wouldn't even miss us, but if he did, I was hoping that the snow would cover our tracks. I know it was risky to leave the crash site, but we couldn't stay and take the chance."

"Did you know the man who was murdered?" Deborah asked.

"Not really, but he and the killer were sitting in front of me. I heard them fighting off and on during the trip.

The killer was in some kind of financial trouble, I think. Anyway, the other one knew. I don't know why it mattered. Then we crashed. I woke up to see the first one strangling the other one… I assume to keep him quiet."

"Dear Lord," Deborah said, then got to her feet. "I need to tell the men. Will you be all right?"

Molly nodded.

"I won't be long," Deborah said, then ran from the room.

Evan was bare to the waist and down on his knees, holding Johnny's limp body in the tepid water. His muscles were trembling from exhaustion but he wouldn't give up his son to anyone. Mike was slowly adding hot water to the tub, in between rubbing Johnny's feet and legs to aid his circulation, when the little boy began to come around. First his eyelids fluttered; then he started to moan.

"Dad! He's coming around!" Evan cried.

"He's talking. What's he saying?" Mike asked.

"Blow the whistle," Johnny mumbled.

Evan swallowed past a knot in his throat as he lifted Johnny from the water and held him close against his bare chest.

Mike wrapped him in a towel as Evan kissed Johnny's cheek.

"It's all right, little man. It's Daddy. I found you. Granddad is here, too. We're all here, son. You don't have to be afraid anymore."

A frown spread across Johnny's forehead, then he opened his eyes. Evan held his breath, afraid that his eye patch and scars would frighten him even more.

"Daddy?"

Evan nodded. "Yes, son, it's me. Daddy. I know I look a little—"

"I told her you would come. I told her to blow the whistle and you would come and you did!" he said, then rose up far enough to reach his father and wrapped his arms around Evan's neck.

Evan was so moved he didn't trust himself to speak.

"Hey, buddy, it's Daddy Mike," Mike said, and gently patted the little boy's back.

Johnny grinned at Mike over Evan's shoulder, then suddenly realized he didn't know where he was.

"We're in a house?"

"Yes. It belongs to a nice lady who helped us find you."

Johnny frowned. "Where's my Molly? Did the bad man get Molly?"

Evan pulled back and stared at his son as if he'd never seen him, then glanced at his Dad.

Mike caught Evan's gaze and shrugged.

At that moment there was a knock at the bathroom door. It was Deborah.

"I need to talk to both of you," she said.

Evan was tightening the towel around Johnny as Mike opened the door.

"Johnny's conscious," Mike said.

Deborah glanced over Mike's shoulder and got a glimpse of a slender face and blue eyes.

"That's wonderful," she said, then took hold of Mike's shoulders to emphasize her words. "I need to talk to you."

Mike frowned. "What's wrong?"

"Has Johnny said anything to you about—"

"About a bad man?" Mike said.

Deborah's eyes widened. She nodded.

"Just that there was one," Mike said. "What don't we know?"

"They witnessed a murder," Deborah said. "It's why they ran. After the crash, one of the survivors killed another, then left the cabin. Molly was afraid that if he came back and found out he had two witnesses, he'd kill them, too."

Evan heard her, but he could hardly wrap his mind around the words. Not only had his son endured a crash, but he'd had to witness his grandparents' deaths and then a murder? It seemed impossible to grasp.

"Is that true, son?" Evan asked.

Johnny turned and hid his face against his father's neck.

"It's okay, honey," Deborah said. "You're not in trouble. Besides, Molly already told us everything."

Johnny looked up. "I wanna see my Molly."

"She's in the bathtub getting warm, just like you did," Deborah said.

Johnny started to cry. "Did the man hurt her, too? He did, didn't he? I wanna see her. I wanna see my Molly!"

Before they could answer him, Molly emerged from the bedroom on the run. She had wrapped herself in an oversize bath towel, unintentionally revealing the depth of her own injuries.

Evan forgot to breathe as she ran into the room. When he saw the extent of her wounds and remembered that she'd ignored her pain to save his son, he was speechless.

Unaware of Evan's scrutiny, Molly ran to the child.

"Look, Johnny. I'm here. The man didn't get me. I'm fine. We're both fine, just like I promised, okay?"

The relief on the little boy's face was obvious. He went from Evan's arms to Molly's without a thought for the fact that he was abandoning his father for what amounted to a total stranger.

The towel slipped a little as Molly took Johnny into her arms, but she didn't notice. Instead, she took him into Deborah's room, sat down on the bed and began to rock him against her.

Johnny went limp and started to cry.

"I'm so sorry," Molly said as the others came in. "He was such a brave little soldier, but it was such a terrible thing for a child to see."

Evan was silent. Seeing his son in another woman's arms was something of an emotional shock. He wouldn't have been surprised if Johnny had pushed him away. It had been a long time since they'd seen each other, and he hardly looked like the daddy that had gone away. Still, he wouldn't have expected his son to have bonded so quickly with a woman he barely knew. It made him wonder how badly Johnny missed having a mother—and how special this Molly must be to have made such an impression on his son.

"It's all right," Evan said, then sat beside her. Slowly he leaned over and began rubbing Johnny's back.

"It's all right, Johnny. It's okay to cry, and you know what? I'm so proud of you for remembering the whistle. If it hadn't been for your whistle, we might not have found you."

Johnny snuffled a little bit more, but he was listening intently. "Really?" he asked.

Evan nodded. "Really."

Johnny leaned back in Molly's arms and this time thoroughly assessed his father's face.

"Is that eye gone?" he asked, pointing to the patch.

"Yes. Does it scare you?" Evan asked.

Johnny frowned. "No. Did it hurt?"

Evan sighed. Truth hurt. "Yes."

Johnny leaned forward and traced a little finger down the path of scars on Evan's face. "Daddy, did you cry?"

"Yes."

Johnny seemed to wince, then crawled from Molly's lap to Evan.

"I'm sorry those bad men hurt you. Maybe it was the same bad man who was on our plane."

Evan's stomach knotted. "No, I think it was a different one, but you need to know that you're safe. That man can't ever hurt you."

Johnny sighed, and then finally relaxed as Deborah interrupted.

"I'm sure James has heated the soup by now. How about we all get some warm food in our stomachs?"

"Yeah, sure," Evan said. "Give me a few minutes to get a shirt and find Johnny some clothes."

Deborah glanced at Molly's bare shoulders and then pointed to the dresser.

"I'm taller than you are, but we're about the same size. Help yourself to whatever clothes that you need."

"Thank you," Molly said.

"I'll help James with the food," Deborah said.

"I'll go with you," Mike offered.

As soon as they were out in the hall, Mike grabbed Deborah by the arm.

"Wait," he said.

She stopped.

He took her by the shoulders.

"Lady, you are something," he said softly. "My family is still intact, thanks to you."

"I'm just happy I was able to help," she said, and started to walk away, but he wouldn't let her go.

"In the beginning, I gave you a hard time, and for that, I'm sorry," Mike said, and took a step closer.

Deborah felt her pulse quicken. Was this it? Was this the moment where everything changed?

"It's nothing that hasn't happened before," she said.

Mike cupped the side of her face and stared, taking in every tiny facet of her features, including the new bruise and scratches, until he was certain he had them memorized. Then he leaned forward.

He heard her swift intake of breath.

Felt a muscle jump at the side of her jaw.

And then he kissed her—gently, because of her swollen lip and sore nose, and tenderly.

Deborah felt his hands go from her shoulders to her

waist. He pulled her close, then closer still, until there was nothing between them but heat.

Deborah could have resisted, but she knew it was futile. She'd already seen what would happen between them, and she gave herself up to the passion.

Moments later, they stopped. Mike groaned beneath his breath and then let her go.

"I didn't know that was going to happen," he said.

Deborah sighed. "I did," she said softly, and then walked away.

Mike felt as if he'd been sucker punched. She was something, this woman. Then he started to grin. What else, he wondered, did she already know?

8

The soup James had chosen was a hearty vegetable beef. He'd made bread-and-butter sandwiches to go with it, and opened two cans of fruit cocktail for dessert. The group ate hungrily as they filled James in on the news. To say he was shocked to hear what Molly and Johnny had endured was putting it mildly.

"Eat first," Deborah said. "Then we'll call the police about the murder." So they did, following her directions, just as they'd followed her up the mountain.

All through the meal James kept looking at his great-grandson in dismay. It was a tragedy that he'd seen death in more than one fashion, and at such an early age. He was, however, proud of the little guy, and he made sure Johnny knew it.

"You're quite a little soldier, aren't you, son?" James asked.

Johnny swallowed his mouthful of soup and then grinned. It was an incongruous expression, considering the cuts and bruises on his face.

"Am I really? As good as my daddy?" he asked.

James smiled. "Yep, I'd say so. What do you think, Evan?"

Evan couldn't quit looking at his son. When he'd been deployed, Johnny had been a toddler. While he was proud of the little man Johnny had grown into, he regretted missing those special steps in his son's development.

"I was always proud of him, and I'm proud of him still," Evan said.

Johnny beamed, then glanced at Molly, making sure she was smiling, as well. It was clear that following the trauma of the crash and his grandparents' deaths, Molly Cifelli had become his touchstone to safety.

"Dad… Molly is a good soldier, too. She took good care of me."

Everyone smiled as they looked at Molly, making her blush.

"We did what we had to, didn't we, Johnny?" she said.

He nodded, then scooped up his last spoonful of soup before asking for more.

"Absolutely," James said, and ladled another cup into Johnny's bowl. "Want another bread-and-butter sandwich with it?"

"Just the soup, please," Johnny said, and dug in.

Deborah stayed silent as she watched the O'Ryans interacting with one another. To a person who spent the majority of her life alone, the O'Ryan invasion seemed oddly comfortable.

She watched Molly, too, wondering what it would be like to be that age and still believe that everything was possible. Deborah had lost that hope the day she'd "seen" her father and the other miners die.

Molly seemed comfortable around the men, which meant she probably belonged to a warm, loving family like the O'Ryans. Deborah's parents had been good to her, but neither of them had been the kind of person who did much hugging or kissing. Her mother had remarried when she was ten, but her stepfather had been leery of a little girl who "saw" things.

Because of her gift, Deborah had grown up feeling as if she was always on the outside of life and looking in. Although she'd long ago accepted her lot, there was a part of her that wished she could belong to a family such as this.

She sat for a few more moments, then got disgusted with herself for being so melancholy when there were things to be done. She picked up the phone, then frowned when she heard only static. "Bad connection," she said. "I'll try again later."

She picked up her bowl and carried it to the sink as the others continued to eat and talk, then ran a sink full of hot soapy water in preparation for dishwashing.

She turned off the water and then, even though it was dark, glanced out the window over the sink and made a face at her own reflection. To her surprise, a second reflection suddenly appeared behind her.

It was Mike. Her heart skipped a beat as she quickly looked away.

"Need some help?" he asked.

"Thanks, but I've got it," she said.

He set a stack of dirty dishes on the counter, then rolled up his sleeves. "Nonsense," he said, and thrust his hands into the soapy water.

Deborah started to argue, then stopped. Just because she was used to doing everything herself, that didn't mean she couldn't accept help graciously.

He put the dishes into the soapy water, then reached for the dishcloth. Without talking, Deborah stepped up beside him and rinsed and dried as he washed. She'd already kissed him, so she knew what it felt like to be held in his arms, but she couldn't help wondering what it would be like to lie with him, body to body.

His shoulders were wide and his legs were long. She noticed the faint scattering of gold-tipped hairs on his forearms, as well as the firmly-toned muscles, and then it occurred to her that he most likely looked like that all over. The thought brought a shiver that Mike quickly noticed.

"Cold?" he asked.

Deborah paused, then looked up at him. "No."

Once again Mike felt knocked off balance by the look in her eyes. A little frustrated, he grabbed a stack of soup bowls and thrust them into the water, then began to wash.

Darn this woman. Why didn't she talk? They'd shared one hell of a kiss already. The least she could do was pretend she'd liked it.

"Oh…I did," Deborah said.

Mike froze. The spoons he was washing slipped from his hands into the water. "Did what?"

"Liked it."

The hair stood up on the back of Mike's neck as he locked onto her gaze. For a moment, he felt weightless—almost numb—and then the feeling passed. There was no other way to explain what had just happened but to accept the fact that she'd read his mind. It should have given him the creeps, but there was a part of him that was intrigued.

"Besides beautiful…what the hell are you? A witch?"

Deborah's eyes narrowed. "I thought we had already covered this territory. I'm not a witch. I'm not weird…at least, not from my perspective. I just know things that most other people don't."

He took a deep breath and then exhaled slowly.

Suddenly a hard gust of wind blew against the house, rattling the windows. It startled everyone into motion.

Johnny had all but fallen asleep at the table, but the noise reminded everyone of the lateness of the hour. Evan slid his arms around his son and picked him up as Deborah dried her hands and then pointed down the hall.

"There are three bedrooms, plus a sofa in the living room that makes into a bed. The wall heaters in each bedroom are on. Adjust them to suit yourselves. I'm going to try and call the sheriff. He needs to know that we've found the missing survivors, as well as what they saw."

"And I should try and call Tony," Mike said. "Dad…I gave you the number. Do you still have it?"

"In my coat pocket," James said.

Mike left the room while Deborah helped James clear the rest of the table, then he finished washing up. When he was done, he drained out the water and wiped down the countertops.

"Thank you," Deborah said. "I don't know when I've had such great company."

James shook his head. "Lord, girl...we're the ones who're thankful. Is there anything you need done before you go to bed? How about wood for the fireplace?"

"That would be helpful," she said.

"How much do you want?" he asked.

"Oh...maybe four or five logs to get us through the night. They're just outside the back door, to the left."

"Yes, I saw them earlier. Won't take me a minute," he said, then added, "Tell the boys to save some hot water for me."

She watched the big white-haired man move easily through the rooms as he went to put on his boots. She wondered about his life. He wore a wedding ring, and he'd mentioned someone named Trudy, then shut down so fast it had been startling. He was very competent in the kitchen, as if he'd been on his own for some time. She knew Evan was a widower, and while Mike hadn't mentioned a woman, instinct told her he was unattached, as well. As a whole, she decided, the O'Ryans were a remarkable group of men—even the youngest, who'd inadvertently saved his own life, as well as Molly's, with the whistle his father had given him.

When James went out to get wood, Deborah found

herself alone. She headed for the phone, although she didn't hold out much hope of getting through. It was difficult to get a connection when there was any kind of storm in the mountains. And even though the snow had stopped falling, the winds were fierce and rising, ensuring that whatever snow had fallen would be in drifts by morning. Still, she had to keep trying until she got through.

She also wanted to let her neighbor, Farley, know that she was home, so he wouldn't come over to do her chores. She knew the hour was late for phone calls, but Farley only had one phone and turned the ringer off at night, so calls wouldn't wake the houseful of kids. She would leave a message on his machine, which he would get when he woke up, and the deed would be done.

But first she had to call Sheriff Wally Hacker's office.

Amazingly, the phone was working again, and there was an answer on the third ring. She recognized the voice of Paul Porter, the night dispatcher.

"Sheriff's office," he said.

"Paul…it's Deborah Sanborn. Can you hear me okay?"

"Sheriff's office? Hello? Hello?"

Deborah sighed. She could hear him, but he obviously couldn't hear her. She tried again, this time speaking louder.

"Paul! It's Deborah Sanborn. Is the sheriff in?"

"Miss Sanborn? Is that you?"

"Yes! Is the sheriff there?"

"You say you're wanting to talk to the sheriff?"

"Yes!" she said. By now she was shouting.

A few moments passed, and then she heard the sheriff's voice. "Deborah...that you?"

"Yes!" she shouted. "Can you hear me?"

"Barely," he said. "Are you all right?"

"Yes, we're fine. We're all fine."

"We? You still with the O'Ryan family?"

"Yes. We found the survivors. Did you hear me? We found the survivors."

He was shouting, too. "Survivors? You say you found them?"

"Yes," Deborah answered.

"Thank God," he said. "Hey...where are you?"

"Home. We're home."

"Anyone need medical help?"

"No, but—"

The line began to crackle and hiss, as if someone had set it on fire; then, suddenly, it went dead.

"Damn," she muttered, and hung up the phone.

At least they knew the survivors had been found and were alive.

Within moments, Mike was back.

"Did you get through?" he asked.

"Sort of. Wally couldn't hear much of what I was saying, but he heard enough to know Johnny and Molly are alive and safe. We'll have to wait until the storm passes and the phone comes back on to tell him about the murder." She frowned and glanced nervously toward the dark windows. "I don't like to think about a killer on the loose out there and no one knows it."

"One step at a time," he said, then added, "I couldn't get a signal to call Tony," he said, holding up his cell phone.

"I'm sure Wally will get word to him, and probably to your grandfather, too. For now, it's the best we can do. The phone's dead again."

Mike nodded. "Good enough," he said, then before he could say more, his father was at the back door. Mike ran to open it, then took several of the logs from his arms.

"In the living room," James said as Mike lightened his load.

"Right behind you," Mike said as he kicked the door shut, then followed his father into the living room before stacking the logs by the fireplace.

"Did you get through to the authorities?" James asked.

"Sort of," Deborah said. "They know we're okay, but the line went dead before I could tell them about the murder."

"Everything in good time," James said, then laid one of the logs on the already burning fire. "If it's okay with you two, I'm going to wash up and find a place to sleep."

"I'll share a bed with you," Mike said.

"Good enough," James said. He had started out of the room when he stopped, turned around and came back.

"Did you forget something?" Deborah asked.

"Yes, ma'am, I did," he said, and kissed her forehead, then gave her a big hug. "Sleep well, angel, and God bless you."

Deborah blushed. She'd never had so much positive feedback.

"Thank you," she said. "Oh…if you need extra blankets, there are plenty in the linen closet in the hall."

He nodded. Moments later, he was gone.

"I better go check on Evan," Mike said.

Deborah rolled her head wearily, then smoothed the hair away from her face.

"And I need to check on Molly. She can share a bed with me."

The moment she said it, she could tell by the look on Mike's face that he was thinking about sharing her bed, too.

She arched an eyebrow.

Mike looked shamefaced, then grinned. "Well, it's your own fault for butting into my thoughts."

Deborah chuckled. "You're right. Sorry. I'll try to do better."

"No need trying to improve on perfection. I'm thinking that you're already as good as it gets."

This time Deborah laughed aloud.

"I'm betting you're not so bad yourself," she said.

Mike's smile stilled as his eyes darkened.

"If you're ever interested in finding out, it's your call," he said.

"I'm going now," Deborah said, and left facing an unfamiliar ache of longing.

Molly went to change while Johnny was talking to Evan about Frank and Shirley Pollard's deaths. She'd borrowed a long flannel nightgown from Deborah, and a pair of warm, wooly socks, as well. She brushed her hair out and left it down, rather than pull it up in the usual ponytail she wore to bed. She came out of the bathroom just as Johnny was asking Evan a question, and paused by their bedroom door to listen.

The little boy was wearing one of Deborah's T-shirts while his own clothes were being dried. It fell below his knees, but it was clean and soft and smelled good. Evan was bare chested, holding very still as his son ran his forefinger down the heavy braid of scarring on Evan's shoulder, tracing the shape as it curled beneath his arm and onto his rib cage like a thick, red snake.

"What did this, Daddy?"

Evan hesitated. How did you explain shrapnel from a roadside bomb?

"A sharp piece of metal."

Johnny nodded. "Did you fall on it, Daddy?"

Evan stifled a shudder, remembering the deafening blast and the screams from the other men in the truck as the hot pieces of shrapnel sliced through their bodies, then the horrifying silence that came after. The scent of burning flesh, hot metal and blowing sand was etched in his memory as vividly as the scars he bore.

"Something like that," he finally said. "Now, no more questions. It's time you got some sleep, buddy."

Johnny's eyelids were drooping as Evan pulled back the covers.

"Here you go, son."

Johnny rolled over, wincing slightly at the bruises

and cuts on his ribs and legs, then stopped in the middle of the bed.

"Scoot over a little, buddy," Evan said. "You get one side. I get the other."

Johnny frowned, turned toward the door and spotted Molly.

"No, Daddy. You sleep on one side of me. Molly sleeps on the other. We keep each other warm, don't we, Molly?"

Molly glanced at Evan, then blushed at the thought of being in the same bed with the man, even with a child between them.

"Yes, we did," she said. "But you don't need me to do that anymore. You have your daddy and Deborah's nice warm house. You'll sleep just fine without me."

Johnny's lower lip quivered as his eyes filled with tears.

"But what if I can't sleep? What if the bad man comes?"

Evan looked uncomfortable. Did his son doubt his ability to protect him because of his healing wounds?

Molly sat down on the side of the bed and held out her arms. Johnny crawled out from under the covers and into her lap, then curled up like a baby.

"Sweetheart, listen to me for a minute, okay?"

"Okay," he said, but his voice was still trembling.

"Your daddy was a soldier. He knows how to protect you twice as good as I ever could. So do your Daddy Mike and your Granddad James. They're all here in this house tonight, under the same roof, and they're not going to let anything happen to anyone. Right, Daddy?"

Molly looked to Evan for support.

Evan mouthed a thank-you as he leaned over and stroked the back of his little boy's head.

"That's right, son. We won't let anything happen to you, and that's a promise."

Johnny was silent for a few moments, then he sat up in Molly's lap and looked his father straight in the face.

"But, Daddy, you didn't see him. You don't know what he looks like, but me and Molly do. That's why she has to sleep with us. If the bad man comes and I'm asleep, Molly can wake you up and tell you he's here."

Evan sighed. He didn't want to argue the point with a little boy who'd been through so much.

"It's okay," he said softly. "You and Molly can have the bed, and I'll—"

"No!" Johnny wailed. "You have to stay, too. Please, Daddy, please. I'll sleep in the middle, and I promise not to kick or take up much space."

Deborah walked in just in time to realize there was a situation in progress, and it was obvious from the looks on Molly's and Evan's faces that they were at a loss as to what to do. Maybe she could help.

"So, young man, it sounds to me like you have a really good plan," Deborah said. "I was going to ask if your Molly would like to come sleep in my bed with me for tonight, but I think you have the better idea."

Molly's eyes widened. "I wouldn't presume to—"

Evan spoke at the same time. "I could just—"

Deborah held up her hand. They both stopped talking.

"For pity's sake, people. He's the best chaperone anyone could have, and he obviously needs to know the two people he trusts most are close at hand."

Evan sighed. "You're right. It's not a problem with me, if Molly is okay with it."

Molly wouldn't look at him. "Of course it's okay with me. Johnny and I have come this far together. I don't see what's wrong with spending another night with my new best friend."

Johnny threw his arms around her and hugged her neck, then crawled from her lap to his father's arms.

"It's okay then, right, Dad? You can have my pillow. I don't need—"

"Oh, I think I can come up with a spare pillow," Deborah said. "Be right back."

By the time she'd gone to the linen closet and back, Molly and Johnny were under the covers, and Evan was standing at the side of the bed. All the lights were out except the bedside lamp.

"Thank you," Evan said as he took the pillow she handed him, then looked down at the pair in the bed. "For everything."

Deborah nodded and smiled. "You're welcome. Sleep well."

Evan nodded, then shoved a weary hand through his hair. "Thanks to you, we'll all sleep well tonight."

"It's my pleasure, believe me," Deborah said, and closed the door behind her as she left.

Evan placed his pillow on the bed, then headed to the bathroom to clean up. A few minutes later he was back, wearing a pair of old black sweatpants and a faded black T-shirt. Without looking at Molly, he sat down on the side of the bed and pulled off his eye patch.

The wind whistled around the eaves of the big old house, but the walls were sturdy and the rooms were warm. He turned off the lamp, then crawled beneath the covers and rolled onto his side. There were a few moments of restless shifting before he found a comfortable spot.

Johnny's little backside was resting right in the curve of Evan's lap. Evan shifted until his arm was free of the covers. Without thinking, he laid it across the covers over Johnny's body so that his little boy would feel his father's presence, even as he slept. As his hand inadvertently connected with Molly's, he realized she had done the same thing.

She flinched at the unexpected contact, then tried to pull away.

"It's okay," he said softly, patting her hand and arm. "Stay where you are."

"Only if you do, too," she whispered.

There was a brief moment of silence, then a sigh as Evan laid his hand right next to Molly's.

"Sleep well, lady, and once again, thank you for saving my son's life."

"You're welcome," she answered.

Johnny heard their voices but was too close to sleep to chime in. For the first time in two days, he felt as if his world was beginning to right itself. He was really sad about his grandparents, and his daddy didn't look quite right. But when he closed his eyes, Daddy still sounded the same, and Molly was still there—strong and smart and smelling really good. He snuggled just a little bit farther beneath the covers and sighed. Maybe it really was going to be all right.

Deborah's bath had been far shorter than she would have liked, but there wasn't enough hot water left for a good soak, so she'd settled for just getting clean.

Her feet were starting to feel normal, but her face still burned. She'd rubbed plenty of moisturizing lotion onto her skin, but it was going to take more than one dose to get her past the chafing the cold had caused.

Her pink flannel nightgown was hanging on a hook on the bathroom door. She took it off the hook and slipped it over her head, relishing the familiar softness and warmth against her skin. She stepped into some house shoes, gave her hair a good brushing, then left it down.

Even though she was sure that Evan and Molly were fine, she thought she would check in on them and grabbed her robe from the foot of the bed as she left her room.

The house was quiet except for the intermittent snoring of someone down the hall. It was coming from the room that James and Mike had taken. She smiled to herself, wondering which one it was. It only took a few moments to see that Johnny's compromise was working. Evan and Molly were lying facing each other, with Johnny nestled right in between. Her vision blurred when she saw that they were sound asleep with their fingers entwined. Even asleep, their intent to protect the boy was still strong.

Quietly she closed the door, then moved toward the kitchen, making sure the back door was locked. She glanced at the clock. It was almost four in the morning. She sighed. Three hours' sleep, and then she would have to be up doing chores, if only so she could let Farley know she was back and he didn't have to come by anymore. The dog and cats could wait a bit for their food, but her old cow wouldn't appreciate a late milking.

She started into the living room, then gasped when she saw a shadow move between the front door and the sofa.

"Who's there?" she called, then watched a figure emerging from the darkened room.

"Sorry," Mike said as he walked into the light. "I was just putting the fire screen up."

"Thank you," Deborah said, and added, "I thought you were asleep."

Mike grinned. "You've got to be kidding. Didn't you hear Dad snoring?"

Deborah smiled. "Well, yes, actually I did hear something. I wondered which one of you it was. Now I know."

"Just so you know...I don't snore," Mike said.

"I'll file that information away for future reference."

Mike grinned again.

Deborah stood for a moment, absorbing this man and his energy.

"What?" Mike asked.

She shrugged. "Sorry, I didn't mean to stare. I just find it remarkable that you all look so much alike. Dark hair, blue eyes, and you're all so tall. Who's tallest?"

"Grandpop," Mike said. "He's also the oldest, at eighty-five. I think he's about six foot six."

"Oh, my," Deborah said. "And here I thought James was big."

Mike smiled. "Yeah. You know how tough it is for a boy to want to be as big as his dad and never quite make it?"

"But you're tall, too," Deborah said.

Mike moved a little closer.

Deborah wished he'd had the foresight to put on a T-shirt like Evan. It was distracting to see such broad shoulders, all that warm, tanned skin and flat belly, and not think of what the rest of him might look like.

"Um, I was just going to bed," she said. "So…I guess I'll see you in the morning?"

Mike stopped just short of touching her. He wanted to, but he could tell she was uneasy.

"Count on it," he said, then pointed to the couch. "If you need me, I'm bunking down on that couch. Just holler. I'll come running."

"I'll get you some sheets and blankets, then," she said, and hurried down the hall to the linen closet.

Her hands were trembling as she pulled out a pair of clean sheets and a pillowcase. As she was reaching for the blankets, Mike stepped up behind her.

"I'll get that," he said, then reached up over her and

pulled a couple of blankets down from a shelf above her head.

Deborah handed him the sheets without looking at him.

"I'll get an extra pillow from my closet, then help you make your bed."

She left before Mike could tell her he was capable of making the bed by himself, and he decided to keep quiet just to be able to spend a few extra minutes alone with her.

Deborah hurried back to the living room carrying the pillow, only to see that Mike had already pulled out the sofa and was putting on the bottom sheet.

"Here, I'll do the other side," she said, and grabbed the loose sheet and began tucking it into place. "I'll be up pretty early, and I'll try to be quiet, but just in case, I'm apologizing ahead of time for the noise."

Mike frowned. "Up early for what?"

"Chores," she said. "I have animals to tend to and—"

He took the sheet out of her hand and turned her toward the hall.

"Damn, woman, if I had known you weren't going to get any sleep at all, I would have nixed the help. For God's sake, go to bed. I can do this."

"It's okay," she said, "I'm used to—"

Mike circled her, then stopped when they were face-to-face. There was a long moment of silence as their gazes locked. The tension between them was palpable.

Deborah's heart started to pound.

Mike's eyes narrowed as he slid his hands beneath her hair and cupped the back of her neck. He could feel the thunder of her pulse beneath his fingers. When he leaned forward to kiss her, he felt it skip.

Their lips conformed to each other's almost instantly, but the hunger in the kiss unsettled them both. Within seconds of making contact, they had pulled away.

"Go to bed," Mike said.

Deborah turned and walked away without answering, but not because she was angry. She left because she knew if she opened her mouth to say anything, it would be to invite him to come with her.

9

Wally Hacker glanced at the clock as he hung up the phone, then turned to the dispatcher.

"Paul, put out the word that the missing passengers have been found. The damn phone cut out before I could get any details, but Miss Sanborn said they didn't require emergency treatment, so I trust they're going to be okay."

"Yes, sir. Right away," Paul said, then added, "That Deborah is somethin', ain't she, boss?"

Wally nodded. "'Something' isn't quite the right word, but you're right on about her being special. Oh…by the way…find the number for that guy from the FAA. What's his name? Antoine Devereaux. I want to call him myself."

Paul shuffled through some papers, found the list he'd been given and wrote the number down for the sheriff.

"Here you go, sir."

"Thanks. Now, go make those calls. If any of those TV or newspaper people call here, forward the calls to my office."

"Yes, sir," Paul said, and got down to business.

Wally carried the phone number into his office, then sat down behind his desk before he dialed the phone. He said a quick prayer as he made the call, hoping it would go through. The last thing he wanted was to have to go out at this time of night and drive up to the crash site to talk to Devereaux to tell him their three missing passengers had been found safe and sound.

Antoine Devereaux was wrapped up in his sleeping bag and lying on the floor of a large motor home one of the searchers had driven up as close as possible to the site. It was built to accommodate six sleepers. There were at least twelve—maybe thirteen—who'd sought shelter inside on this cold, snowy night.

He'd been lying there for hours, dozing off and on between cursing the sounds and snores of so many people crowded into such a small place, even though he knew it was better than being outside in the snow, where a lot of the searchers had bedded down.

When his cell phone rang, it startled him. In trying to answer it, he dropped it, giving it time to ring four more times before he found it in the dark.

"Devereaux," he mumbled.

"Mr. Devereaux, this is Sheriff Hacker. Sorry to be calling at such an ungodly hour, but I thought you'd like to know that I just heard from Deborah Sanborn."

Tony twisted far enough free of the confines of the sleeping bag to sit up.

"Who? Oh…yeah, your psychic."

Hacker grinned to himself. "Yeah, well, my psychic, as you call her, has found your missing passengers. The phone cut out, but I heard enough to know that they're all safe, and they made it to her house."

Tony was floored. "You're kidding!"

"Nope. I wouldn't kid about something like that," Wally said. "Also…she said they didn't need any immediate medical attention, so we have to assume they'll be all right until we can get to them."

"Well, hallelujah," Tony muttered, thinking of all the people who would finally get to go home. "Thanks for calling. I'll deal with the searchers now and get back with you later to get Sanborn's phone number. I wonder why Mike didn't call me direct?"

"Probably couldn't get through."

"Oh, yeah…didn't think of that," Tony said. "Anyway, thanks for the call, and I'll see you later."

"Any time," Hacker said, and disconnected.

Tony dropped his phone back in his pocket and then made his way up from the floor to a light switch. When he turned it on, a multitude of groans and soft curses could be heard throughout the RV.

"Shut the hell up and listen," Tony growled. "The missing passengers have been found. The searchers need to be notified, but there's a possibility that our cells and handheld radios won't reach them. Even so, they have to be notified before daylight, so they don't head off into the woods again, broadening their search. That means I need volunteers. Get dressed and be ready to go in fifteen minutes."

More grumbles, but they were good-natured. Everyone was pleased to learn the missing passengers had been found. While everyone else was dressing, Tony headed outside.

It was only a few hours before daylight. The sky was a murky black. No stars were visible, and if there was a moon, it was hidden by the clouds he had yet to see. The few lights that had been strung up around the area were powered by the generators Tony could hear running. It made getting around the vehicles much easier than if he'd had to do it with only his flashlight, but it also made the air smell of fuel, instead of mountain.

Bits and pieces of the crashed plane had been hauled here to be taken away to a warehouse, where the plane would be reconstructed in hopes of finding a reason for the crash. It would be days before everything was removed. Reflections from the artificial lights shining down on the chunks of ripped and curled metal gave the area a macabre appearance.

As he walked, a couple of armed guards nodded at him from a distance. He waved and kept on going toward the communications van. One quick knock to signal his entrance and he was inside.

The techie on duty had been asleep. Tony didn't say anything as he moved to a coffeepot and poured up what looked like black syrup into a foam cup.

"Jesus, Carter, when was this made?"

Carter ran the end of a pen through his hair to scratch his scalp. No need messing up a perfectly good do by disarranging the pointy little spikes.

"I couldn't say," he said as he waved a hand toward the minifridge. "I'm into soft drinks myself."

Tony winced as he took his first sip, then stirred in some sugar.

"Maybe this will help," he said as he took a second drink, which turned out no better than the first, just sweeter. "Nope, that didn't work, either," he said, and abandoned it for a Coke from the fridge.

"So…what's up, boss?" Carter asked.

"I need you to call in all the searchers."

Carter's face fell. "Don't tell me it's bad news."

"Just the opposite," Tony said. "The missing passengers have been found alive and well. Tell everyone to come back in at daybreak."

"Yes, sir!" Carter said. "That's the kind of news I like to send."

Tony grinned. "Oh, yeah, I hear you loud and clear."

Tony downed his Coke, tossed the empty can in the trash and then left the van. He was halfway back to the motor home when someone called out his name.

"Hey, Devereaux! Wait up!"

Tony stopped and turned around as a man ran out of the shadows from between a row of parked cars. It wasn't until the stranger stepped into the glow of the overhead lights that Tony realized who it was. He frowned as the man started pummeling him with questions.

"So, Devereaux, you're up early. What's going on? Anything you can tell me? Any news from the searchers? Did you find the missing passengers? Are they dead? They are, aren't they?"

Tony shoved his hands in his coat pockets to keep from putting them around the reporter's neck.

"Morrison, right?"

The reporter nodded. "Yeah…what can you tell me?"

"That it's friggin' cold out here," Tony said, and headed for the RV.

"Damn it, man…all I want is an answer."

"To which question?" Tony asked as he reached the door.

Morrison cursed.

"That wasn't a question," Tony said, and disappeared into the RV, firmly shutting the door behind him.

But Morrison wasn't giving up that easily. He stood for a minute to make sure that Devereaux was safely inside, then headed for the communications van.

He walked up the steps leading into the van, then hesitated before firmly gripping the door latch and easing it open a couple of inches. It was just enough to hear what the man inside was saying. He listened until he was certain of his information, then slowly closed the door and headed back to his car, grinning all the way.

Inside the RV, Tony had handpicked the nine people he wanted to follow up.

"Go over to the communications van. Carter is on duty. Find out which groups are nonresponsive. Take snowmobiles, go to their last known locations and send them in." Then he pointed to a tall middle-aged woman who'd been with the FAA almost as long as he had. "Bonnie…you're in charge. Coordinate who's going in which direction. The rest of you, partner up and let's get this done."

"Yes, sir," the woman said, and headed out the door. "Come on, guys, let's get to the mess tent. I might even be persuaded to make a pot of fresh coffee before we disperse."

There was a general round of good-natured ribbing about the quality of her coffee as the group filed out, but it was with a far better attitude than when they'd come in. Dead and dying passengers were common at a crash site, but it was rare that they went missing. Knowing that the trio were no longer at the mercy of the elements made everyone feel a lot better.

Once the RV was quiet, Tony dug through the mini-kitchen for some coffee to make a fresh pot. There was none. Cursing the situation in general, he followed the others back outside. Bonnie's coffee wasn't all that great, but it was better than none.

It was the lead news story on all the morning talk shows and the perfect lead-in to *USA Morning*'s already scheduled feature on holiday miracles. With only days until Christmas, what could be more miraculous than to survive a plane crash, get lost in the Appalachians during a snowstorm, then be found alive and well? The names of the missing passengers had been on everyone's lips since the crash, and pictures were every-where of Senator Wilson at work on Capitol Hill, Molly Cifelli in her college graduation cap and gown, and Johnny O'Ryan in his most recent school picture. A couple of news crews had even done their research and found out that Johnny O'Ryan was the son of an American soldier, fresh from the Iraqi war, then gone on to learn that Evan O'Ryan was only the latest in a long line of O'Ryans to have served their country in fine military fashion. When the story hit the news that Johnny O'Ryan was the son of an American soldier who'd been given an honorable discharge due to extensive injuries, teddy bears began showing up at the sheriff's office in Carlisle—all for a little boy who'd gotten lost on his way home for Christmas.

Everyone wanted an interview with the survivors, but their location was still vague, and the prediction of another storm in the area limited the possibilities of getting to them.

Wally Hacker had the presence of mind to go to the motel where Evan had taken a room, and he notified Thorn that not only was his family safe, but that his great-great-grandson had been found.

Thorn thanked the sheriff profusely, and once he was alone in the motel room again, wept tears of relief. He tried to call James personally, but the call wouldn't go through. Still rejoicing in the good news, he went into the bathroom to shave.

The mirror kept fogging over as he dragged his razor through the shaving cream and stubble on his face. If he squinted, he could almost pretend the years hadn't marked themselves so drastically upon his features. Not that he minded getting older. It was just difficult to believe he'd lived eighty-five years, when he still felt young inside. The blessing was that there was a comfort within him now that had nothing to do with knowing the men in his family were still intact. It came from the bond he'd had with his wife. Even in death, she had just proved to him that she was never far away.

He rinsed the razor beneath the small flow of hot water, then took another swipe on his cheek as the steam continued to rise between him and the mirror. When he was done, he wiped his face free of any remaining shaving cream, then spoke, as if his wife were standing right beside him.

"So, my darling Marcella, once again I am humbled by your diligence," he said softly. "Thanks to you, our little Johnny has been found."

At that point he finished dressing, then grabbed his coat and wallet. For the first time in days, he felt hungry. It was time to get something to eat.

Darren Wilson was unaware of the news. In fact, he was so damned miserable that he would have welcomed being found just to know he would also be warm. Even if it was in a jail cell.

Instead he woke up alone, still hungry, still freezing—and still in a butt-load of trouble.

He pulled what was left of the energy bar from his pocket and took a small bite. He chewed three times on one side of his mouth, and then, although it hurt like hell, three times on the other side before he swallowed. He kept going until he'd eaten another third of the bar, leaving him with one third left to go. He folded up the paper around it and put it back in his pocket, repeated the mouth-rinsing technique that he'd used the night before, then got up and peed—marking the white snow in three places with urine. Only then could he relax.

His spirits were low when he resumed his hunt, but his attitude changed when he soon found tracks. Something deep in his brain registered that there were too many tracks for only a woman and a child, but all he noticed was that he was no longer the only person alive on this mountain. It was enough.

He locked onto the trail, and despite the fact that it led upward, he followed the footprints relentlessly. Whatever happened later was beside the point. He just needed warmth and food and shelter.

Farley Comstock woke up and groaned, thinking of the trip he had to make up to Deborah's place. Even though she gave him milk and cream in return for firewood, the thought of having to hike through the snow to milk that damned cow was enough to send him back to bed.

On a good day, he didn't like to milk. On a day when the weather was so miserably cold, he would have tried to talk his wife into making Kool-Aid for his nine kids to drink. However, his wife was close to giving birth again, and when she got like that, all her mothering instincts kicked in. She would have given him hell for even suggesting Kool-Aid, although he didn't know why. He'd grown up drinking it, and it hadn't hurt him none.

He made a face in the mirror as he finished shaving, ignoring the two missing teeth in front on his lower jaw, and slapped some after-shave on his skin to close the pores. He would much rather have grown a beard in winter to keep his face warm, but his wife didn't like facial hair any more than she liked Kool-Aid. Still, she was a good wife and a good mother, and if the worst thing she demanded of him was to shave and make sure her kids had milk to drink, he considered himself a lucky man.

He wiped his hands on a towel, then quietly exited the bathroom and tiptoed down the hall. If he was lucky, he would get the fire going good and maybe get in a cup of fresh coffee before everyone woke up and he had to head out to see to Deborah's cow.

Farley liked his quiet times. There just never were enough of them anymore to suit his ways.

He laid a couple of logs on the fire, then turned up the thermostat on the floor furnace and headed for the kitchen. The last thing he expected was to see a half-frozen and bloody-faced stranger standing there, eating fistfuls of jelly sandwiches like they were going out of style.

"Hey!" he yelled out. "What the hell do you think you're doin'?"

Darren Wilson turned abruptly, a half-eaten bite of sandwich still dangling from the corner of his mouth. As a politician, he'd always been concerned with pre-senting a good face to the public. He would have been horrified had he been able to see himself through Farley Comstock's eyes.

But he was starving and in trouble, and at the moment, he couldn't have cared less what he looked like. He grabbed the rifle he'd found hanging above the back door and pointed it at Farley.

"Sit down and keep quiet," he mumbled, while chewing his food in alternating sequences of three.

Farley dropped into a chair, his mouth open, his eyes wide with shock. He couldn't get past the fact that there was a man in his kitchen stealing food.

"If'n you're hungry and all...then eat what you want," he said. "There ain't no call to pull a gun for the food."

Darren felt guilty for the act, but sometimes a man had to do what a man had to do.

"Just shut up," Darren muttered, and stuffed the rest of the sandwich into his mouth.

Farley watched the man eat, noticing that he was particular about the way he chewed, and tried to figure out how to get the gun away from him before the first of his nine kids woke up. After that, there was no telling what might happen.

There were days when Farley himself considered shutting all nine of them up in the chicken house just for an hour's peace and quiet—and he loved his kids. No telling what this stranger would do when faced with Farley's nine offspring. Whatever he did, it wouldn't be good—not when he was holding a gun and eating all the bread and jelly. Farley, knowing his kids, figured they were gonna ignore the rifle and take offense over the fact that their bread and jelly was gone.

Darren had come upon the farmhouse by accident. Earlier, he'd been blindly following the tracks he'd found, stumbling and falling and cursing the world in general, when he realized that the forest had gone silent.

The birds he'd been hearing, the off-and-on complaints of squirrel chatter, even the occasional shriek of a hawk overhead, were all suddenly gone.

It was then that he'd stopped and looked—really looked—at the land in which he'd been walking.

At first he'd seen nothing except the thick growth of trees and snow as far as the eye could see. He was still looking around when he caught movement from the corner of his eye. When he realized it was a mountain lion, and that the lion was looking back at him, he all but lost it.

He remembered once reading that if confronted by a bear in the woods, the worst thing you could do was turn and run away. He didn't know if the same applied to mountain lions, but he wasn't going to take a chance and be wrong, only to be eaten.

Slowly, he looked around for something that would serve as a weapon and saw a large branch that had fallen from a nearby tree. Without taking his gaze from the lion, he walked slowly over to the branch and picked it up. The moment he had it, he held it over his head, giving the animal the false impression that he had suddenly grown several feet taller.

The mountain lion watched, its belly growling audibly from hunger. Then its eyes narrowed nervously as it hissed a sharp warning.

Darren saw the mouthful of sharp teeth and shivered.

"Get!" he yelled, and swung the limb in a large circle above his head.

The cat's eyes caught the movement. Its ears went flat against its head as it slipped a couple of steps backward. Again it hissed, and then growled.

Darren was so pissed off to be in this situation that before he thought, he growled back.

The cat went flat, then, seconds later, leaped up and ran away. The moment it showed its back to Darren, Darren peed his pants. It wasn't something he was proud of, but it was either cry or pee. His bladder won out.

As the warm urine ran down the inside of his leg, it occurred to him that it was the first time he'd felt warmth since the plane had gone down. He began to curse as he stared in the direction the cougar had gone, making sure that it didn't decide to come back.

And while he wasn't giving up on trailing the woman and the kid, he had no intention of following that damned mountain lion up into the trees, even though the tracks he'd been following led the same way, so he was forced to take another direction.

He soon found himself on a snow-covered one-laned road and only a few yards away from a small frame house. Relief swept through him as he headed toward it with single-minded intent. There was a thin spiral of smoke coming out of a chimney, and the early-morning sounds of a bunch of chickens waiting to be fed coming from a small red shed out behind a barn.

Smoke meant warmth. Chickens meant food.

At that point, he didn't care who saw him. He just

needed to eat and get warm—maybe get some dry clothes and some medicine for his aches and pains.

It never occurred to him that he would wind up taking a family hostage. But when the morning began to take a turn in that direction, he was already too far in to pull back.

Now that he'd been confronted by the owner of the house, he felt backed into a corner. He swallowed the last bite of sandwich and shifted the rifle to a more comfortable position, which happened to coincide with a line right toward Farley Comstock's head.

Farley was sweating right down to his socks, but when the man reached for the bread and jelly again, Farley felt it only fair to warn him.

"Say, mister…if you're hungry…you might think about letting me wake up the wife. She'd be happy to cook you up some eggs and biscuits, maybe a little sausage and gravy to go with 'em. But you don't want to be eatin' up all the bread and jelly. The kids won't like it."

Darren frowned.

"I don't give a good goddamn about what your kids like or don't like. I haven't eaten in days. I have the gun. I'll eat what I please."

Farley shrugged. "Don't say I didn't warn you."

Darren was in the act of slapping another spoonful of jelly on a slice of bread when he heard the first set of footsteps coming down the hall. He frowned.

Farley spoke up. "I'm tellin' you now, mister, that if you even point that gun at one of my kids, I'll have to hurt you."

"You keep your kids out of my way and they'll be fine," Darren muttered.

As he was saying it, he kept hearing more and more footsteps—running. By now, he'd lost track of how many people he'd heard coming down the hall. He was expecting more than two, but not the herd of children still in pajamas and nightgowns that hit the kitchen running.

"Jesus!" Darren yelled. "How the hell many kids do you have?"

All nine of Farley's kids saw the stranger at the same time that they realized he was into their bread and jelly. They paid no attention to the fact that he looked like something out of a nightmare, or that he was holding their daddy's gun. They began to scream.

"Daddy! Daddy! That man's eatin' up our bread and jelly!"

Darren actually flushed, then he swung the rifle toward them.

"Get back, you brats! All of you. Get back or I'll shoot your daddy dead."

The two smallest ones started to wail, but not from fear they were about to lose their daddy. It was the loss of bread and jelly that had sent them over the edge.

Their wails were like nothing Darren had ever heard. He threatened, he shouted—he even fired a shot up into the ceiling, which did nothing but set the other seven children to screaming and wailing, as well.

At that point, a very pregnant Ruth Comstock came waddling into the room with a pistol in her hand.

Darren's eyes bulged.

"What the hell's going on here?" Ruth cried.

Then she saw the stranger holding Farley's gun, saw the mess he'd made of her kitchen, knew he was responsible for her babies' tears and raised her pistol. She fired before Darren could duck.

Fortunately for him, her aim was off.

The bullet shattered the wall next to him. He would have raised the rifle and shot back, but he hesitated about shooting a pregnant woman. Before he had time to reconsider his moral issues, Ruth Comstock had shot at him again.

This time the bullet ricocheted, sending a shower of wood splinters into the side of his face.

"Oh, hell! Wait! Lady! Stop shooting! Stop shooting! I only wanted—"

The third shot sailed past his waist and hit the doorjamb. At that point he realized she was lowering her aim. Fearing that the next shot would catch him right in the balls, he turned on one heel and went out the kitchen door as fast as his bum leg would carry him.

He knew she'd followed him out onto the porch, because he could hear the wails and shrieks of all those kids. The way he figured it, the only reason she stopped was because she'd finally emptied her pistol while he was in retreat. He thanked God for her bad aim and kept on running.

Farley was somewhat taken aback that his Ruthie had been the one who'd saved the day—and the bread and jelly. Ruthie, however, was so overwhelmed by what had just happened that she announced she was going into labor, and went back to bed.

Farley tried to call the doctor—hoping to talk him into a half-price vasectomy after the baby was born—but the storm had knocked out the phones. So, with all thoughts of Deborah's cow gone from his mind, he told the older kids to mind the younger and went up to see to the birth of his tenth.

10

As exhausted as Deborah had been when she finally went to sleep, her internal body clock had gone off, even if the electric alarm had not. She sat up and then scooted to the side of the bed, feeling for her house shoes with her eyes still closed.

She staggered into the bathroom and came out a short time later, wide awake, teeth brushed and hair piled up on her head. She rummaged through her closet, choosing a pair of black pants and a pink cable-knit sweater. She dressed quickly, adding thick wool socks, then headed for the kitchen. She made coffee, then, while it was brewing, retrieved her hiking boots from the hearth where she'd left them last night to dry out. They were a bit stiff, but warm, as she slipped them on. An unintentional shiver ran up her spine as she thought about going back out into the cold.

She looked around for Mike as she went into the living room and glanced toward the sofa. Last night he'd threatened to sleep in here. Quietly she tiptoed closer, then peered over. He was still there—flat on his back and sound asleep, with his arms thrown over his head. In repose, his features were almost beautiful. The coals in the fireplace were still glowing a bright, fiery red, casting shadows of light and dark upon his face. She thought long and hard about leaning over and kissing his softly parted lips, then told herself she'd been alone too long.

Reluctantly, she turned away and moved toward the fireplace, walking softly so as not to wake him. Puppy, who had made her bed by the fireplace, lifted her head and looked sleepily at Deborah, who bent down and patted the dog's head, then quietly lifted the fire screen and set it aside to lay a fresh log on the grate. The embers flared and soon caught. Satisfied that she'd set the house in motion for the day, she replaced the fire screen, gave Mike a last wistful glance and turned her attention toward the chores. Puppy followed her out of the room, her little toenails clicking on the hardwood floors as they entered the kitchen.

Mildred, the milk cow, would be waiting at the barn, as would the barn cats. So many chores. So many house-guests. At least she would be able to tell Farley she was back when he showed up.

Ah, well… I always have plenty of solitude. A little change is good for the soul.

Even though the house was quiet, it felt different—more alive. What was strange was that the energy from her unexpected guests was imbuing her with the same feelings. She couldn't remember when she'd felt this excited about a day, which didn't say much for her social life. It was pitiful to admit that five strangers in her home had taken on monumental proportions of importance. Despite her proclivity for solitude, she was looking forward to what might unfold as she stepped outside.

The cold hit her like a slap to the face, sharp, biting and deceptively deadly. Still, it was nothing to what Molly and the boy had endured. Thank God they'd found them when they had. She didn't think they would have survived another night without fire. Anxious to get the chores over with and get back inside, she picked up the milk bucket and headed toward the barn.

The crust on the snow crunched with each step she took, leaving perfect footprints from the house to the barn. Mildred heard her coming and bawled a welcome. Puppy woofed a soft hello back to the cow. Buttercup, the yellow barn cat, bounced out of a nearby storage room and wound herself around Deborah's ankles as she entered the barn.

"Good morning, Buttercup. How are the kids?"

As if on cue, four half-grown kittens came piling out of the same storage room and began mewing loudly.

"I hear you," Deborah said. "Just give me a minute, okay?"

She hung the milk bucket on a nail and went into the tack room to get cat food. When she turned around, Puppy was sitting in the doorway, watching her intently.

"Yes, Puppy, I see you. You're gonna get your food, too."

Having said that, she took the sack of dry cat food

and filled three bowls. Two for the cats and one for Puppy. Puppy had been hanging out with cats most of her life and preferred to eat what her buddies ate. The way Deborah looked at it, Puppy was entitled to likes and dislikes, just like anyone else.

Mildred bawled again, only softer and in a lower tone. Deborah smiled as she filled a big grain scoop with sweet feed and put it in the manger. The old cow moved into position as calmly as she did every morning, eager to eat and to be relieved of the milk Deborah was after.

Half wondering where Farley was, Deborah took the milk bucket from the nail, moved a small milk stool into position and sat down. As always, she rubbed Mildred's belly a couple of times, talking softly to her as she warmed her hands before touching the cow's udders. Mildred munched slowly on her food, satisfied with what was going on. Deborah stroked the cow's belly, reminding her what was about to occur, then pulled gently on two of the tightly swollen teats a few times, alternating strokes until Mildred's milk began to flow.

Steam rose instantly as the warm milk hit the cold bucket. Deborah's breath mingled with the steam coming from the cow's warm belly, mixing familiar scents she'd known since childhood. Even though the cold made the chore uncomfortable, there was something satisfying about the routine. When Deborah was with the animals, the rest of the world and its troubles fell away. There was nothing to worry about, no one to save, no visions to endure. And so she sat, her forehead resting against Mildred's side, squeezing the teats in strong, steady strokes until they were flaccid and the bucket contained all Mildred's morning milk.

Deborah scooted the stool back, then got up, taking the bucket with her as she went. She paused long enough to pour the cats a bit of the fresh milk. They crowded around the bowl and drank until their treat was gone, then climbed up in the stack of hay bales and disappeared.

Puppy gazed longingly at the high-stacked bales, then woofed once before turning to look at Deborah.

"Come on," she said. "You can go back in by the fire."

Puppy wagged her tail and then led the way out of the barn. Deborah glanced at the sky as she hurried toward the house. It was overcast again. A sign of more snow. Smoke from the fireplace rose high above the roof, only to disperse into the atmosphere. The scent of burning wood and fresh pine from the nearby trees was strong in the air. She could almost taste the hot coffee waiting for her inside, and then remembered she would not be eating breakfast alone.

Unconsciously, her steps lengthened. By the time she reached the back porch, she was breathless. She reached for the screen door, then jumped when it opened before her.

"Oh!"

Mike reached out, took the bucket from her hands, then took her by the arm and helped her up the steps and inside the screened-in back porch. When the old collie bounded in between them, he grinned.

"Well, hello there, girl. You and Deborah have been up awful early." Then he looked at Deborah. "What is it you call her?"

"Her name is Puppy," Deborah said as she stomped the snow off her boots.

"Puppy?"

Deborah shrugged. "What can I say? Once upon a time, it fit."

Mike arched an eyebrow, then slid an arm around Deborah's waist and pulled her to him.

She didn't resist.

"Don't spill the milk," she whispered.

"Wouldn't think of it," he said. And then he kissed her.

His lips were firm and warm, and he tasted slightly of coffee. Deborah wanted so much more of him than just the kiss, but it wasn't going to happen. Not yet.

When she moaned beneath her breath, Mike's mind went blank. Her lips had been cold, but they were warm now, and yielded to his demand without caution. It would be so easy to forget where they were, or that they weren't alone.

He couldn't believe how quickly this attraction had happened, but he wasn't going to question a good thing. It had been years since he'd been this out of his head for a woman, and he didn't want to mess up. He wanted Deborah in every way a man could want a woman. Just when they were at the point of forgetting propriety, Puppy barked.

Deborah drew back reluctantly, then glanced at the dog and smiled.

"She wants in by the fire."

Mike sighed, then reluctantly turned Deborah loose.

"And you probably do, too. What do I do with this?" he asked, holding up the bucket of milk.

"Give it to me. I'll strain it up out here, then wash the bucket inside."

"I can help," Mike said.

"Have you ever done this before?" she asked.

He paused, then grinned. "Done what?" he asked.

Deborah made a face at him.

"I never did get the hang of flirting, so quit it. We're talking about straining milk, not having sex."

"I don't know what you're talking about," Mike said.

"You forget who you're talking to," Deborah said. She took the milk out of his hands and poured it through a strainer into a large crock jar, then covered the jar with a clean cotton cloth and carried the bucket inside to wash.

The warmth of the house was almost intoxicating.

"Ooh, it feels good to be warm," Deborah said as she took off her coat and hung it on the hook by the back door. "Who's up besides you?"

Mike's grin widened.

When he didn't answer, Deborah looked up. Immediately, it dawned on her what she'd said.

"I'll rephrase the question. Who's awake besides you?"

"Everyone, or I'd offer to—"

Deborah laughed out loud. She had never had these kinds of conversations with a man, and yet instead of offending her, his ingenuous honesty just struck her as funny.

Mike watched the surprise, then the delight, spreading across her face and ignored the ache of want in his belly. She was so pretty when she let down her guard, and her laughter…God, it was a force of nature.

"You need to do something with your hands besides what you're thinking," Deborah said, and handed him the milk bucket and the strainer. "Here…please wash these well with hot, soapy water. You can hang them on the nails just outside the kitchen door."

"Yes, ma'am," Mike said, and pretended dismay at being misunderstood.

Deborah laughed again, only softer.

"You are such a fake," she said. "But a lovable one, nonetheless."

Mike paused. "Am I? Am I really?"

"Really what?" Deborah muttered as she poured herself a cup of coffee.

"Lovable?"

Deborah paused in the act of stirring sugar into her coffee and looked up at him. The fun in his voice and expression was gone. She sighed.

"Something tells me I'm going to regret being so open with you, but yes…you are a lovable man, Mike O'Ryan."

He nodded, then straightened his shoulders as if he'd just been divested of a huge weight and headed for the sink.

Deborah took a sip of her coffee, added a bit more

sugar and stirred, then sipped again. It was perfect. As soon as Mike took the bucket and strainer to the back porch, she washed her hands, got a package of bacon from the fridge and began fixing breakfast. While Mike went outside to bring in more firewood, she began frying bacon. In the middle of taking the last perfectly fried strips out of the skillet, she heard Johnny squeal. The sound was unfamiliar, and she couldn't tell whether it was panic or pleasure, so she hurried to the living room to investigate.

He and Puppy had found each other.

James was stirring the fire, and Mike was standing by with a fresh log to put on the fire as she came into the room.

"Is everything all right?" Deborah asked, somewhat shocked by her old dog's puppy-like behavior.

"Good morning," James said. "Compared to the past two mornings, this one's a beaut."

She wouldn't look at Mike for fear he would make her blush, but she knew he was looking at her and remembering their kiss.

Johnny squealed again as Puppy nosed the spot beneath his ear and then licked his chin.

At that point Evan came running. He'd managed to pull on his jeans, but he was still wet from his shower. The minute he entered the living room, his gaze went straight to his son.

"Johnny?"

Johnny rolled over on his back and then looked up. "Dad! Look at the cool dog!"

Evan breathed a sigh of relief, then thrust his fingers through his hair, combing it away from his face. Without his eye patch, the devastation of his injuries was accentuated, yet he couldn't have cared less. He'd heard what sounded like a scream and reacted.

"Jesus," he muttered. "My heart nearly stopped."

"I'm sorry," Deborah said. "I didn't know she would get so excited. I can put her outside."

"No!" Johnny cried, and threw his arms around the old collie's neck. "No, Dad, please! We'll be quiet. I promise."

Evan knelt at his son's feet, then ruffled Johnny's hair.

"It's okay, son," he said softly. "I overreacted." Having apologized to Johnny, he then smiled at the old dog. "Hey, girl. What's your name?"

"Her name is Puppy," Deborah said.

"That's a cool name," Johnny said, and then picked up the dog's front foot and shook it, as if it was a hand. "Hello, Puppy. My name is Johnny. Pleased to meet you."

Puppy woofed, as if acknowledging the introduction, which made everyone laugh. Satisfied that all was well, Johnny grinned and resumed his wrestling match with the dog, who seemed to be enjoying it as much as he was.

Evan went back to finish dressing, while James and Mike returned to the fire.

It occurred to Deborah that one of her new guests was missing.

"Has anyone seen Molly this morning?" she asked.

Both men shook their heads. It was Johnny who answered.

"She's still sleeping," he said.

Deborah frowned, wondering how the young woman could sleep through all this.

"I'll just peek in on her before I finish making breakfast," she said.

As Johnny said, Molly appeared to be sleeping. Evan had obviously slipped out of bed when his son had awakened and carefully covered her back up. Her dark hair was fanned across her pillow, her body curled into a ball beneath the covers.

Deborah started to back out of the room when something caught her attention. Frowning, she moved closer, then stopped at the bedside to look closer.

Molly's cheeks were bright red, as if she'd gotten overheated. That in itself wasn't so unusual, except that the room was fairly cool.

Lightly, she laid the back of her hand against Molly's forehead. She was burning up.

"Evan!"

The bathroom door flew back. Evan was standing in the doorway, completely dressed, eye patch and all. When he saw Deborah leaning over the bed, he frowned.

"What's wrong?" Then he realized her attention was on Molly. "Molly? Is something wrong with Molly?"

"She's burning up with a fever. Did you notice anything during the night? Was she restless? Did she get up very often?"

Evan rushed to the bedside.

"Sick? She's sick?"

"Or hurt. It could be an infection. We paid so much attention to Johnny last night that I'm afraid I neglected to check her as thoroughly." Her frown deepened. "Still, I helped her into the tub and didn't see any deep cuts or puncture wounds."

"What do we do?" Evan asked.

"I need to check her. If you would just leave the—"

"You'll need help turning her over. Besides, she put herself in harm's way for my son. I'm not leaving her."

Deborah didn't argue. He was right about one thing: she would need the help.

"Okay," Deborah said. "Let me check her stomach first. If she has internal injuries, I think her belly will be distended."

"Jesus," Evan muttered, and helped Deborah pull back the covers.

He was all but holding his breath as Deborah made a thorough check of Molly's body. Seeing the slender limbs so battered and bruised made him sick, imagining the blows she must have suffered to get this way. When Deborah pulled the nightgown up a bit farther, they both gasped at the size of the bruise just above her rib cage.

"God…what could cause that?" he asked. "Can you tell if her ribs are broken?"

"Not much telling what she hit…or what hit her," Deborah said. "As for her ribs…they feel okay. There's nothing obviously wrong. That's not to say she might not have cracked ribs, but nothing feels out of place."

"Thank God," Evan said.

"Exactly," Deborah said. "Now…help me roll her onto her side."

When Molly didn't once object to being disturbed, Evan feared the worst.

"Shouldn't she be talking to us, or objecting to being undressed…or something?" he asked as he helped Deborah turn Molly over.

Deborah started to answer, then gasped.

"Oh, Lord," she said, and leaned closer, feeling along the wound on Deborah's back.

"What?" Evan asked.

"Here…down low on her back. I don't know why I didn't see this last night."

Evan shifted position so he could see better. There was a dark streak just beneath the top layer of her skin, while the area around it was a swollen and red.

"What the hell is that?" Evan asked.

Deborah pushed gently at the streak. It didn't move.

"I'm not sure," she said. "But there's something under her skin."

"I'm going to get Dad," Evan said.

"No. Stay here with her," Deborah said. "I'm going to get my first aid kit. I'll tell him."

"What are you going to do?" Evan asked.

"Whatever that is, it isn't supposed to be there, so we need to get it out."

Molly moaned.

Deborah glanced at her nervously, then ran from the room, leaving Evan and Molly alone.

Evan felt the heat emanating from her skin, and wanted to pick her up in his lap and rock her as he had his little boy. She'd come out of that crash with injuries like this and yet she'd never said a word. Her whole focus had been on keeping herself and Johnny alive.

He pulled the covers back up over her body, then sat down on the bed beside her. Without thinking, he reached for her hand. When her fingers curled around his, his belly knotted. Had she heard them talking about her, or was that just reflex? Was she scared? God knew he was. He smoothed the hair back from her forehead, then cupped the side of her cheek.

"Molly, can you hear me?"

A tear slid from beneath her eyelids and onto his fingers.

"Ah, honey…don't be afraid. You're not alone. You were there for my son. I'm here for you."

When she heard his voice, she took a slow, deep breath, then tried to reach the place on her back that was inflamed.

"Somethin'…hurts…."

Evan laid a hand on her arm.

"We know, Molly. We're going to make it better."

Her eyelids fluttered; then, slowly, she opened her eyes.

"No, no…go 'way. Leave me 'lone. Don't wanna die."

Evan's gut knotted. She must think he was the killer. "It's okay, Molly. It's me. Evan. You're safe, and I promise I won't let you die."

Seconds later, Deborah came rushing back into the room. Mike was right behind her.

"Where's Johnny?" Evan asked.

"Dad's with him," Mike said. "What's going on here?"

"Molly was injured in the crash, and she never said a word. We should have known. We should have asked, but we were all so focused on Johnny…."

Mike heard the guilt in Evan's voice.

"As you should have been," Mike argued, as he moved closer to the bed, then reached for the covers. "Let me see the wound." He winced as he saw the inflammation. "Damn. That's a mess."

"Here," Deborah said, handing him a couple of large bath towels. "Scoot these beneath her."

Mike unfolded the towels, then tucked them under Molly, who felt the pressure and tried to roll over.

"No, Molly. You need to lie still. Can you hear me, honey? It's Deborah. You need to lie still so I can doctor your wound."

"Hurts," Molly mumbled.

"I know, and I'm so sorry I didn't see it before."

Both men moved aside to give Deborah some room. She doused a handful of cotton balls with alcohol, then thoroughly swabbed the area.

"What do you think that is?" Evan asked.

"It could be almost anything," Deborah said, then dug through the first aid kit. "Damn," she muttered.

"What's wrong?" Evan asked.

"I had a can of freeze spray. I wanted it to deaden the area around the wound, but it's not in here."

"So what are you going to do?" Mike asked.

She glanced around the room, then up at the window. The frost patterns were heavy on the glass, reminding her of what lay outside.

"The snow! I'll use snow. Mike, there's a large dishpan on a table on the back porch. Would you please pack it with snow? We'll use it in lieu of the spray. It's not great, but it's better than digging into her back with no painkillers."

"God Almighty," Evan muttered.

It reminded him too much of how soldiers were patched up in the battlefield, which didn't make sense, because this wasn't Iraq. They were in this great old house, only days before Christmas. It was snowing. A day for making snowmen and snow ice cream with Johnny, not digging what amounted to shrapnel from Molly's back.

Unaware of his son's black mood, Mike ran to do Deborah's bidding. "I'll be right back," he said.

"Everything okay?" James asked as Mike hurried past the living room.

Mike glanced at Johnny, then shook his head.

James got the message and quickly refocused Johnny's attention on the fact that Puppy wanted to play with a chew toy that had been in her bed by the fireplace.

The air outside was already swirling with fresh snowfall as Mike quickly filled the old dishpan. His fingers were so cold they were numb as he carried the pan full of snow back inside.

"Here we go," he said, and set the pan on the side of the bed.

Deborah scooted the pan onto the towels at Molly's back.

"Here…both of you. Grab a handful of snow and hold it on the wound. When the snow starts melting, grab another handful and do it all over again."

All three of them thrust their hands into the snow, grabbed it by the handful and then pressed the snow against the wound.

Even though Molly was hovering close to unconsciousness, she reacted to the harsh cold by grimacing, then moaning as she helplessly tried to move away from the pain.

Evan hated to be causing her discomfort, especially when she didn't understand what was happening.

"I'm sorry, honey," he said softly as he laid one handful of snow after another against her skin. "So sorry…but you'll feel better soon."

When Molly's skin was ice cold, Deborah moved into place. She put on a pair of latex surgical gloves, then poured alcohol over a small scalpel.

"Hold her," Deborah said, and quickly made a shallow incision down the length of the wound.

Molly's weak cry of distress hurt all the way to Evan's soul. Seeing the quick flow of blood made him flinch. So red against skin so white.

Deborah's hands were quick, her movements sure, evidence of her emergency training. Once she had an opening large enough in which to maneuver, she grabbed a large pair of tweezers and thrust it into the slit she'd made in the skin.

"Can you tell what it is?" Mike asked.

Deborah's frown deepened as the tweezers fastened on something, then slipped off just as quickly.

"Darn it," she muttered, and tried again, maneuvering the tweezers through the welling blood until she felt them catch. "There. Whatever it is, I have hold of it."

Molly moaned again and flinched. The motion caused the tweezers to slip again.

"Oh, no," Deborah said, then looked up at Mike. "Hold her tighter," she snapped.

"Sorry," he said.

Evan was shaking from empathetic pain.

"God in heaven…let this be over," he whispered.

Deborah grabbed a handful of gauze pads and swabbed the blood away from the incision, then tried again.

"Okay, okay, I've got it," she cried. "Hold her…hold her…yes, good girl, Molly. Just a little bit more."

The men watched in disbelief as Deborah pulled a piece of metal out of Molly's back. It was a little larger than a half dollar and about three inches in length, and appeared to have been ripped from its point of origin. The edges were ragged, yet sharp as a razor.

"I can't believe she's been walking around with that in her back," Mike said.

"I can't believe we didn't see it sooner," Deborah said.

Molly cried out again when the alcohol hit the open wound, but Deborah kept working. As soon as she'd cleaned the area, she doused it with antiseptic, then threaded a surgical needle and quickly stitched it closed.

Molly moaned with every thrust of the needle into her skin. Tears spilled from under her eyelids as Evan reached for her hand. Her fingers curled around his and her nails dug into the palms of his hand, but he wouldn't let her go.

"There, it's done," Deborah suddenly announced. When she swabbed off the area one last time with antiseptic, Molly went limp.

"Now she passes out," Evan muttered.

Deborah covered the stitches with a light bandage, pulled down Molly's gown, then rocked back on her heels and started to shake.

"Good job, lady," Mike said softly.

"Thanks to all of you," Deborah said. "Still, I wish we had some antibiotics."

Evan looked up. His face was grim and pale, as if he'd endured the pain of every stitch with her.

"I do. I have some," he said.

Mike frowned. "You can't give her medicine you need to be taking."

Evan glared. "I not only can, I will. I'm healed in every way that matters, and I have them to spare."

As Evan went to get his pills, Mike removed the damp and bloody towels and the pan of melting snow. When he came back, Deborah was sitting on the side of the bed and staring down at the floor.

"Are you all right?" he asked.

Deborah sighed, then looked up. "I haven't had to do anything like that in years."

"You've had some training, haven't you?" he asked.

Deborah nodded. "When you live this far away from medical help, sometimes knowing what to do makes all the difference between life and death."

"Molly was fortunate," he said.

Deborah didn't say anything as she reached for the object she'd removed from Molly's side.

"Can you tell what it is?" Mike asked.

She ran her fingers up and down the bloody metal, then looked up.

"Not really," she said, and then her eyes suddenly lost focus as her head dropped downward.

Snapping trees.

Plowing through the snow.

Falling—falling.

Something coming toward her.

Turning away—pain ripping through her side.

Deborah gasped, then inhaled deeply as the images fell away.

"It's a piece of the outer hull," she said, then dropped it in the waste basket beside the bed.

Mike picked up a wet cloth and gently washed the blood off Deborah's fingers.

"You know something, woman?"

She looked up. "What?"

"Any man would be damn lucky to have you at his back."

The compliment caught her off guard. She started to say thank you, then realized if she spoke she would cry.

"Here are the pills," Evan said as he came back into the room.

They looked at Molly, then at the pills in his hand.

"Now we're going to have to wake her up to take them," Mike said.

"Better that than let the infection take a firmer hold," Deborah said.

"I have some water, too," Evan said, and began to issue orders. "Dad, lift her head up from the pillow."

Mike slid his arm beneath Molly's shoulders, then gently raised her up enough so that she wouldn't choke when she swallowed.

"Molly? Molly, it's me, Evan. You have to open your mouth for me. You have a fever, and I have a pill for you to take. Do you hear me? Open your mouth."

To everyone's surprise, Molly responded. Evan slipped the pill in between her teeth, then thrust the glass of water up to her lips.

"This is water. Drink some of it, Molly." He tilted the glass enough for a little bit of the water to pour into her mouth. "Swallow it, Molly. Swallow the water so the pill can go down."

She choked, and as she did, a little of the water ran out of her mouth and down her chin.

Evan frowned and quickly tilted her chin back just enough so that the pill and water wouldn't come out.

"No. Swallow the water, Molly. Swallow it now."

This time she did.

"It's down," Mike said as he felt Molly go limp.

"Thank goodness," Deborah said. "Now we need to just let her rest."

"I'm staying here," Evan said.

Mike glanced once at Evan, then down at Molly, and finally nodded.

"That's probably a good idea," he said. "Call if you need help."

Evan nodded, but he was so focused on Molly's pale face and the tears on her cheeks that he never knew when they left the room.

11

Johnny was still in the living room when Deborah walked through. They'd all been watching a newscast earlier, but little had been mentioned of the crash. Either they'd missed an earlier broadcast, or the weather was slowing down the gathering of new information. He was sitting on the floor near the fireplace, watching cartoons on television while Puppy lay with her head in his lap. Deborah smiled to herself. She wasn't sure, but Puppy just might have dumped her for a younger playmate.

She was still chuckling as she walked into the kitchen, where James was pouring himself a cup of coffee. She smiled wider when she realized Mike was right behind her.

The sparkle in her eyes was intoxicating, he thought, and he wished he'd been the one to make her smile. "What put that pretty smile on your face?" he asked.

"Johnny and Puppy. I think they're falling in love."

"I can understand how that might happen," Mike said.

Deborah looked nervously from one O'Ryan to the other, as if she'd only just realized she might have done better to leave all of them out in the snow.

"Let's eat," James said. "I'm starving."

Deborah smoothed her hands down the front of her shirt, although she was still a little rattled.

"Um... I'll just..."

"Sit," James said. "You've already cooked the bacon, and the toaster is cranking out toast just fine. If I can't scramble a few eggs, then I don't need to be sharing your food. Go get the others and tell 'em to hustle or it'll all be cold."

"Johnny is the only one not here. Evan is staying with Molly. We'll save some food for them."

"Good enough," James said. "I'll cook the eggs now. Go get Johnny boy...and tell him to wash his hands and face. He's kissed the dog as much as the dog has kissed him."

"And what's wrong with that, I'd like to know?" Deborah asked.

Both men turned and looked at her, then burst out laughing.

"Ah, woman, where have you been all my life?" Mike asked, and went to get Johnny.

Deborah blushed, then was disgusted with herself. That was something better left to innocent young things, not semiworldly women with psychic abilities.

Mike soon came back with Johnny, who quickly noticed that his dad and Molly were missing.

"Where's Daddy? Where's Molly? They have to come eat with me."

Deborah could tell by the pitch of the little boy's voice that he was nervous, but Mike seemed in control.

"Molly doesn't feel well, and your daddy is staying with her. You sit and eat, and when you're through, we'll go see them, okay?"

"No," Johnny said. "I want Daddy and Molly to eat with me."

Mike shoved a hand through his hair in frustration. "Look, Johnny…you can't—"

Deborah decided to help before it became a big deal. She felt his panic. The least she could do was take the edge off his fear.

"I know what, Johnny. I'll go sit with Molly so your daddy can come eat with you. When you're through, you can both come and sit with Molly for a while and I'll eat, but only if you promise to leave some food for me. What do you say?"

"All right," Johnny said, and then looked up at Mike, making sure his grandfather wasn't going to challenge his decision.

"Thanks," Mike said as he seated Johnny at the table. "That's another one we owe you."

Deborah shrugged it off with a slow, secretive smile. "I'll collect before you leave."

The hair rose on the back of Mike's neck as she walked out of the room. What the hell had she meant by that?

* * *

Evan was trying to remember what his wife had looked like, but every time her face finally came to mind, her features morphed into Molly's. He felt guilty and, at the same time, realized he was feeling more than gratitude toward the woman who'd saved his son's life.

The fact that she was moaning beneath her breath from time to time made him nervous. They needed to get her to a doctor, but it didn't appear as if that would be possible until the weather cleared. As he sat watching, she pushed at the covers, then cried out when the movement caused her pain.

"I'm sorry, honey…so sorry," Evan said softly as he pulled the covers back over her.

A tear slid out from beneath her eyelid and was on its way down the side of her nose as the bedroom door swung open. Evan forced himself to look up.

It was Deborah. She laid a hand gently on his head, then let it slide, stroking down the back of his neck as she spoke.

"You need to go eat breakfast with your son. I'll stay with her until you've both finished, then you and Johnny are going to visit Molly together."

Evan stood abruptly. "What happened?"

"Nothing big. Johnny's just feeling insecure right now, and I can't say as how I blame him. He needs to know that he's safe, and your presence confirms that for him."

"Jesus," Evan said, then pointed at Molly. "She's crying in her sleep. Do you think she's in bad pain?"

"Is she restless?" Deborah asked.

"Some."

Deborah sighed. "For now, she's had all the pain medicine and antibiotics we can give her. We'll know more later. Just go eat with your son—and save me some bacon and eggs."

Evan managed a smile. "Yeah…okay. Once again, the O'Ryans owe you a debt of gratitude."

"Like I told your dad, I'll collect in due time."

With one last glance at Molly, Evan hurried out of the room.

Deborah sat down on the side of the bed long enough to feel Molly's skin. It was still hot to the touch, but the medicine hadn't really had enough time to work.

She straightened the covers, then lightly brushed Molly's hair away from her face.

"You don't know it, but you're certainly stirring up a lot of emotions with the two youngest O'Ryans. Better be careful, or you're likely to find yourself permanently attached."

Deborah went into the bathroom and brought back a cool wet cloth and laid it on Molly's forehead. It wasn't much, but it might give her some comfort from the fever.

And so she sat, alternating wet cloths and hoping that the snow would soon stop. She would feel a whole lot better once she knew that Molly and Johnny had seen a doctor and been pronounced fit.

The quiet in the room began to lull Deborah into a false sense of well-being. All she could hear was the soft ticking of a battery-powered clock hanging on the wall and the occasional sound of sleet hitting the windows on the other side of the room. After laying a fresh cool cloth on Molly's forehead, she walked to the window and looked out.

The sky was gray and dismal. The air was full of swirling snowflakes. There was a faint draft coming from the upper left-hand corner of the window, and she made a mental note to recaulk it soon.

The tracks she'd made going to the barn and back were almost obliterated. The chance of communicating with the outside world was, for the moment, slim, and there was nothing anyone could do about it. Still, she felt nervous and wasn't sure why.

It wasn't until she turned away from the window that the vision began, and it came so abruptly that she lost her sense of balance and fell to her knees.

She could feel the nubby texture of the carpet beneath the palms of her hands, but what she was seeing had nothing to do with her room or, for that matter, even her house.

His heartbeat was erratic. His breathing was shallow and rapid. She could feel panic welling up in his chest as he gazed about at the wall of trees surrounding him.

She never knew when she realized she was not only looking at the killer, she was simultaneously inside his mind, and the knowledge was sickening. She felt his disregard for human life as vividly as if she'd been a witness to murder herself, and she felt his pain and knew he, too, was trying to recover from the crash.

He turned away and started walking. Suddenly it dawned on her that if he kept moving at that angle, she would see his face.

Closer and closer he moved. Deborah's pulse rate accelerated. She inhaled slowly, trying to direct the vision, and then gave it up as a lost cause. As always, she had no power over what she saw.

The tension was building in her belly. A few more steps, then she would be able to see him.

She saw him pause. She held her breath.

He wiped a shaky hand across his eyes. When he looked up, she realized she was looking straight at his profile.

He had a long, narrow face, with small light eyes and a nose that appeared to have recently been broken. His hair was awry and stiff with dried blood—hiding most of its mousey-brown shade. His clothes were covered in snow, and there was several days' growth of beard on his face. He would have been an ordinary man—except for the cruel twist to his mouth.

And it was that mouth she was watching. His lips were moving, but she couldn't hear his voice. She didn't know what he was saying, had somehow lost his thoughts, but he was bitterly angry, and she could feel that frustration.

She didn't see Mike come into the room with a plate of food, didn't hear him cursing softly, didn't feel him helping her to her feet. She was too focused on watching for a frontal view of the man's face.

Just a step more, a little to the right, just a fraction of a step more and—

There! She saw him. Watched as he carefully traced the cuts and bruises on his face, then lightly ran a practiced finger down the crooked length of his nose. Then, to her surprise, she heard his voice, as plain as day.

"Damn it, Wilson, if you don't get rid of your witnesses, you will rot in hell."

Deborah gasped, and as she did, the vision disappeared and she suddenly realized that Mike was holding her and staring intently into her face.

"What did you see?" he asked.

Deborah swayed.

Mike groaned, then took her in his arms.

"This is crazy," he muttered as he cupped the back of her head with his hand and pressed her cheek against his shoulder. "I can't believe I'm even asking you this."

"The killer. I saw the killer," she said as she pulled away from his embrace.

"Where is he? What's his name? Maybe we can get through to—"

Deborah grabbed him, her fingers unintentionally digging into the muscles of his forearms.

"He called himself Wilson, but whether it's a first or last name, I don't know. I don't know where he is, either, but I know what he's doing."

"What? Is he headed out of the country? Damn this storm. We can't let him get away."

Deborah glanced nervously at the bed where Molly was lying, then lowered her voice.

"He's not going into hiding," she whispered. "He's looking for Molly and Johnny."

"You mean he's actually trailing them?"

She shivered, as if a cold wind had suddenly blown down her neck.

"Yes, or trying to. He needs to make sure there are no witnesses to what he did."

Mike heard her words, but it was like listening to them from the other end of a long tunnel. It didn't seem possible that this was happening, that the danger wasn't over.

"He's coming to kill them?"

She nodded.

"And you saw this?"

"Yes."

"Then we're one step ahead of him, because, thanks to you, we know what the devil looks like."

Deborah's eyes widened as a sudden knot pulled at her stomach.

"You believe me?"

"Devoutly," he said.

He *did* believe her. She could see it in his face. A huge weight rolled off her shoulders. This was more than she'd ever hoped for.

"What do we do first?" she asked.

Mike pointed to her swiftly-cooling breakfast.

"First you eat, then we make plans."

Deborah nodded as she picked up a fork.

Darren Wilson got up. His head was throbbing and he was in a world of pain. Once he'd relieved himself by peeing in three separate spots, he sat back down on the fallen tree to assess his options.

Thanks to Alphonso Riberra and the crash and his injuries, his plan to escape to the Bahamas was in ruins. If he managed to live through this hell, he wasn't sure if he would ever have the guts to get on another plane, let alone dodge Riberra's bad guys, who would be looking for him—and Riberra's money.

Breakfast had come and gone. Molly woke up to find Evan dozing in a chair by the side of her bed. Johnny was asleep, stretched out on the covers beside her. He was still wearing the old T-shirt he'd slept in last night, but with a little smear of grape jelly on the front. The wool socks he was wearing were pulled up past his knees. His bruises were a darkening purple, but she knew the pain in his ribs was easing with each passing day.

She felt light-headed and a little bit sick to her stomach, but the pain in her back didn't seem quite as bad.

"Evan?"

He rose with a jerk.

"Molly? Are you in pain? What do you need?"

Surprised by the depth of his concern, Molly wondered what she'd missed.

"I don't feel so good," she admitted.

"You had a fever," Evan said as he laid the back of his hand against her cheek.

"My back…"

Evan cupped her face. "Why didn't you tell us you had been injured?"

"What do you mean?" she asked.

"Jesus, lady, you walked around with a piece of metal in your back for days and got an infection. Don't tell me you couldn't feel it."

Molly's eyes widened in disbelief as she reached toward the pain in her back.

"I felt pain, all right, but I hurt all over. It's impossible to distinguish where pain starts and stops."

Evan grabbed her hand, gently stopping her from disturbing the bandage Deborah had put on the wound.

"Deborah performed minor surgery on you a few hours ago. The metal is out. You have some stitches, so no touching, okay?"

"Lord," Molly muttered, then glanced down at Johnny and stroked his hair. "Is he all right?"

"He's okay," Evan said. "Just worried about you. I hope you don't mind, but after what you two went through, you've become his touchstone to sanity."

Molly's eyes filled with tears. "Mind? Of course I don't mind. He's a pretty special little guy."

Evan sat down on the side of the bed, then realized Molly was staring intently at him. Instinctively, he turned the injured side of his face away from her.

"I guess I must look pretty scary," he said.

"Not scary." Then her eyelids fluttered, and she closed her eyes. "Never scary…just hurt," she mumbled.

Evan swallowed past the knot in his throat, then

reached for the pills, shaking a painkiller as well as another antibiotic into his palm.

"Molly…you need to take these pills before you go back to sleep…okay?"

She struggled to open her eyes, but the only thing she managed to open was her mouth.

Evan slipped the two capsules between her teeth, then reached for the water on the table.

"Sip slowly, so you don't choke," he warned, then slipped a hand beneath her head and raised her up enough for her to drink and swallow.

Once she'd finished, he eased her back down and straightened her covers. He was just about to go back to his chair when Molly's fingers curled around his arm.

"Stay," she whispered.

A small pain twisted itself through Evan's belly. Stay? The more he was around her, the more appealing that idea became.

"Yeah…sure," he said softly, then made a place to lie down by scooting Johnny into the middle of the bed.

Molly opened her eyes once to catch Evan staring intently at her. With the eye patch and the scars, he could have passed for a Hollywood version of a pirate, but she knew better. He wasn't just a man who'd come home from a war. He was a father who'd kept a promise to his son.

She smiled, then reached for his hand. Only after she'd threaded her fingers through his did she finally relax. The medicine was working its magic as her eyelids grew heavier and heavier. Finally, she slept.

Evan watched her closely until her breathing slowed and her skin grew cool. When he was certain that her fever was abating, he closed his eyes. At once, he felt himself falling into another nightmare filled with blood and bombs and the never-ending sounds of dying soldiers. His body twitched uncontrollably as he struggled to get out of the way of an approaching tank. Just at the point where the tracks were about to crush him into the desert sand, he felt Molly's fingers tighten their hold. It was exactly what he needed to come back to reality. He shuddered, then slowly relaxed and remembered that he was safe in bed with his child—and this woman.

12

Deborah, Mike and James were huddled together near the fireplace. Purposefully, they kept their voices low so as not to wake the sleeping trio down the hall.

James had been shocked by Deborah's prediction that the killer was coming to make sure there were no living witnesses to what he'd done and had immediately tried to call the sheriff's office down in Carlisle, but to no avail.

The television was on, but no one was paying it much attention. They were so intent on trying to figure out what to do next that they didn't hear the sound of little footsteps coming down the hall. They didn't even know Johnny was anywhere around until they heard him moan.

Deborah jumped and turned around as Mike flew out of his chair and ran to Johnny, who had his Elmo toy stuffed under his chin and his eyes squeezed shut. He was trembling so hard that when Mike picked him up, Mike thought he was ill.

"Hey, little man...what's wrong? Tell Daddy Mike. Are you sick?"

The Elmo toy fell to the floor as Johnny threw his arms around Mike's neck and hid his face in the curve of his grandfather's neck.

"What in hell?" James asked as he laid a hand on Johnny's back.

"I don't know," Mike said. "He doesn't feel feverish."

Deborah laid her hand on the back of Johnny's neck to check his body temperature and was immediately sucked into the panic he was feeling.

"Oh, dear," she said softly, and turned to Mike. "Something has frightened him."

Mike's frown deepened. "Is that so, Johnny? Did something scare you?"

Johnny nodded but wouldn't look up.

Mike hugged Johnny closer, thinking that he'd probably had a bad dream.

"Was it a dream, son? Did you have a bad dream?"

"No," Johnny said.

"Then what? You know you can tell me. I won't let anything hurt you."

Johnny lifted his head, peering over Mike's shoulder to the television in the corner of the room, then pointed.

They all turned around, looking for something that might have frightened a child, but saw nothing out of place.

"What are you pointing at?" Deborah asked.

Johnny cupped his hands and then held them up to Mike's ear and whispered so softly that Mike had to strain to hear.

"Him," Johnny said. "It's him."

Mike's frown deepened. "Him? What 'him' are you talking about, honey?"

Johnny's eyes welled. Moments later, tears spilled down his cheeks.

"The man from the plane. The one who killed his friend."

Mike's arms subconsciously tightened around his grandson as he stared at the television screen.

"Are you talking about someone on the television?" Johnny nodded.

"Who the hell is that?" Mike muttered as he sat down in front of the television, then cradled Johnny in his lap.

Deborah ran to turn up the volume, then they watched in silence, listening to the interview in progress. The only person on camera at that point was Senator Patrick Finn's wife. She was wearing black and obviously in mourning. The journalist talking to her was commiserating with her on the death of her husband in the Kentucky plane crash. They'd just asked her if she'd been in touch with Senator Darren Wilson's family, since they all knew by now that Senator Wilson had been found, along with the missing woman and boy.

"Of course we're happy for Senator Wilson and his family," Mrs. Finn said, stifling a fresh set of tears. "I'm sure they consider Darren's rescue nothing short of a miracle, especially at Christmas."

As she spoke, the picture cut to a photo obviously taken on the steps of Congress in Washington, D.C. It was a picture of several senators standing around some foreign dignitary. The camera closed in on Patrick Finn, then on the man on the other side of the dignitary, identifying him as Senator Darren Wilson. As the interviewer continued to talk, a comment was made regarding the odds of two senators having been on the same flight.

"Jesus H. Christ," James muttered. "That's Darren Wilson. He's a senator from Texas."

Deborah stiffened at the name "Wilson," then hurriedly shoved a blank tape into the VCR and hit record. She'd seen the killer's face, but it looked nothing like the well-dressed cosmopolitan man in the photo.

"Why are you doing that?" James asked.

"For Molly," Deborah said. "When she wakes up, I want to see what her reaction is."

"Good thinking," Mike said.

"Will he hurt me, Daddy Mike?"

The fear in his grandson's voice was palpable. It made Mike angry all over again.

"No. Never."

"But he—"

"Look at my face, Johnny."

The little boy shuddered, then fixed his gaze on his grandfather's face.

Mike's eyes were cold and narrowed. The muscles in his jaw were tight and twitching, and there was a slight tic in the muscles near his left eye.

"Have I ever lied to you?" Mike asked.

Johnny took a deep breath, then exhaled on a long, shaky sigh.

"No."

Mike hugged him close.

"Okay, so remember that. When Daddy Mike tells you something, he means it. I've said I'll keep you safe, and I will, won't I?"

Johnny nodded.

"Good. Now, are you hungry, buddy?"

Johnny shrugged.

Mike pushed the issue, knowing that an ordinary task was what Johnny needed to change the focus of his thoughts.

"I saw some cookies in Deborah's cookie jar."

Johnny almost smiled.

"They're pretty good," Deborah added. "Maybe you'd like some chocolate milk with them?"

The little boy's expression lightened a little bit more. "Maybe I could dunk my cookies in the milk?" he said hopefully.

Deborah smiled.

"Is there any other way to eat a cookie? Of course you can."

Mike could feel the tension in Johnny's body easing with every breath.

"Would you like to come with me?" Deborah asked. "Daddy Mike needs to put some more wood on the fire. When he's done, he can come in the kitchen and have cookies, too. Okay?"

"And chocolate milk?" Johnny added.

"And chocolate milk," Deborah promised, then took the little boy out of Mike's arms.

Mike mouthed a silent thank-you to her as she took the child out of the room, then he turned and looked at his dad.

"What in the hell are we going to do about this?" he asked.

James's hands were curled into fists. His expression was stern, his chin jutting mutinously. He didn't know that, at that moment, he and Mike looked almost exactly alike. He did know, however, that they were both capable of doing whatever it took to protect the ones they loved.

"We've got to get hold of the authorities," James said.

"Let's try the phones again," Mike said.

James reached for the phone, then hurried into the kitchen, Mike on his heels. "Deborah, what's the number to the sheriff's office?"

Deborah rattled it off as she mixed a glass of chocolate milk and set it in front of Johnny.

"Thanks," James said, and punched in the numbers as he left the room.

Mike winked at Johnny, took a cookie from the cookie jar, then followed his dad back into the living room. Unfortunately, their attempts to get through proved as useless as they had before.

"Damn this weather," James muttered as he laid the phone back in the cradle. He'd gotten nothing but static for his trouble.

Mike swallowed his last bite of cookie, then dusted the sugar from his hands.

"Let's confirm this with Molly, then go from there," Mike said.

"What if she's too sick? I hate to wake her," Mike said.

"She can always go back to sleep. This is serious, Dad. Waiting is no longer an option."

James sighed, then nodded. "You're right. So…who tells Evan?"

"I will," Mike said. "Be right back."

Mike could hear Johnny talking to Deborah about the merits of peanut butter cookies over chocolate chip and grimaced as he hurried down the hall. That a child should have been subjected to these horrors was disgusting. That it was his own grandson made it even worse. A child Johnny's age shouldn't have to be concerned with anything more serious than learning to tie his shoes, not worrying if he was going to be murdered in his sleep.

When he got to the bedroom, he paused, hoping he would hear voices. It would be far preferable to interrupt than to wake them, but as he'd just told his dad, they were left with no other choices.

He knocked once, then eased the door open.

Evan had heard the knock and was already rolling over to the side of the bed when Mike walked in.

"Hey, Dad…what's up?" Evan asked, then realized Johnny wasn't in the room. "Is Johnny with you guys?"

"Yeah, he's in the kitchen with Deborah," Mike said. "He's fine, but we need to talk. Something new has come up."

Evan glanced at Molly, then slipped out of bed.

"Let's talk out there," he said, pointing toward the hall. "I don't want to wake her."

"Sorry, but that's why I'm here," Mike said. "We have to wake her. There's something she needs to see…something she needs to verify before we make any more decisions."

Evan frowned. "She's still running a fever. I don't want to—"

"I'm awake. What's wrong?" Molly asked, and tried to sit up, but when she raised her head, the room began to spin. "Yikes," she muttered. "That wasn't a good idea." She lay back down.

"Dad, can't this wait?" Evan asked.

"Johnny just said he saw the killer on television."

Evan flinched as if he'd just been punched. "What the hell?"

"Are you serious?" Molly asked.

"It really scared him," Mike said.

Now Molly was struggling to sit up again. "Is he still on the TV? Can I see? I need to see."

Evan grabbed her by the arm as she tried to get up, then steadied her as she sagged against him.

"Deborah taped it," Mike said.

"If you're determined to go, you're not walking," Evan said, and before she could object, he picked her up in his arms. "Don't wiggle or you'll mess up your stitches," he said.

"I'll be still," Molly whispered. "But I need to see."

"Then hang on, girl," Evan said, and followed his father back into the living room.

Deborah had rewound the tape, and they were all waiting for Molly's arrival, except for Puppy and Johnny, who were in the kitchen. Johnny was at the table drawing pictures, while Puppy sat beneath, licking at his feet. Johnny's laughter drifted through the house.

"I'd guess that's a sound you never get tired of," Deborah said as the others entered the room.

When she saw Molly, she quickly made a place for her on the sofa.

"Put her here," Deborah said, and tossed some throw pillows on the floor.

Evan lowered Molly onto the sofa. Her pallor was obvious, as was the tremble in her voice when she said, "Quit fussing and let me see."

Deborah punched the play button on the remote and then waited.

Almost immediately, a man's image filled the screen.

"Lord have mercy," Molly whispered, then looked up at Evan. "It *is* him! That's the killer."

"Do you know who he is?" Mike asked.

"I heard the other man call him Darren."

Mike's eyes narrowed sharply. "And what did this Darren call the other man?"

Molly frowned, trying to remember. It was hard to put the pieces of the past two days together and have them make sense. She closed her eyes, trying to focus on the times she'd heard them arguing. And then it hit her.

"Oh! I remember! It was Patrick. He called him Patrick."

James stood abruptly. "Christ Almighty!" he cried. "That's the other senator. Senator Patrick Finn. We're talking about powerful men here, not just one pissed-off guy knocking off another."

Mike nodded. "Waiting is no longer an option. We've got to let the authorities know that Wilson is a killer," Mike said. "It's the only way we'll be able to make sure that Molly and Johnny are safe."

"We could try to drive down," Deborah offered. "I have a four-wheel-drive SUV, but I can tell you that, in weather like this, we're more likely to go off the side of the mountain than make it down to Carlisle."

Mike moved to the window, then thrust his hands into his pockets, watching in frustration as the snow continued to fall. There was enough wind with this storm that the snow was blowing from north to south, creating drifts against the side of the house that were window high.

"Unless someone's grown wings since I last looked, driving anywhere is not an option."

"How does Farley get back and forth?" James asked.

"Farley has a four-wheel-drive truck, and his place is less than a mile from here. The driving from here to there isn't so risky, but in this kind of weather, the rest of the way down the mountain is dangerous."

Deborah got up, stirred the coals in the fireplace, then stepped aside as Mike laid two fresh logs on the fire.

She watched the play of muscles beneath the sweat-shirt Mike was wearing, then shook off a small lecherous thought and returned to the problem at hand.

"I've lived here all my life. I know the mountain as well as I know the inside of this house. I could hike down the—"

"No," James said abruptly. "I'm the one who's going down."

Mike frowned. "No way. If anyone goes, it's going to be me."

James frowned back. "Why you?"

"Because I'm younger and—"

James eyes narrowed angrily as he thrust both hands through his hair, spiking it even more than normal.

"I'm going to assume you didn't mean anything personal by that remark, and I'm well aware of your age. I was there when you were born, remember?"

Mike sighed. "Look, Dad. I didn't mean to imply that you can't—"

"That's good," James said. "Because I not only can, I am. I'm fit and strong, and I have as much survival training as you have…maybe more." Then he looked at Deborah. "Anything you want to tell me before I leave…like maybe it's all going to be okay?"

Deborah grimaced. "I wish I could, but for now, I'm just as much in the dark about all this as you are."

Mike put a hand on his father's shoulder. "Come on, Dad. At least wait until the morning. If you start now, dark is going to catch you before you get all the way down."

James shook his head. "I can make it to the crash site before dark. I'll either stay there with the workers or catch a ride down. I'll be fine, and you know it. Besides,

I want to check in on Dad. He's still there in that motel, probably worrying himself silly."

Mike wanted to argue, but he knew what his father was saying was the truth. James was as physically fit as he was, and it was imperative that the authorities know that Senator Finn's death wasn't due to the crash, and that the other missing passenger was the killer.

"I'll fix some food and hot coffee for you to take," Deborah said.

James grinned. "A real picnic," he said, then added, "I'm going to change. It won't take more than a few minutes for me to get ready."

"I won't keep you waiting," Deborah said, and hurried into the kitchen, leaving Mike and James alone.

James saw the look on his son's face. "I'll be fine," he said.

Mike nodded. "Yeah, I know."

"You're needed here, and you know it. Evan is still not up to par, and now he has to set aside his healing time to be strong for Johnny and that girl. I think he's a little bit intrigued by her."

"Yeah, you may be right," Mike said, remembering the concern on Evan's face when he'd come in to eat breakfast.

"So what do *you* think about her?" James asked.

"I think it's too soon to worry about stuff like that," Mike said.

James shook his head. "It's never too soon to worry about falling in love."

Mike frowned. "Don't you think you're getting

ahead of yourself?" he asked. "They barely know each other."

"You say that, and yet you're pretty smitten with the little witch who's in there making my coffee."

"She's not a witch," Mike muttered.

James grinned. "See what I mean?"

"By what?" Mike asked.

"You're defending her."

"I'm not defending anyone," Mike said. "I'm just grateful, that's all."

"Yeah, and I'm a bleeding Republican, too."

Mike laughed in spite of himself. An O'Ryan had yet to be born who would claim a connection to the Republican party. It had something to do with their ancestors and Ireland and staying true to the working class.

"Point taken," Mike said.

"Good thing," James said. "I was running out of arguments. Now, excuse me, son. I have to change, then load up the backpack. I gave my flashlight to Johnny. Lend me yours."

"Yeah, sure," Mike said. "Come on. I'll help you."

By the time the coffee was made and the thermos had been filled, James reappeared in the kitchen. Deborah handed him the coffee, which he promptly put in the backpack.

"Take your cell phone," Deborah said. "The closer you get to Carlisle, the more likely that it will work."

"It's right here," James said, patting a zippered pocket in his parka.

"Be careful," Deborah said. "And it's easy to get disoriented up here, especially after the sun goes down, so when it gets dark, stop. Otherwise, you're likely to find yourself falling somewhere you can't get out of."

"I will," James said, and headed for the living room, where Mike was waiting by the door. "I trust you're going to be on your best behavior," James said to him, then winked at Deborah, who pretended she didn't know what he was talking about.

"I'm not making any promises," Mike said.

James shook his head and grinned at Deborah.

"You watch him, girl. He's hell on wheels when he gets himself started."

Deborah pursed her lips, then frowned at the both of them. "I'm sure I'll be fine."

"You take good care of my boys," James said, giving Mike a big hug. "And that includes you," he added.

"We'll be fine," Mike said.

"I'm counting on that," James said, and then kissed Deborah lightly on the cheek. "God bless you, honey," he said softly.

"God bless you, too," she said, and then stood in the doorway and waved until she could no longer see him.

When she closed the door and turned around, she caught Mike watching her.

"What?" she asked.

He didn't say anything for a few moments. Finally, he just shook his head.

"I'm going to check on the others," he said, and disappeared down the hall, leaving Deborah on her own.

She locked the door out of habit, then stood for a few minutes, trying to decide what to do next. It wasn't until her gaze fell on the bare mantel over the fireplace that she thought about all of the Christmas decorations up in the attic. The least she could do was bring them down. Decorating the living room would give Johnny something to do.

She could hear Mike moving around in the room where James had been sleeping and guessed he was moving his sleeping quarters from the living room couch to the bed. She walked past without stopping, well aware that he was capable of making her lose all focus.

As she started up the attic stairs, a strong gust of wind blasted the north side of the house, causing an eerie whistling sound. The farther up the stairs she went, the louder the sound and the colder the air became.

Two steps from the top, she reached for the light switch and flipped it on, immediately illuminating the large open area. Neatly labeled boxes were stacked along the walls. An old trunk was to her left, and a dusty wardrobe that used to be in her parents' room was on her right. Directly in front of her was an old dress form. She had vague memories of watching her grandmother fitting a new dress to the buxom form.

She hadn't been up here in almost a year, but it was too cold to linger. She distinctly remembered transferring the Christmas decorations to three large clear plastic tubs with red lids. Now all she had to do was find them.

It took a couple of minutes before she spied them stacked one on top of the other and partially covered with an old drop cloth. She tossed the cloth aside and began to drag the three tubs toward the doorway. She was so focused on moving them that she didn't hear the footsteps coming up the stairs behind her.

"Dang, woman…it's cold enough to hang meat up here."

Deborah turned abruptly. "Oh! Mike! You startled me."

"Sorry, honey. I didn't mean to. Here…let me do that."

Deborah stepped back. "Gladly," she said, and then held the door open. "The contents of the one on top are breakable. We'll have to take them down one at a time."

"Got it," Mike said, and picked up the top one first. "What's in here?"

"Christmas decorations," she said. "I thought Johnny might enjoy them."

Mike stopped, set the tub down and turned around. For a few seconds he just looked at her, as if he couldn't believe she was real, then he took her by the shoulders. Before she knew it, he was kissing her. It lasted just long enough to derail her good sense, then he turned her loose.

"What was that for?" she muttered, although she didn't really give a damn about his reason. She was just happy he'd done it.

"For being you," he said, then picked up the tub of decorations again. "Where do you want this?" he asked.

"Maybe the living room to start with," she said.

"Consider it done," he said, and started down the stairs.

She watched until she was sure he'd cleared the steps safely, then she picked up a box and started down behind him.

He met her halfway down, took the box from her and then sent her packing.

"I'll get these," he said. "You go down and get warm."

Deborah touched his face, then laid her hand in the middle of his chest. She could feel the rock-steady beat of his heart. Between that and the love she'd seen him shower on his family, she knew this man was a man you could count on.

"Mister…you're something special," Deborah said softly.

Mike leaned into her touch, savoring the moment.

"No, ma'am," he said. "You're the one who's special, and just for the record, I'm really sorry I gave you such a hard time about your gift. You saved my son's family, and you're still protecting us."

"I suppose you're worth the trouble," she said, and leaned forward.

This time she was the one who initiated the kiss. Their lips met, then curved to fit. Deborah felt the tug of passion between them and gave back as good as she got. It wasn't until Mike moaned beneath his breath that she made herself stop.

She pulled back, looking him square in the face. His

eyes were dark with passion, his lips slightly parted, on the verge of saying something they might both regret.

"Tonight," Deborah said, and then walked away.

All the breath left Mike's body. By the time he could think, she was gone, and when he carried the last of the decorations into the living room, she and Johnny were already digging through the boxes. After the fear they'd seen on Johnny's face earlier, if he could have, he would have given Deborah the world for the sheer joy that was there now.

And there was no doubt in his mind as to what she'd meant. The difficulty was going to be in waiting until everyone else went to bed to take her up on her invitation.

13

James left the warmth of the Sanborn home without thought for his own comfort. He had a pistol in his pocket, as well as his cell phone. Eventually he would walk to a place where he could get a signal, and when he did, he would let the sheriff know he was coming and what was going on.

As for the pistol, he wouldn't have a problem using it if the need arose. It had taken him years to learn to live with what he'd experienced in Vietnam, but not once in his life had he felt guilt. When called upon, he'd served his country with passion and pride—he could give no less to his family.

Given all of that, he still couldn't get past the horror he'd seen on Johnny's face when they'd aired the picture of Senator Wilson. No child should ever have to witness a murder, let alone fear for his life because he thought the murderer was coming after him. It was all he needed to keep him walking, with no thought for the wind and weather.

As he walked, he kept going over Deborah's advice,

making certain he stayed true to the obvious path the road took going down the mountain, even though it might appear, from time to time, that he was taking the long way down.

The cold wind and blowing snow were distracting, and more than once, he realized he'd strayed. Each time, he had to stop and reassess his location before continuing.

He'd been on plenty of maneuvers during his years in Vietnam, and he'd taken more chances with his life then than he would ever have imagined. But this was different. This time he didn't have the option of going off half-cocked and hoping everything worked out to his advantage. It was his responsibility to get the information about Patrick Finn's murder to the right people before Johnny and Molly were put in jeopardy again.

And as he walked, with only the sound of the wind for company, he couldn't help but think of his Trudy back in the nursing home. He wondered if she missed him, then struggled to swallow past the knot in his throat. She didn't, and he knew it. How could she miss someone she no longer remembered? He missed *her*, though—more than he had words to express.

Deborah had cautioned him about getting lost, but his Trudy had been lost for years. All her memories of their life together were gone, lost within the confusion that had become her world. When he let himself think of her, it was like trying to breathe underwater. It was a combination of panic and fear, coupled with the positive knowledge that his next breath would be his last. How could someone who'd been so vital to his life still be alive but in essence already gone? The loneliness of his world was impossible to describe.

He shuddered as a blast of wind tore through the trees lining both sides of the road, but his discomfort wasn't from cold, it was from the pain of how Trudy's life was ending. Still, he couldn't afford to waste time and energy on the ending of one life, though ever precious to him, when he was trying to save the lives of two people who had yet to live it to their fullest. Determined to do what had to be done, he lowered his head against the wind, put one foot in front of the other and focused instead on the miles he was putting behind him.

Darren Wilson's social calendar was always full, especially during the holidays. He liked the parties. But unless something drastic happened, he would never attend another party again as long as he lived. Which might not be very long.

Right now, he was trying to backtrack to the place where he'd walked up on the mountain lion. It was there that he'd lost the trail he'd been following. Looking back, he suspected that the tracks he'd seen earlier in the day were from a search party. He feared that the woman and kid had been found. What he still didn't know was if the pair had just wandered away from the crash site on their own or if they'd witnessed what he'd done and were running away from him. If he only knew that one truth, he could go about the business of getting himself found and out of these godforsaken mountains.

He wouldn't let himself consider that he'd been over-looked. Surely the search parties were still out. They would have to know he was missing, too. He'd been listed on the passenger manifest. Even if they'd already found the woman and kid, the body count would still be off by one. He just needed to find out who, exactly, was looking for him—the police or the rescue party.

Full of pain and self-pity, he continued to slog through the woods. He kept thinking back to that house he'd broken into. Except for the fact that his belly wasn't so empty, it had been a complete mistake. The couple had probably reported the break-in to the au-thorities. If a search party found him up here like this now, it would only be a matter of time before they figured out he'd also been the thief. He could blame it on being out of his head from the wreck and starving, but how could he explain the fact that he'd taken the farmer's rifle? If he was so innocent and lost, he would have begged the farmer to take him into town, not stolen a gun and run for his life.

While he'd been running from the gunshots the woman had fired at him, he'd taken the rifle without conscious thought. But having it now, he had to admit how much better he felt, just knowing the weapon was in his hands. He'd already fired it once, so he knew what kind of kick it had. It shamed him somewhat to know that he'd let a pregnant woman and a roomful of kids back him down, but he'd just learned the hard way that a pissed-off mother with a loaded gun who was protect-ing her family was more dangerous than any bad guy could ever be. He considered himself fortunate to have gotten away unharmed.

Shouldering the burden of his circumstances, he put his head down against the blowing wind and kept on walking. At times the snow was up to his thighs, but in most places it was just below his knees. The wind and the cold cut through his clothing like knives, and he could no longer feel his feet. If only he could catch a break. What was happening wasn't fair.

He was pushing aside some low-hanging branches when he stumbled across something buried under the snow and fell. The rifle went flying out of his hands and hit the side of a tree trunk. Were it not for the fact that Darren reached out, instinctively bracing himself for the fall, he would have dashed his head into the same tree trunk and ended it all right there. As it was, he fell through the snow, landing on his elbows first and jarring his body all the way to his back teeth. Pain shot through him in waves as the fall reinjured his bruised ribs and once again sprained the knee he'd been favoring ever since the wreck. His nose started bleeding again, as did a large scratch he'd just put on his face.

He rolled over on his back, holding his belly and writhing in pain. Finally he managed to sit up. As he did, he heard something above him hiss, then growl.

He was grabbing for the gun as he rolled. There was a blur of snow and the color of light brown fur in the air above him as he pulled the trigger.

The shot went off. Snow fell down on his face from the tree limbs above his head. Frantic, he dug quickly to clear his vision, only to see that he was, once again, alone.

He got up, holding the rifle at the ready, searched a full three hundred and sixty degrees around himself and at first saw nothing.

Then he saw the blood drops on an undisturbed span of snow and frowned. Whatever it was, he'd hit it.

"Good," he muttered, thinking of that big cat. "It's your own damn fault. Now go off somewhere and die, and leave me the hell alone."

Brushing himself off and swiping at the blood on his face with the back of his hand, he stood tall as he surveyed the area once more. He would never have considered himself a woodsman, but, by God, he was doing all right.

The burst of faith in himself came with renewed hope that he could prevail over this ever-looming disaster. He hadn't thought of Alphonso Riberra in hours. There was much more to consider than owing money to a gangster. He needed a warm place to sleep, and some food, and the notion of heading down the mountain in hopes of being found sounded better all the time.

The hell with witnesses. Maybe his return would be hailed as a miracle. Lord knew it would be a great hook come reelection time. And it was too bad about Patrick, but he should have minded his own damn business.

Convinced that everything was surely going to work itself out, Darren decided to look for a place to wait out the night before walking down the mountain. A short while later, as he was searching for a place to spend the night, he suddenly realized he was seeing intermittent movement through the trees to the east. Thinking of the search parties, he began to run. It was time to end this trek. He wanted to be found.

James O'Ryan was moving at a quick pace. His hands were in his pockets, his dark blue sock cap on his head. As he walked, he tilted his head slightly down and to the side, away from the brunt of the wind. His heartbeat was rock-solid, and his legs felt strong, his steps sure and steady. Each warm exhalation that mingled with the cold air formed a small cloudlike puff of condensation in front of his face.

He had no idea how far he'd come, but he was keeping an eye on what was left of the daylight. He was so focused on his mission that he didn't hear anything but his own footsteps until it was almost too late.

The first time he realized someone was running up behind him was when a pair of quail suddenly flew up and out of some bushes that he'd already passed. He stopped to see what had startled them, and as he did, he heard the footsteps in the snow behind him. As he turned around, he automatically shaded his eyes against the evening sun. The first thing he saw was a running man, dragging one leg as he went. At the same time, it registered that the man was carrying a rifle. Automatically, his hand went to the pistol he was carrying.

"Hey! Hey! Wait up!" the man called out.

James stared. The longer he stood there, the more things didn't seem right.

The man was wearing mismatched clothes that were

covered with stains, most of which looked like dried blood. His face was a mass of bruises, and there were several days' worth of whiskers on his face.

It wasn't until he came closer that James realized he'd seen him before—on the evening news, listed as one of the three people missing from the downed passenger plane. Anger filled him, knowing that this was the son of a bitch who'd been after Molly and Johnny.

He dug in his pocket, pulled out the pistol and took aim.

"Stop there!" he yelled.

Darren stumbled in midstride. The man had a gun!

"Wait!" Darren called. "I just need—"

"Toss your rifle aside and drop to your knees!" James yelled.

Darren groaned.

He didn't know how it had happened, but obviously the word was out. That bitch of a woman and the kid had seen him, all right, and from the way this guy was acting, they had blabbed the story all over the place.

Which left him with exactly no options. He sighed. Today was not the day he was going to get rescued after all.

He raised the rifle and fired off a shot. To Darren's surprise, he hit the target—and at quite a distance.

James felt the lead tearing through his clothes and into his side. In the back of his mind, he was thinking that he'd felt like this before—in a jungle in Vietnam, many years ago. He thought of his son and knew Mike would blame himself for this for the rest of his life. He fired back, but at this distance, the shot was off.

Then everything went black as he hit the ground.

The shots echoed from one side of the hills to the other, ringing in Darren's ears to the point that for a few seconds, he heard nothing else. Then, when he finally realized he'd just shot a perfect stranger without knowing if there were others like him close by, he turned on his heels and ran into the trees, then up the mountain, away from town and from search parties— away from warm food and dry clothes and a soft place to sleep.

He'd made his bed—snow that it was—and now he was going to have to lie in it.

Deborah stood at the window overlooking her front yard. It had been hours since James had left, and she couldn't help worrying. The weather was terrible. The electricity had gone off an hour ago, right in the middle of the news broadcast. She'd quickly gathered up oil lamps and candles in preparation for nightfall. In times past, she would just have gone to bed early. But tell a bored five-year-old it was time to go to bed before dark and they would all have a fight on their hands.

She could hear the others in the kitchen, laughing and talking. About an hour ago they'd found her old checkerboard and checkers. After that, they'd disappeared into the kitchen, and she hadn't seen them since. The sound of their laughter left her feeling lonely and empty. She didn't know what was wrong with her, but she couldn't relax. Something bad was going to happen. She could feel it in her bones.

The clock in the hallway chimed the hour. It was four o'clock. Another hour or so and it would be dark.

She glanced at the stack of empty boxes near the doorway, then at the Christmas decorations they had put up. Besides her small tree, they'd found two artificial wreaths, a clump of plastic mistletoe and a plastic Santa, complete with sleigh and eight reindeer.

Johnny had been fascinated with the sleigh and reindeer, and had played with them all afternoon. At the moment they were lined up on the coffee table, as if in preparation for takeoff.

Molly was still in bed, but her fever was almost gone. The minor surgery she'd endured and the antibiotics they'd poked down her were doing the trick. Mike, Evan and Johnny were the ones making all the racket in the kitchen. Deborah would have liked to go join them, but she knew if she didn't go do the evening chores right now, it would be dark before she was done.

She hurried down the hall to her room—thankful she was back to take care of things herself, since something must have happened to Farley—changed her jeans for a pair of heavy wool pants, and then went toward the kitchen.

"Hey," Mike said as Deborah entered the room. "We wondered where you were. I'm afraid we've just about eaten all of your cookies."

Deborah smiled. "We'll make more, if need be," she said, and sat down on a chair near the back door and began putting on her work boots.

"What are you going to do?" Evan asked.

"Chores," she said. "It won't take long, and I need to finish before dark."

"I'll help," Mike said.

"No need," Deborah said. "I do this all the time. Oh…just so you know, there's an oil lamp in that corner cabinet. You might want to light it now, before dark catches you."

"Good idea," Evan said, and retrieved the lamp, then lit it quickly. "Hey, Johnny, no cheating," he called.

Johnny laughed and put his checker back where it had been.

Mike frowned. She was trying to put him off, but he wasn't having any of it. "I know you're capable of just about anything, woman, but since we're here, I'll help."

She stood up and reached for her coat and scarf.

"Okay, if you want."

"I want," Mike said shortly, and grabbed his own coat and gloves. "Be back in a little while, buddy," he said to his grandson.

Johnny grinned, then jumped his dad's checkers.

"King me!" he crowed.

Evan pretended great dismay, when in truth he was in awe. While he'd been gone, his little boy had grown up. Not only did he know how to play checkers, but he was actually good enough so that Evan didn't have to let him win. He'd already won once on his own, fair and square.

"I'll get even with you. Just wait and see," Evan warned.

Johnny's giggle of delight followed Mike and Deborah out the door.

The cold wind seemed to cut straight through their clothing. Within seconds of emerging from the warm house, Deborah found it difficult to walk in the drifting snow.

"Good grief. We almost need snowshoes," she muttered as she slogged her way through.

"Here, hold my hand," Mike said.

Deborah looked at him, then grinned. "I can walk just fine. You're just trying to flirt," she said.

Mike chuckled. "And not doing a very good job of it, it seems."

She opened her mouth, ready to launch a retort, when the ground went out from under her. One minute she was standing up, and the next thing she knew she was on her belly and fighting for her life. She could feel the sharp tear of flesh at the back of her neck and smelled the coppery scent of her own blood.

"Oh God, oh God," she cried, and she pushed herself up on her hands and knees.

Mike grabbed her and helped pull her the rest of the way up.

"Are you all right?" he asked.

She pushed him away as she turned toward the house. "The gun! I need to get the gun!" she cried, and began to run.

Mike looked around frantically, trying to see what had gone wrong.

"Deborah! What is it? Why do you need a gun?"

But she didn't stop to answer. Within seconds she was up the steps, on the screened-in back porch, then dashing into the house.

Evan and Johnny were still playing checkers when she burst into the room. When she went flying past them, leaving a messy trail of melting snow, Evan jumped up and followed her down the hall, then into her bedroom.

"What's wrong? Is it Dad?"

"No, no, he's fine," she muttered, but when she backed out of the closet, she was carrying a gun.

"Is it the killer...the man from the plane?"

"No, no," she muttered as she dashed past. Her boots made loud thumping sounds as she ran down the hall.

He followed her through the house and would have followed her outside onto the porch, but Johnny, who'd gone pale at the sight of the gun, ran to Evan, then clung to him in fear.

Deborah hit the snow running and would have run right past Mike, but he grabbed her by the arm and stopped her.

"What the hell is wrong?" he asked.

"In the barn...hurry..." she said, and took off toward the barn, plowing through the snow as fast as she could run.

Powdery clouds of it flew up behind her as her feet cut through the depth, coating the back of her coat and the legs of her pants. As she neared the barn, she heard the desperate sounds of a barking dog and Mildred, the cow, bawling as loudly as she knew how.

"Oh, no...Puppy!" she cried, and flipped off the safety of the rifle she was carrying.

Mike heard the commotion in the barn only seconds after Deborah and realized that whatever was wrong was happening in there. When he saw her shift her rifle from one hand to the other, his heart skipped a beat. What in hell did she know that he didn't?

The wounded cougar had taken refuge in the barn. It was cold, hungry and injured. Blood dripped from its shoulder onto the hay as it clung precariously to the rafters, waiting for a chance to pounce. It could smell the fear of the other animals that were sheltered beneath the broad roof, but their fear was nothing to the fear and hunger the big cat felt as its lifeblood dripped onto the ground.

The cow was bawling in fright. The old barn cat had taken her kittens and disappeared into a crawlspace in the barn floor. The cougar knew that, to get to the cow, it was going to have to go through the dog. Normally that wouldn't be a problem, but the injured shoulder and loss of blood had weakened it, so it had been forced to take refuge in the rafters and was now waiting for the perfect moment to strike.

Deborah dashed into the barn and headed toward Puppy as fast as she could run. She saw the blood on the ground only seconds before she saw the cat. It was already in a crouching position and ready to leap when she swung the barrel of her rifle upward.

Two shots rang out just as Mike dashed into the

alleyway of the barn. He saw a shadow of something drop from above Deborah's head, then saw her stagger backward as it landed on her. When he realized it was a cougar, and that she wasn't moving, his heart nearly stopped. He grabbed at the animal and began dragging it away from her.

"Deborah...sweetheart..."

Her eyes opened, and she grunted as she tried to catch her breath.

"Get it off me!" she cried, but Mike was already in the act.

"Jesus," he muttered, as he pulled it aside, then stared down at the big cat, taking in its size, as well as the injured semicaked blood around its shoulder. "Look. It had already been shot."

She squinted a little as she leaned down for a closer look. "It's still fresh, though...someone shot it earlier in the day. Maybe Farley."

She poked the animal with the barrel of her rifle, then set the gun aside and caught Puppy as she launched herself at Deborah, who was laughing and petting her old dog as Puppy alternated between licking her face and growling at the dead cat.

"Yes, you're a great watchdog," Deborah said over and over as she patted Puppy's head. "You did a good job, girl. A good job."

The dog wiggled herself in pure joy, then began circling the carcass, sniffing and growling while the hair stood up on the back of her neck.

"You knew, didn't you?" Mike asked.

Deborah hesitated, then nodded. "Yes."

"How? What did you see?" Mike asked.

"It wasn't as much what I saw as what I felt."

"Like what?" Mike persisted.

"Pain in the back of my neck and blood running down my face."

Mike looked as if she'd just slapped him.

"What do you mean?"

"I mean…that if I hadn't gone back to the house to get the gun, it would have attacked me as I entered the barn. From the way I felt when I fell, I think I was dying."

"Dear God," Mike muttered as he pulled her up and into his arms.

For a moment they just stood there, wrapped in the comfort of each other's presence and relieved that they were still alive; then Mike cupped her face and ever so gently centered his mouth on her lips. They were cold, and her body was trembling, but there was nothing hesitant about her response. She wrapped her arms around his neck and kissed him back, soundly and thoroughly. When they finally stepped back, it was Mike who was trembling. He shook his head in disbelief as he kept touching her, unable to believe she was still in one piece.

"I saw you," he said. "I saw you fall, and when you got up, it was like watching someone I didn't know. I'm a witness to your ability, and I still don't understand how it works."

"Join the club," Deborah muttered.

Mike gave her one last hug, then pointed to the nearest stack of hay bales.

"Why don't you go sit over there and let me do whatever it is that needs to be done while you catch your breath."

She hesitated, but only briefly. "Yes… I think maybe I will," she said, and sat down on the hay bales before she fell down. Her legs were trembling, as was her entire body. She felt as if she might throw up but was too weak to give it a try.

"What first?" Mike asked.

She pointed to the big cat. "Drag it out of the barn."

"Does it matter where?" Mike asked.

She glanced at Puppy, then sighed. "Yes, probably. It will take you a bit longer, but if you could get it as far as the trees beyond the corral, it would be better. Scavengers will take care of the carcass, but I don't want them any closer to the place than necessary."

"Will do," he said, then pointed at her. "You stay seated. I'll feed the animals just as soon as I get back."

"I'm really okay," she said. "Just a little bit rattled."

"*Rattled* is a small word for going head to head with a cougar."

She grinned. "Welcome to my world."

"Lord," Mike muttered as he grabbed a length of rope, looped it around the dead cat's head and took off out of the barn with it, leaving a long drag mark in the snow as he went. Puppy followed, sniffing and growling with every step.

14

Feeding Puppy and the cats, then milking a cow, seemed somewhat anticlimatic after killing a cougar, but it went a long way in settling Deborah's nerves. Mike was at the back of the pasture, dragging the carcass away, when Evan appeared at the door of the barn. She stood up, saw the concern on his face and felt a sudden burning in the back of her throat. Too much sympathy had always been her downfall.

"What in blazes has been going on out here?" he asked.

"I killed a mountain lion," she said, and then started to shake and sat back down on the bales of hay.

Evan's expression went slack. "The hell you say."

She shrugged, then nodded.

"Where's Dad?" he asked.

Deborah pointed toward the back of the barn. "Dragging the carcass away."

"Jesus," Evan muttered, then squatted down in front of her. "Are you all right?"

"Yes," she said, and then burst into tears.

He sat down beside her, put his arm around her shoulders and just held her while she cried.

By the time Mike got back, Deborah had pulled herself together and was scooping Mildred's sweet feed into a bucket. Evan was nowhere in sight.

"Evan was here," she said.

Mike nodded. "I guess he heard the shots and came to see what was happening."

"I guess," Deborah said, and poured the feed into Mildred's manger. "I told him we were fine."

The cow moved into place without urging. She was calmly chewing her first bite when Deborah pulled up the milking stool and sat down.

"What can I do?" Mike asked.

"Pour some cat food into those two bowls, then dump the ice out of their water bowl and fill it up with fresh water."

"Will do," Mike said.

When he was done, he picked up the rifle, gave the barn loft another long look, then sat down.

Deborah's hands were still trembling, but the routine of her evening chores had gone a long way toward calming her. The scent of warm milk, the intermittent mewing of the cats and Puppy's cold nose on the back of her ear reminded her that all was well with her world. Sadly, the O'Ryans couldn't say the same.

"Do you think James is okay?" she asked.

Mike glanced out at the gathering darkness and tried not to think about the number of things that could go wrong on a trip down the mountain. But then he made himself relax. His dad was a law unto himself. He'd survived four years in Vietnam and countless years afterward without going off the deep end as so many of his compatriots had done. He was as tough as they came. A little walk in the snow would be nothing to a man like him.

"Yeah, I'm sure he's fine," he said, then remembered who he was talking to. "Do you have a reason to believe otherwise?"

She glanced up at him and almost smiled.

"No...no, nothing like that. I was just thinking about him, that's all."

"Okay," Mike said. "You think about him, and I'll think about you."

A little embarrassed, Deborah quickly finished milking. Very aware of Mike's gaze, she shakily poured a bit of warm milk into the cats' bowls, then gave the barn one last glance, checking to make sure the doors on the grain bins were secure and the animals were set for the night.

"Are we done?" Mike asked.

Deborah took a deep breath, then turned around and stared him straight in the face.

"We haven't even started."

Mike's heart skipped a beat. He shifted the rifle from one hand to the other as he watched the play of emotions on her face.

"Deborah..."

"Yes?"

"How far are we taking this?"

She took so long to answer that Mike started to wish he hadn't asked. Then she lifted her chin, as if bracing herself for rejection.

"How far do you want it to go?"

Mike touched the side of her face, frowned at the small scratch the cougar's claw had left on her chin, eyed the bits of hay caught in her hair, then pulled the hood of her coat up over her head.

"You know something, lady…for the first time in my life, I don't have an answer. If I told you what I'm feeling, I'm afraid you'd send me packing. We've only known each other three or four days, but it seems like I've known you forever. I know that when I saw that cougar leap toward you, my heart stopped."

He leaned forward.

Deborah's lips parted.

They could feel the warmth of each other's breath against their faces as the kiss began. Heightened by the danger they'd endured, the passion between them exploded.

"I want you, Deborah…more than I can ever remember wanting a woman."

Deborah looked at him closely, watching his mouth form the words that would change her world.

"I want you, too," she said. "As for where this is going…who knows? I'll take what I can get."

"Good enough," he said softly.

Deborah glanced toward the house, its outline blurring in the coming darkness.

"Let go inside," she said, and picked up her bucket of milk.

Puppy appeared from behind a stack of hay bales, nosed two of the kittens back into their bed and then led the way home.

By the time Mike and Deborah left the barn, long purple shadows had stretched as far eastward across the snow-covered yard as they could go without disappearing into the trees.

Deborah carried the milk. Mike carried the gun.

Johnny met them at the back door, big-eyed and full of questions, as Puppy slipped in between them and headed for the fireplace in the living room.

"Daddy said you killed a mountain lion. Did you really kill a mountain lion? Did it eat the barn cats? Is Mildred okay?"

Deborah was a little taken aback, but Mike picked up the slack.

"Yes, Deborah shot a mountain lion. The barn cats are fine, and so is Mildred. Something smells good. What's for supper?"

"Daddy made soup. He made some corn bread, too, but it's burned on the bottom. What did you do with the dead mountain lion?"

"Soup sounds good, and we'll just leave the burned parts of the corn bread in the pan. I dragged it away."

"It's canned vegetable soup. Will Puppy eat burned cornbread? Why didn't you bury it?"

Deborah laughed.

Mike and Johnny stopped talking long enough to look at her.

"What's so funny?" Mike asked.

Deborah just shook her head. "Do you know how alike you two are?"

Evan looked over his shoulder as he was stirring the soup.

"I've been telling Dad the same thing ever since Johnny learned to talk."

Deborah was still smiling as she grabbed the empty milk crock and went out onto the back porch to pour out the milk. By the time she finished and came inside, the kitchen was empty. She could hear voices in the back of the house and guessed that they were washing up as best they could without water. When the electricity had gone off, the water pump had gone with it. Fortunately for her guests, her penchant for cleanliness was being put to good use. She had several small dispensers of hand cleanser scattered throughout the house and heard Evan telling Johnny how to use it as she hung up her coat. She traded her boots for shoes, then used some cleanser on her own hands. She lifted the lid on the soup pot, gave the contents an appreciative sniff and then replaced the lid before hurrying to her room. The savory scent of the soup, coupled with the corn bread warming in the oven, made her mouth water. It had occurred to her more than once since the O'Ryans' invasion that they were very competent at feeding and caring for themselves. In her experience, men had a tendency to sit and wait for the women in their lives to care for them. She made a mental note to compliment them when they sat down to supper later.

The oil lamp in the kitchen had already been lit, but there were extras in the pantry, as well as some candles. She distributed them throughout the house, then lit them, preparing for the possibility that the electricity would still be off when they went to bed.

When she got to her room, she lit a candle in the bathroom and a lamp near her bed, then she changed out of her work clothes, grimacing at the blood splatters on them.

The weak glow of candlelight cast dark shadows as she glanced around the room. Tonight with Mike was going to be a step in a different direction. Whether or not it was a positive direction still remained to be seen.

A few minutes later, she left her bedroom. As she walked down the hall, she was struck by the life in this old house. It hadn't seen this much excitement in years. When everyone finally left and she was, once again, alone, she knew she would be sorry they were gone.

"There you are!" Johnny said as she walked into the kitchen. "We can't eat until you sit down. So sit down fast, 'cause I'm really hungry. Molly's here. She's hungry, too."

Deborah laughed out loud. It appeared that Johnny O'Ryan was definitely recovering nicely from his trauma.

A little embarrassed by his son's emerging personality, Evan managed a grin.

"Sorry to keep you all waiting," Deborah said as she winked at Johnny. "I'm hungry, too, so let's eat."

"Yay!" he said, and thrust his spoon into the soup.

"Just for the record… I must thank the O'Ryans who keep cooking our meals and cleaning up afterward. It's delicious, and greatly appreciated."

"It's the least we can do after what you've done for us," Evan said.

"And I double the thanks to everyone, since I've been no help whatsoever," Molly said.

"On the contrary," Evan said quickly. "You saved my son's life. In my book, you've earned a free ride from me for the rest of your life."

Molly waggled her finger at Evan.

"Ooh, that's something you should never promise a woman. She's likely to take you up on it."

Evan's expression didn't change as he passed her the butter.

"O'Ryans always mean what they say."

Molly's eyes widened, but she didn't say any more. For a few minutes there was little conversation in the house other than a request for butter to be passed, or a comment on the good taste of the food. It wasn't until their first pangs of hunger had been quenched that they began to talk again.

Johnny, however, was still in the business of eating. He pointed to a jar of honey at the other end of the table.

"Can I have please have some honey?" he asked.

"May I," Evan said, absently correcting him as he reached for the honey.

Johnny beamed. "Yeah, Daddy, you can have some, too."

Evan grinned as he passed the honey to Johnny, who proceeded to string it over a small piece of corn bread. When he missed the corn bread, he tried to catch it and managed to get the rest of it on the table and himself.

"Here, son, let me help you," Evan said as a thick drip of honey took a swing off the plate onto the table.

Without thinking, Molly took her napkin and helped by wiping the honey off Johnny's fingers. Deborah saw the way Mike was watching them and wondered if he had the same impression about the trio as she did. Whether they knew it or not, they had the makings of a family going on.

Mike caught her gaze, arched an eyebrow, then shrugged, as if to say that whatever happened between them was none of his concern.

Deborah watched the play of emotions on his face while thinking how much her mother would have liked this man and smiled.

Mike's first reaction to her smile was curiosity. "What are you thinking?" he asked.

"That you look a little bit like Tom Berenger."

Mike looked confused. "Who?"

"The actor?" Molly asked.

Deborah nodded.

"Good grief," Mike muttered.

Evan grinned. "Don't tell him that. He's got a high enough opinion of himself as it is."

"Ooh, you know what, Deborah? I think you're

right," Molly said. "Hey, Mike, may I have your autograph? Make it out to Molly, with love, Tom."

Mike tried to glower, but Johnny's curiosity kept the moment light.

"Hey, Daddy Mike, what's a *ottagraf,* and who's Tom?"

At that point, even Mike had to laugh.

"Who's Tom?" Johnny asked again. "Is it Tom Bunyan from my storybook?"

"The name is Paul, not Tom," Evan said.

Johnny appeared more confused than ever. "Tom's name is Paul?"

"I'm out of this conversation," Deborah said.

She was still grinning as she got up from the table and began carrying dirty dishes to the sink. Mike grabbed a handful and followed her. Before she knew it, he had her pinned against the sink.

"Look what you started," he said, nodding toward the table where Johnny was still talking in high gear.

Deborah turned around. They were body to body—face to face. She could feel the warmth of his breath against her cheeks; then she looked up and forgot what she'd been going to say. The glitter in his eyes was a promise of the night to come.

"I...uh..."

He grinned. "Now you know how *I* feel," he said softly. Before she could answer, he brushed a quick kiss across her lips, then left her standing there as he went back to the table for more dirty dishes.

"Daddy Mike! You kissed Deborah! Why did you

kiss Deborah? Is it love? You're not a'post to kiss girls 'less you love 'em."

"And who told you that?" Mike asked.

Johnny took a big bite out of his honey-covered corn bread, then proceeded to talk while trying to chew.

"Um, my friend Dewey. Dewey says you're not a'post…"

"The word is *supposed,* not *a'post,* and don't talk with your mouth full," Evan said. "And besides that, you ask too many questions. Leave Daddy Mike's kissing business to Daddy Mike, okay?"

Johnny eyed the adults dubiously, well aware that their silly smiles hid a secret they weren't willing to share, but before he could voice another opinion, the electricity flickered, then came back on.

"Yay!" he cried. "Now can I watch cartoons?"

"Not can, son…it's 'may I watch cartoons,'" Evan said, having another go at correcting his son's grammar.

Johnny looked at his daddy and grinned. "Yeah, sure, Daddy. You can watch 'em with me. I'll tell you what's happening on the side of the TV that you can't see."

Evan suddenly realized Johnny believed that because his father had a patch on one eye, he could only see half of what was before him.

"I can see just fine, son," Evan said softly. "So let's go wash the honey off of your mouth and hands, and then we'll watch those cartoons together." He paused at the table, then held out his hand to Molly. "Maybe Molly would like to come with us."

"I'd like nothing better," she said softly, and after a

quick thank-you to Deborah for her meal, followed them out of the room.

"Molly is falling in love," Deborah said.

Mike nodded. "I think Evan is, too."

The silence that followed lengthened noticeably.

"Now that we have power again, I'm going to finish the dishes," Deborah said, and began running water in the sink.

Mike walked up behind her, reached over her shoulder and turned off the tap.

"No. I'm going to do the dishes. You're going to go take a long, leisurely bath."

"But I—"

Mike took her by the shoulders and turned her around to face him.

"Look at me," he said.

Deborah sighed, then lifted her chin. "What?"

"After the evening you've had, don't you think you deserve a little babying?"

"I suppose," she said softly.

"So take a bath, damn it."

The gruffness in his voice was offset by the tenderness of his touch.

She grinned. "Don't mind if I do." Then she added, "See you later?"

His eyes darkened. "Count on it."

A shiver of longing swept through her. It had been ages since she'd felt a connection this strong with anyone. She wanted it to happen. She did. She just wasn't sure if she could remain heart-whole once he was gone.

* * *

James regained consciousness in a world of hurt. Groaning, he rolled over on his back only to realize that the first star of evening was already out. In a panic, he pulled himself up by sheer will. After packing his glove against the wound in his side to stanch the bleeding, he knew he had to get moving.

Two brutal hours later, by his best estimate, he decided he should be coming up on the crash site any time. He was weak from loss of blood, and light-headed to the point of hallucinating. Twice he'd thought he'd seen his own mother down the hill from him, urging him forward, and both times, it had given him pause for thought. He'd never believed in ghosts until today.

He needed some first aid, a shot of codeine for the pain ripping up his side, a cup of hot coffee, a steak cooked medium rare and a long, hot shower, and in that exact order, but not until he'd warned the authorities about Darren Wilson.

Not for the first time, he wondered how hard a sell it was going to be, trying to convince the law that a senator of Wilson's stature was also a murderer. However, there was the bullet hole in James's side, Molly's testimony regarding what she'd seen on the plane and an autopsy on Patrick Finn that should prove his cause of death. Plane crash victims didn't die of strangulation.

He glanced at his watch, then looked up, judging the wind by calculating how fast the long, stringy clouds passing in front of the half moon were moving. The sky was littered now with stars, but only a few were clearly visible through the growing cloud cover.

He continued to move, ignoring his pain and sloughing through the snow as if it were nothing. Within a few minutes he saw what appeared to be lights flickering in the distance. He stopped, staring intently through the darkness until he was sure that what he was seeing was real.

"Talk about timing," he said softly, then fixed his gaze on the glow and moved forward with a prayer of thanksgiving on his lips.

Evan had wrestled Johnny in and out of the bathtub, then dressed him in his sleep shirt before getting into the bath himself. As he rinsed off the soap, he thought of Molly. He'd left her and Johnny in bed, reading a storybook. It had been touching to see his son nestled within Molly Cifelli's arms, Elmo tucked under his arm and his eyelids at half mast as she read.

It crossed his mind that he might be just the least bit jealous of his son's place in that bed. It had been a long time since he'd thought of another woman as anything but a way to pass the time. But Molly was different. Trouble was, so was he. He couldn't imagine a woman feeling anything for him but pity.

Struggling with a feeling of despair, he quickly dried off and then put on the T-shirt and sweatpants he used for sleeping. He glanced at his reflection as he left the bathroom, then looked away. If he couldn't stand to look at himself, how did he think anyone else would?

But when he came out of the bathroom, Molly looked up, and the smile she gave him stopped him in his tracks. Johnny had fallen asleep with his head pillowed on her breasts. The sight brought tears, blurring his vision. He'd once seen a painting in a museum called *Madonna with Child*. In this moment, it was like seeing it all over again.

"So…he finally gave out," he said softly.

Molly nodded. "I didn't want to wake him, so I was waiting for you to help me move him."

"Sure thing," Evan said, as he put one knee in the middle of the mattress to brace himself, then leaned down and slipped his hands under his son.

At that moment he looked up. Molly was only inches away. His gaze centered on her lips, slightly parted and too damn close to ignore.

"Ah, Molly," he said softly, and with his son still in his arms, he moved his head three inches to the right and kissed her.

Molly moaned beneath her breath. She'd been dreaming of this moment ever since she'd first seen his face—his beautiful, tortured face.

When Evan finally pulled away, he saw she was crying.

"Jesus, don't cry," he muttered.

Together, they put Johnny to bed, then, as always, turned toward each other. With the boy in the middle, they reached for each other in the dark, and when their fingers touched, they let them entwine, then closed their eyes and slept.

* * *

Mike made the rounds of the house, checking to see that the doors were locked. He laid a couple of fresh logs onto the fire, then paused, listening to the silence. All he heard was the fire as it crackled and popped as the logs caught. The sound was a comforting reminder of how blessed they were to be inside. At the same time, he thought of his dad, then shoved the worry away. James was most likely sitting inside a cop car having some hot coffee, or already on his way down to Carlisle to join Thorn in the motel. He couldn't let himself dwell on maybes.

He watched the fire until he was certain the wood was burning, then put the fire screen in place. As he did, a cold wind buffeted the sides of the house, rattling a loose pane in a window somewhere toward the kitchen. A faint howl rode with the wind, reminding him of the dead cougar he'd dragged into the woods. Wolves had obviously found it. Whether it was fair or not, the circle of life continued to play itself out. One thing dies so that another might live.

Thank God it wasn't Deborah who'd been sacrificed tonight. Thank God, thank God.

He took a deep, shaky breath, then combed his fingers through his hair.

She was waiting for him down the hall.

Suddenly he couldn't get there fast enough.

Deborah's bath had turned into ritualistic foreplay. The warm water and the soft, silky bubbles eased the weariness of her body and soothed the cold-chapped surfaces of her skin. She soaked until the water cooled, then got out and dried quickly. It didn't take long to slather herself with moisturizer. But instead of dressing in her usual flannel nightgown, she chose a soft fleece robe and stayed naked underneath. The robe was blue, the same color as her eyes, and the hem brushed the tops of her bare feet as she walked. She'd piled her hair up on top of her head during the bath and had yet to take it down, although long, ash-blond tendrils were dangling about her neck.

She was turning back the covers of her bed when she heard footsteps coming down the hall. She stopped, then turned to face the doorway, unaware that she was clutching the edge of the bedspread in her hand.

Her heartbeat accelerated. Her legs went weak.

The door opened.

Mike was silhouetted in the light from the hall.

"You still sure about this?" he asked.

"Yes. Aren't you?"

He walked inside, closed the door behind him, then took her in his arms.

"I've never been more sure of anything in my life," he said softly. He paused, splaying his hands across the back of her robe, then down to her hips. "Are you naked under this?"

She smiled.

"Lord," he muttered, then picked her up and carried her to the bed. "Give me five minutes to shower," he said.

"Four," Deborah countered.

He did it in three.

* * *

Deborah had turned out all the lights in the bedroom, so when he came out of the adjoining bath, he had to stand for a moment until his eyes adjusted to the darkness.

"Mike?"

The way she said his name made the muscles in his belly tighten. "Yeah?"

"Can you see?"

"No."

"Then follow the sound of my voice."

Unerringly, he turned slightly to the right and walked eight steps before he saw the outline of the bed. Before he could go farther, Deborah came to meet him.

Automatically, he mapped the shape of her body as she leaned into him. He felt her arms around his neck and the soft jut of her breasts against his chest as he pulled her close.

They fit as perfectly as if they'd been measured beforehand—toe to toe, heart to heart, mouth to lips. Mike tunneled his hands through her hair and felt the pins holding it up on top of her head. One by one, he did a slow, thorough search until he managed to pull them all out, then dropped them on the floor as her hair tumbled down over his arms.

15

"Like silk," Mike whispered as his hands mapped the contours of her body.

As soon as his eyes had adjusted to the darkness, he picked her up and carried her back to the bed, then laid her down and stretched out beside her. When she turned toward him and wrapped her arms around his neck, the knot that had been in his belly disappeared.

Their lips met, then their bodies melded. There wasn't an inch of skin that remained untouched on either of them as they made the jump from sexual tension to the real thing. The scent on her body was elusive, but tantalizing—something that smelled like mint with a touch of spring.

She was soft, slender to the point of fragile, and yet he'd never known a less fragile woman in his entire life. She seemed dauntless—even fearless—and then there was that part of her that he would never understand.

Deborah felt as if she'd been living her entire life for this moment and this man. Her body felt raw. She craved his touch, and yet it was close to painful. Every time his hand touched her skin, her body vibrated like a guitar string that had been strung too tight. She wanted more. She wanted *him.*

Finally Mike rolled onto his back, taking Deborah with him. When she straddled his legs, then rocked back on her heels, he reached for her breasts. They filled the palms of his hands—a perfect match. Her hair was thick and soft, and fell to the middle of her back. Mike tangled his fingers in the length, then tugged gently until she submitted.

Deborah gave up her dominance by leaning forward and then stretching herself along the length of his body. Within seconds he rolled again, this time taking her under. She reached for him, feeling the strength of the muscles along his shoulders as his head dipped toward her. She felt the warmth of his lips along her skin, on her lips, in the curve of her neck beneath her chin, in the valley between her breasts. When his tongue circled the outer surface of her navel, she shuddered from want.

"Mike…please…" she whispered, then fisted her hands in his hair and tugged gently.

He moved back up her body, then rose up on his elbows to look down at her in the dark. It was like looking at her through a sheer curtain. Even though he could see her, the outline of her features was slightly blurred.

"You are so beautiful," he said softly.

The words filled Deborah's heart, but she wanted more. She wanted the emptiness of her life to go away, if only for one night. She locked her legs around his back, then arched upward.

"Make love to me, Michael. Don't make me wait for you any longer."

So he did as she asked.

Their joining was more than either of them had imagined. For Deborah, it was knowing that she'd been born to love this man. For Mike, it was a feeling of coming home. When they began the dance of love, time stopped. All sense of themselves as individuals became lost in the act of making love.

The room stood in darkness but was tempered in warmth. The gentleness of their lovemaking was slowly moving into a frenzy they wouldn't have stopped, even if they could. All the power of Mike's body was focused into a pinpoint of energy, an energy that grew with each thrust.

Deborah took everything he gave her without thought, riding the feeling that continued to swell, pushing her past thought into a moment of insanity. Moments became minutes, and the minutes passed without count. Nothing mattered but the goal just out of reach.

The climax came suddenly and without warning, shattering Deborah to the core. Only seconds separated them as Mike followed suit.

He'd been in control from the moment he'd slipped inside her to the exit of the last thrust. But when he began another downward stroke, he felt himself coming apart. He tried to maintain the motion but lost it—and himself—inside her. Swept away by wave after wave of helpless release, he could do nothing but ride the feelings all the way down.

When it was over, they lay weak and spent in each other's arms. No words were spoken. No sounds were made as Mike reached down, grabbed the blankets and pulled, covering himself and Deborah.

And so they slept, with her head pillowed on his chest and his arms holding her close while danger came up the mountain.

James didn't know the setup of the crash site, but it stood to reason that the place with the most lights was probably a command post, and he headed toward it with single-minded intent.

He didn't know how weak he was until he found himself staggering. As he did, the lights of a vehicle passed behind him on the road. He spun around, intent on hailing the driver, but was too late to be seen. He stood in mute frustration, watching the taillights of the vehicle disappearing down the makeshift road.

"Hey! Who's there?" someone called.

James turned back to the site, breathing a quiet sigh of relief. At last, a warm body and hopefully some means of communication.

"O'Ryan!" he called. "I'm coming in."

He walked into the lights as a pair of guards came to meet him.

"Hey, mister…where the hell did you come from?" one of them asked.

James pointed up the mountain.

The guard was at first taken aback, then realized who James must be.

"I know who you are. You're one of the men who found those three missing passengers, aren't you?"

James flinched. It was the first time he realized the world thought *they'd* found all three.

"I need to talk to the sheriff," he said.

"Man, what a crazy stunt that was. You're lucky you didn't get lost, too."

"We had a good guide," James said. "Can you tell the sheriff I need to—"

"Come inside and get warm," the other guard offered.

James sighed with frustration. These two didn't do much listening.

"Do you have a working phone in there?"

"Yeah, why?"

"I need a doctor, and I need to get in touch with the authorities."

"What's the doctor for?" the guard asked.

"I've been shot," he said, and swayed where he stood.

"Well…for the good Lord's sake, why didn't you say so?" the guard cried, and headed him toward the rescue station.

Within minutes James was cradling a cup of hot coffee while the guard was cleaning the entrance and exit wounds in his side. Another guard had come in with them, called the local sheriff's office down in Carlisle and, as the phone started ringing, handed it to James.

James took it, sipping coffee as he counted the rings. Finally someone answered.

"Sheriff's office."

"This is James O'Ryan," he said. "My grandson

was one of the survivors of the crash. I need to talk to the sheriff."

"I'm sorry, Mr. O'Ryan, but Sheriff Hacker isn't here. Can one of the deputies help you?"

He frowned. "Where is the sheriff?"

"I'm not sure."

"Then I need the number for the state police."

The dispatcher rattled off a number. James hung up, then made a second call. Within moments, he was connected.

"I need to speak with an investigator," James said.

"Who's calling, please?"

"My name is James O'Ryan. I have information about a murder."

It was the magic *M* word that got the attention he needed. Seconds later he was explaining why he'd called to a man who'd identified himself as Sergeant Burl Tackett.

"So who's dead?" Tackett asked.

"Senator Patrick Finn. He—"

"This is not the time of night to be making prank calls. We already know Senator Finn is dead. He died in a plane crash."

"No, he didn't," James said. "He was alive after the crash, then murdered."

Tackett wanted to hang up. He didn't want to play this game, but part of his job was handling the nutcases who called.

"And you know this because…?"

"There were three survivors on that plane. A woman

and a boy witnessed the murder, then ran away from the crash site to keep from being killed themselves. It's why they got lost on the mountain. They were afraid for their lives."

Tackett's frown deepened. As crank calls went, this one was a bit more detailed.

"The other missing passenger has been tracking them all over the mountain, trying to find them to shut them up. He shot me as I was coming down to find the authorities to tell them what's been happening."

Tackett's attitude shifted.

"He shot you? Where did he get a gun?"

"I don't know. But he shot me and I passed out. When I came to, I walked on down the mountain to the crash site. That's where I'm calling from."

Tackett was making notes quickly now. "So where are these two witnesses?"

"They're snowed in at Deborah Sanborn's home near the top of the mountain, which is above where the crash occurred. As soon as weather permits, we'll be bringing them out."

"Exactly who are these witnesses?" Tackett asked.

"A young woman named Molly Cifelli, and a little boy named Johnny O'Ryan."

Tackett paused, tapping the end of his pen against the paper as he reread the last name.

"That last one any relation to you?" he asked.

"Yes. My great-grandson."

"And exactly who did these two witnesses say killed Senator Finn?"

"The other survivor…Senator Darren Wilson."

"The hell you say!" Tackett shouted.

James heard anger, doubt and frustration in the man's voice, and couldn't blame him for any of it. The story was far-fetched, but he had to make Tackett believe.

"Look, all you have to do is autopsy Senator Finn's body. The two witnesses claim he was strangled. That shouldn't be hard to prove."

Tackett's instincts kicked in. As far-fetched as this sounded, he was beginning to believe it. But along with a sense of urgency, there was a problem. It had been several days since the crash. He didn't know how many of the bodies had been released to relatives, but if Finn had already been sent to a mortician to be embalmed, they might have lost their only way of proving this man's claims.

"I want to talk to these witnesses," Tackett said.

"Then pray for the weather to clear. I came down from the house on foot in a snowstorm. It's not snowing now, but there's no way they could walk out. Miss Cifelli is injured, and Johnny is too small."

"Too small? How old are we talking here, mister?"

"He's five."

"That's too bad," Burl Tackett said, thinking if the kid *had* witnessed a murder, that was a horrible thing for a child to see.

"What about getting a chopper in to take them out?" Tackett suggested.

"We're talking four people to evacuate, not just two,

and when I left, the weather was too inclement for any kind of evac, whether by land or air."

"I thought you said there were only two other survivors besides Wilson. Who else are we talking about?"

"The other two are my son and grandson, who happens to be Johnny's father. There's no way they would let that little boy leave that mountain without them."

"They couldn't walk out like you did?"

"My son could, but my grandson, Evan, who's Johnny's father, is still recuperating from wounds suffered in Iraq. He made it up the mountain during the search, but it took everything he had in him to do it. I would hate to put him through that kind of rigorous march again."

"I see," Tackett said. "Do you have a phone number where you can be reached?"

"We have a room at the Carlisle Motel in Carlisle, Kentucky. You can reach me there. The room is in Evan O'Ryan's name. Also, I'll give you my cell phone number."

Tackett wrote everything down, then added, "We'll be in touch," and hung up.

James returned the phone to the cradle, then leaned back as the guard finished taping the bandages in place. Having overheard everything James said, both guards were staring at him in disbelief.

"You claiming Finn was murdered?"

James nodded.

"That other senator killed him?"

"That's right," James said.

"Man… I'm glad I'm not on that detail," the guard said. "Can't you just see the shit hitting the fan when they go to arrest a senator?"

"I need a ride down into Carlisle," James said.

"I'll take you," the guard said. "I'll come back to get my buddy here when our shift is over."

By the time they pulled to the curb at the sheriff's office, James was shaking from pain and exhaustion. "I think you're going to have to help me," he said.

The guard jumped out and steadied James as they entered the building.

Paul, the night dispatcher, took one look at the bloody clothes and the bandage on the big man's belly and jumped up to help.

"Find the sheriff and get him here ASAP," the guard said.

Paul got on the radio and began to call.

James stared through the windows to the café across the street. It appeared to be open, but he didn't know for how long. If Thorn was still up, they could talk over some hot food. He reached into his pocket, pulled out his cell phone and called the motel. To his relief, the call went through.

Thorn had been watching television when the phone rang. He answered absently.

"Hello."

"Dad! Hey, Dad! It's me. James."

Thorn sat up quickly.

"Son! Where are you calling from? Is everyone all right?"

"I need a ride. I'm down the street at the sheriff's office."

"I'll be right there," Thorn said, and hung up the phone. He was out the door within seconds.

It wasn't any time before James saw a pair of headlights appear at the curb outside. He breathed a quick sigh of relief, then winced from the motion. The door to the sheriff's office swung inward. Thorn was silhouetted in the doorway briefly, then hugged his son.

"By God, it's good to see you." Then he frowned and pointed to the bloody bandages. "What the hell happened?"

"Gunshot. I need to see the doctor to get some antibiotics. Otherwise, I think I'm okay."

"Christ Almighty," Thorn muttered. "Come on. I'll take you to the doctor."

"Can't leave yet, Dad. I've got to tell the sheriff what's been happening."

"Tell me first. And where is everyone else, by the way?"

"They're still on the mountain. As for what's been happening, the other missing passenger is a killer. Molly and Johnny witnessed him killing Senator Patrick Finn."

"Oh, good Lord. I thought he died in the crash."

"Nope. He was still alive when it was over. Molly said Wilson strangled him."

Thorn's eyebrows rose.

"You're saying that Senator Wilson killed Senator Finn?"

"Yes… Then I ran into him on the way down the mountain. He shot me. We've got to get help up to Deborah's house. She believes Wilson is going there to silence his two witnesses."

At that moment Sheriff Hacker came into the office from the back.

"Hey! What's everybody doing out so late?" he asked.

James started talking.

Sheriff Hacker's reactions were instantaneous and unquestioning.

"How's the road up to Deborah's? Can we get up the mountain okay?"

"Not in the dark," James said. "Some drifts are over my head."

"Damn it," Wally muttered. "I've tried for years to get that woman to move down into Carlisle where it was safer, but she won't give that place up. Now look what a mess she's in."

"So is my family," James said.

"Yeah, yeah…I didn't mean to exclude them. It's just that I've known Deborah all my life. She's a good woman. As for your family, I can only imagine what Ms. Cifelli and that little boy have had to face. The kid sees his grandparents die, then witnesses a murder. Sometimes I wonder what this world is coming to." He frowned, then glanced over at the Wanted posters scattered all over the walls. "Maybe I spoke too soon.

Maybe I do understand why Deborah stays up there instead of mingling with us down here."

"Are you done with James?" Thorn asked, eyeing the weary expression on his son's face and the slight slump of his shoulders.

"It was a long walk down," James said. "As much as I hate to admit it, I'm not as young as I once was."

"You've been shot. We're going to the doctor now," Thorn said.

"I'll call the doc and tell him you're coming," Hacker said.

"Just make sure you get to Deborah's house tomorrow morning," James said, then added, "Deborah said that Molly and Johnny are in danger."

Hacker's face paled. "From Wilson?"

"Yes. Right now, they're the only witnesses to a powerful man's sin. You need to get Wilson in custody, then they should be safe."

Thorn frowned. "Are you talking about Deborah…the so-called psychic?"

James quickly came to her aid. "No, Dad, it's Deborah who's half witch and all woman."

"You mean you've bought into it, too?"

James shrugged. "Look, I don't know how to explain it, but she's for real, and I can't believe you're questioning it. You, who started all this because Mom came and told you Johnny was in trouble."

The others frowned, unable to follow the conversation.

Thorn nodded briskly. "Okay, you've convinced me. Now, off to the doctor."

They left the sheriff's office together, and as they walked to the car, James realized how comforted he was by his father's presence. Even at eighty-five, his father was still a power to be reckoned with. As James eased himself into the car, he leaned back with a groan.

"I haven't been this tired and hungry since I don't know when."

"When we're through at the emergency room, I'll get some food to take back to the room."

"That sounds like a deal," James said. "Once we're there, I'll try calling Deborah's house. I'd like them to know I'm okay."

Thorn nodded as they drove away.

"How's Evan doing through all this?" he asked. "He didn't look all that strong."

"He's an O'Ryan. He'll manage."

Thorn relaxed. It was true. Somehow, no matter what life handed them, the O'Ryans always found a way to survive.

Johnny woke up, then sat up. His dad and Mollie were asleep, but he needed to go to the bathroom. He crawled over his dad, then did what he had to do. When he came back, Evan automatically made room for him without fully waking, but Molly came to enough to know that Johnny was back. She slid her arm across his body and hugged him close, taking comfort in the way he relaxed so completely. The last thing she was thinking as she fell back to sleep was how easy it was to love both father and son.

* * *

Deborah, who had never in her life slept an entire night with anyone else in her bed, had fallen asleep in Mike's arms as if it were a common occurrence. Even the rhythm of their breathing was in sync.

Neither she nor Mike was aware, as they slept, of the shift in the weather or the strong winds that came out of the north. They didn't know that, once again, the sky was filled with frozen moisture. But not the large, soft snowflakes they'd had before. This time it was sleeting. Tiny pellets peppered down, covering surfaces with a thin crust of ice and making travel treacherous.

Deborah was lost in a deep, dreamless sleep until a man suddenly appeared in her head. Even though it was dark, she somehow knew he was looking straight at her. Then, suddenly, he was gone.

She sat up with a gasp, hearing the horrific sound of someone screaming and the sounds of limbs snapping from the weight of a falling body, and knew he'd fallen off the mountain.

Mike felt her movement before he opened his eyes, but as soon as he did, he reached for the light. Deborah was wide-eyed and staring at a point on the opposite wall, but he could tell she was locked into a vision. He didn't know whether to touch her or speak, so he waited for her to make the first move.

Deborah was inside the man's mind, feeling the pain and confusion—and the anger. She understood the first two, but not the last. Why anger? Why not fear?

* * *

There was blood. He could feel it running past his ear and down the back of his neck. His knee hurt, too, enough that he groaned when he tried to move.

Damn, damn, damn.

The way he figured it, this was God's way of paying him back for what he'd set out to do.

He leaned forward, then held his breath. His body actually rocked where it had stopped, which told him he wasn't in a secure position yet. He didn't know exactly where he was, but he knew where he wasn't. He was no longer walking on the road toward lights he'd seen in the distance, and he was no longer carrying the rifle.

It only took him a few seconds more to figure out that he was hanging upside down. At that point, he screamed. Only once. But the sound was enough to accentuate the seriousness of his present state.

He didn't know what to do. If he moved and his body slipped from where it had stopped, he might wind up in a worse position. On the other hand, if he did nothing, he would wind up frozen to death. How ironic would it be to finally die on this mountain after surviving that plane crash?

What he needed was some light, but since that was impossible, he was going to have to proceed on feel alone.

There was a large branch to his left. He felt the circumference, decided it was large enough to hold his weight and grabbed onto it for dear life. As he did, his ankle, which had been caught in the V of a branch, suddenly slipped and came loose. If he hadn't been holding on to the branch, he would have plummeted to the bottom of...somewhere. He laughed aloud. Once again, he'd cheated death.

But the humor of the moment soon disappeared. The darkness in front of him was frightening. At the least, he should have been able to see something—trees, snow, anything but this black, bottomless void.

Obviously, he must have gone over the side of the mountain, and, as far as he could tell, the only thing keeping him from falling all the way down was his grip on the tree.

One false move and he would be gone. At that point, he stopped moving and considered his options. It didn't take long to accept that he had none.

He cursed. Once again, by his own bad judgment, his free will had been taken away.

He felt himself slipping again, but this time he was not only holding on to the tree with both hands, he'd dug into the trunk in front of him with the toes of his shoes. As he did, he felt himself gaining ground. Slowly, slowly—inch by inch—he felt and grabbed and climbed up until he realized there was nothing left to hold on to and nowhere left to climb.

Somehow he was back in the same place he'd fallen from. He was too afraid to move, and grateful for the fact that he was on his belly and lying on solid ground. Unable to crawl any farther, he rested his head on his forearm and closed his eyes.

* * *

"Oh Lord, oh Lord," Deborah said, and covered her face with her hands. "He fell. He fell. He went over the mountain."

When Mike heard her, his heart nearly stopped. Thinking only of James, he wanted to weep. Instead, he took her in his arms and held her close.

"Deborah…honey…what did you see? Was it Dad?"

"No, no, it wasn't James," she said, and then covered her face.

"Then who was it?" he asked.

"I don't know. I couldn't tell."

Deborah got out of bed, putting on her robe as she ran through the house to the front door. Mike was right behind her.

She pulled it open, then shivered as sleet blew onto her bare feet.

"Dear Lord. Ice."

"It's sleeting," Mike said.

She closed the door, then leaned against it as the tiny pellets of sleet coating her nightgown quickly turned into water.

After the horror of what she'd seen and heard in her vision, she wanted the subject changed. Despite the fact that it didn't fit the conversation, she said the first thing that came into her head.

"It's too bad I didn't know sooner that I would be having company for Christmas. I would have done a little shopping."

Mike took her in his arms and pulled her close,

resting his chin on the top of her head as she wrapped her arms around his waist.

"I can't think of a place I'd rather be right now than here in this house with you and my family. And thanks to you, my family is still intact."

Deborah pulled back, then looked at Mike.

The intensity in her gaze silenced him.

"If this thing between us is nothing but gratitude, a simple thank-you would have sufficed," she said.

He frowned. "I've been grateful plenty of times in my life, but I never took anyone to bed because of it."

"All right, then," she said, and laid her cheek against his chest where his heart beat the loudest. "I don't have all that much experience when it comes to casual sex. I just wanted to know where I stood."

Mike's arms tightened around her. "I'm sorry for the misunderstanding, but make no mistake…there isn't a damn thing casual about my feelings for you."

"Mine, too," she said, and then turned in his arms until she was standing with her back to his chest and staring out the window.

"Do you think it was Darren Wilson who fell?"

"I don't know. I wish I knew for sure. I only saw the shape of a man, then, after that, just the sounds of screaming and breaking branches."

"Do you think that whoever fell is dead?" Mike asked.

"I can't tell. I don't feel anything anymore."

Mike frowned.

"Then that's good enough for me. Maybe if you

don't feel him, that means the bastard is dead. However, if you get a new vibe that leans toward the opposite theory, don't hesitate to let me know."

"Deal," she said. "Are you sleepy?"

"Wide awake," he said, and then grinned. "Got any ideas?"

"Hot chocolate."

The grin fell flat. "Hot chocolate?"

"Um, yes. Don't you want some?"

"Oh, I want some all right, but it wasn't chocolate that first came to mind."

Deborah poked his bare chest and then winked.

"Well, little boy, if you say please when you tell Santa, you might get both your wishes tonight."

"Have mercy," Mike said, and followed her to the kitchen.

16

State policeman Burl Tackett had known from day one that as an officer of the law, holidays did not apply to him, and this was no exception. After the talk he'd had with James O'Ryan, and then the background check he'd run on him and his family, he knew the man was definitely on the up-and-up. In fact, the entire family seemed nothing short of honest-to-God heroes.

After verifying that, he'd wasted no time in locating Patrick Finn's body. To his relief, it was still in cold storage in a Kentucky morgue.

Despite shock and confusion from the family, he claimed the body and demanded an autopsy be done on the spot to determine the cause of death. The M.E. was pissed but had no choice but to comply.

The findings were shocking. It was just as James O'Ryan had stated. Patrick Finn's injuries from the crash were severe, and there was every chance that he might never have walked again. However, he hadn't died from blood loss or blunt-force trauma due to the crash. He'd died of strangulation. The tiny pinpoints of broken blood vessels in his eyes, along with the crushed larynx and bruising around his neck, were all the proof the medical examiner needed.

Tackett got the information about Finn just as he was leaving for the day, and while he'd opened himself up to the possibility that James O'Ryan had been telling him the truth, hearing the medical examiner tell him the same thing O'Ryan had said was shocking.

"Are you sure?" he asked.

The medical examiner rolled her eyes. "Yes. My colleagues and I, with our years of experience in this profession, agree that Patrick Finn was strangled, causing air to cease flowing to the brain, causing his heart to stop, thereby causing termination of his earthly self. Are we done?"

"So he really was murdered."

Tackett hadn't realized he'd spoken that thought aloud until the M.E. answered.

"He died of strangulation. The rest is up to you."

Tackett frowned. "Are you hedging?"

"No."

"Then could Finn have died in any other way than at someone else's hands?"

"I suppose he could have been caught up in something during the crash and strangled, but that something would have needed ten fingers and the ability to crush the larynx and the larynx only."

Tackett grinned. "Are you being a smart-ass?"

"Yes."

He chuckled. "Good job. Oh…and by the way, Merry Christmas."

"Same to you," she said, and hung up.

Tackett disconnected, then flipped through his Rolodex before punching in another set of numbers. The call was answered on the second ring.

"Federal Bureau of Investigation, how may I direct your call?"

"This is Sergeant Burl Tackett of the Kentucky State Police. I've got a perp who's going to fall under your jurisdiction."

"One moment, please," the receptionist said.

Tackett reached for his coffee, but his call was answered before he had a chance to take a drink.

"This is Agent Farris."

"Farris, my name is Burl Tackett, of the Kentucky State Police."

"Happy holidays, Tackett. How can we help you?"

"Are you aware of the plane crash here in Kentucky a few days ago?"

"Are you talking about the one the two senators were on...with three missing passengers?"

"Yes."

"Did you find your missing passengers?"

"Yes...two of them, at least, and that's why I'm calling. It seems the reason they didn't stay with the plane and wait to be rescued is because they witnessed Senator Darren Wilson murder Senator Patrick Finn and were afraid for their lives."

"That's a heavy accusation. Do you have anything to back that up?"

"Yes, a recent autopsy on Senator Finn confirms

their story. The M.E. just called me with the results of Finn's autopsy. He died of strangulation, all right."

"Do we know why?"

"No. I'm passing on the torch of knowledge in the hope that you can ascertain the answer to that question."

Farris sighed. Just what he didn't want. A great big messy case right before Christmas. It was obvious he must have been a bad boy this year, because this damn sure wasn't on his wish list.

"Say, Tackett…are you being a wiseass?"

"Probably, but I also apologize. Merry Christmas."

"Same to you," Farris said, and then added, "Fax me all the info you have. I'll get to work on an arrest warrant. Oh…do we know where Senator Wilson is?"

"Somewhere up on the mountain above the Carlisle crash site, probably planning on doing away with his two living witnesses. I suggest you hasten your search. When you get some men here, I'll explain in detail," Tackett said.

Farris was already in work mode as he hung up, then dialed his boss's extension.

Tomorrow was Christmas Eve.

Darren stared down at his cracked and bleeding hands, remembering how he'd taken such things as warm clothes and soap and water for granted. And ChapStick. God, what he wouldn't give for a tube of ChapStick. His lips were so dry and swollen, he couldn't bear to moisten them.

He was fed up. Fed up with everything and everyone.

To hell with the cops.

To hell with Alphonso Riberra.

To hell with that meddling woman and kid who couldn't be bothered to die on that plane like everyone else. If they had, none of this would be happening.

He fingered the butt of the rifle lying across his lap, then leaned back against the tree trunk and closed his eyes.

It wasn't long until sunset. If he wasn't mistaken, the house he could see through the trees was sheltering the very two people who could put him on death row. There were too many people living there for him to storm the house, but he would bide his time. And when the time was right, he would take his borrowed rifle and put them out of his misery, then be gone before anyone knew what had happened.

James slept the night through and woke late the next morning to find his dad sitting up in the only chair in the room, reading the paper. A cup of coffee and a slightly greasy brown sack of something enticing sat in the middle of the table. The bandages over the gunshot wound pulled painfully at his flesh, reminding him of how lucky he was to still be breathing.

"Morning, Dad."

Thorn looked up and grinned.

"Good morning, James. You're looking better."

"I hope that's for me," James said, pointing to the sack on the table.

"You mean those two sausage-and-egg biscuits, grape jelly and a large cup of coffee?"

"Way to go, Dad," James said. He winced as he got up, then grabbed a pair of pants and headed for the bathroom. "Be right back."

Thorn grinned, then returned to his paper. A short while later, James was out, washed up and half dressed.

He grabbed the sack and coffee and carried everything to the bed. The coffee went onto the bedside table, while the first sausage-and-egg biscuit went into his mouth. Four bites later it was gone and he was unwrapping the second.

"Looks like I misjudged," Thorn said.

"How so?" James asked as he took a bite of the second biscuit.

"I don't think two are enough."

"Two is plenty," James said as he opened the grape jelly, smeared it on one side of the biscuit, then put it back together, adding a bite of sweetness to the breakfast sandwich.

"What's happening today?" Thorn asked.

"Have you tried to call Mike?" James replied.

Thorn nodded. "Didn't get through. When I was getting breakfast, I heard some of the locals talking about the weather up higher on the mountain."

"What about it?" James asked.

"There was an ice storm. About an inch of sleet on everything by the time it stopped."

James paled. "Damn it. I've never seen such a weather mess. I'm beginning to wonder if we'll ever get our boys off that damn mountain."

"What about the police? Were they going to call you and let you know about the arrest?"

"They can't arrest Wilson until they find him," James said.

Thorn frowned. "Well, they *have* to find him, and soon. We can't have Johnny and that young woman in any more danger."

"He's not particular about who he shoots," James said, patting his bandage. "Evan and Mike are probably in just as much danger as Johnny and Molly."

Thorn frowned. "Well, if that Sanborn woman is as psychic as she claims to be, she should know when he comes around."

"You'd think, but I don't know how all that works," James said. He downed the last two bites of his breakfast, then reached for the coffee. There was an expression on his face that pierced Thorn to the core, and he knew why it was there.

"You need to check on Trudy before we get too involved with other things."

James took a deep breath, exhaling slowly as his shoulders slumped.

"I've thought of little else ever since I got on the plane to come here. I was afraid to leave her alone, and at the same time, afraid she wouldn't miss me at all. I don't know which is worse."

Thorn folded up the newspaper and set it aside.

"I'm so sorry, son. I wish with all my heart that there was something I could do."

James's eyes filled with tears, but his voice didn't waver.

"She's still my Trudy, Dad. I know it, even if she doesn't."

Thorn got up from the chair and moved to the bed where James was sitting. He patted him on the back, then put an arm around his shoulders and gave him a quick hug.

"So you call and check on your girl. Then we'll go from there."

James picked up the phone as Thorn made himself scarce.

Mike woke abruptly. It was difficult to sleep when there was a finger up your nose. He reached out, grabbed his grandson by the waist and pulled him into bed.

"What were you digging for up there?"

Johnny giggled. "Boogers."

Mike laughed out loud as Johnny pounced. The wrestling match was on and that was what Deborah saw as she came out of the bathroom. She was dressed for morning chores, but she would have preferred to be wearing nothing. Last night in Mike O'Ryan's arms had been a taste of heaven. The last thing she'd wanted to do was get up, but she couldn't ignore Mildred's swollen udder or the other animals' needs. And now, seeing that Johnny had snuck into their bed, it was just as well that she'd vacated when she had. It might have been tricky explaining away why she was naked under the covers with Daddy Mike.

Mike was rubbing his knuckles on the crown of Johnny's head when he saw Deborah exit the bathroom.

He could tell by her choice of clothing that she was all about business.

"Hey, gorgeous. Give me a couple of minutes and I'll go with you."

She shook her head and grinned. "No need. I do this every day by myself. Besides, looks like you've got another agenda going right now that's far more important than babysitting me. I'll see you guys later. I'm fine, but Mildred's not."

Mike frowned. "Deborah…wait. I don't want you to—"

She smiled as she interrupted, but there was a sad tone in her voice that pierced Mike to the heart.

"Quit fussing about me, okay? Besides, what do you think I'm going to do when you're gone?"

Mike's frown deepened as she left the room. She'd just voiced a fact he'd been unwilling to face. What *was* she going to do? More to the point, what was *he* going to do? Making love to her last night had been magic. He didn't want to give her up.

"I'm hungry, Daddy Mike," Johnny said.

Mike shifted focus because he had to, but all the while he was dressing, then fixing Johnny some breakfast, he kept watching for her to come out of the barn.

Even though she'd assured him that she no longer sensed danger, he was nervous. They hadn't heard from James, and he kept remembering her claim to have seen someone fall off the mountain. When he finally saw her emerging from the barn, he breathed a sigh of relief.

"Hey, Dad, what are you looking at?"

Mike turned around as Evan entered the kitchen.

"Just checking on Deborah," he said, then pointed to the stove. "Stir that pancake batter for me, will you?"

Evan gave the batter in the bowl a couple of quick stirs, then abandoned it for a cup of hot coffee.

"How's Molly?" Mike asked, as he set a glass of milk down at Johnny's plate.

"She's okay," Evan said, and looked away.

Mike's eyes narrowed. He knew his son. There was something going on that he wasn't talking about.

"Can I have another pancake, Daddy Mike?"

"Sure thing, Johnny boy. Just give me a sec."

He quickly poured some batter on the griddle as Johnny continued to talk.

"Hey, Daddy, I got up and went to the bathroom by myself last night," Johnny said as he stirred his fork through the butter and syrup left on his plate.

"Good for you, son," Evan said.

"You didn't wake up, but Molly did," Johnny said, then held out his plate as Mike slid a freshly cooked pancake into place. "Molly snuggled with me and I slept real good. Me and Molly snuggled a bunch when we were in the snow. It was so cold, but Molly kept me warm."

Evan stopped in the middle of buttering Johnny's pancake, and just sat and looked at his son as if he'd never seen him before.

Johnny pointed at his plate. "Could I have a little more syrup, too, please?"

Evan blinked, then refocused on the task at hand.

"Yeah, sure thing, buddy," he said softly, and poured syrup over the hot buttered pancake. "So Molly kept you warm, did she?"

Johnny nodded, then when Evan slid the plate of food toward him, he attacked it vigorously with his fork. The room remained quiet until Deborah reached the back porch. The sound of her stomping snow and ice off her boots, then banging the strainer against the crock as she poured up the fresh milk, was the signal Mike had been waiting for. He began cooking pancakes again, this time in multiples.

"Evan, go see if Molly is awake. If she doesn't feel like coming to the table, we'll fix her a plate. Either way, hurry back. The pancakes will be getting cold."

The back door opened as Evan left the room. Deborah entered, carrying the bucket and strainer to the sink, then she went back to the door and took off her boots.

"Something smells wonderful," she said.

"Pancakes!" Johnny cried. "Daddy Mike is making you some."

"Yum," Deborah said, eyeing Mike's long legs and broad back as she stepped into her shoes. "Daddy Mike is a whiz at everything, isn't he?"

Mike was already grinning when he turned around. "So I'm a whiz, am I?"

Deborah smiled as she strode to the sink to wash her hands. "You know what today is?" she asked.

Mike leaned close to her ear and whispered softly, "The morning after I rocked your world?"

She laughed out loud and then threw her arms around his neck and kissed him soundly, which surprised the hell out of him. He went back to the stove to turn the pancakes before they burned, hoping that he hadn't turned as red as his son had moments earlier.

"No, what day is it?" Johnny asked.

"It's Christmas Eve," Deborah said.

Johnny's expression fell. "My presents for Daddy were on the plane."

"Then we'll find others," Deborah said.

"Are we going to a mall?" Johnny asked.

Deborah held out her plate so Mike could set a stack of pancakes on it.

"Better than that," she said as she sat down beside Johnny and reached for the butter. "We're going up into my attic," she whispered. "It's full of really neat things. You can pick out something for your daddy and your Daddy Mike, too."

"And for Molly," Johnny added.

"Absolutely," Deborah said. "For Molly, too."

"What about you?" Mike asked.

She looked up at him then, memorizing the habit he had of standing with his weight on one hip more than the other, as well as the way he held his mouth when he was trying not to laugh.

"Oh…you've already given me my present by sharing the pleasure of your company." Then she kissed the side of Johnny's face and picked up the syrup. "If it wasn't for all of you, I would be spending Christmas alone again, just as I have for years."

Johnny grinned, then scooted his chair back from the table.

"Can I be 'scused, Daddy Mike?"

"Yeah, sure," Mike said. "Go find out what's keeping your daddy and Molly for me, will you?"

"Yes!" he cried, and bolted from the room as Deborah dug into her food.

Mike turned back to the stove and started cooking another stack of pancakes but he couldn't get his mind off this woman—or her life. All these years she'd spent up on this mountain—day after day, holiday after holiday—alone.

"Hey, Deborah?"

"Yes?" Then she waved her fork at the food on her plate. "By the way, these are fantastic."

"Thanks."

"So what was it you were saying?" she asked as she took another bite.

He stared at her for a moment, watching the play of light on her features and the way her hair curled around her face when it was damp.

"I was wondering…were you ever married?"

Her expression stilled. "No."

"Why not? You're beautiful and you're smart and—"

"I creep men out," she said shortly, and stabbed another bite of pancake and shoved it into her mouth.

He could tell by the way she was chewing that he'd hit a nerve.

"That's stupid," he muttered. "It's the men who are creeps, not you."

"You say that now, but remember when we met?"

Mike wondered if he looked as guilty as he felt. "What about it?"

"You doubted everything about me."

"But I changed my mind. You made me change my mind."

"So you accept what I am," Deborah said. "Big deal. I'm still going to be the topic of conversation some night when you're out with 'the boys,' so to speak. I can hear it now. 'Say, guys…have you ever had yourself a piece of witch.'"

Mike flinched as if he'd been sucker punched.

"I would never say anything like that about any woman I've ever slept with," he said.

Deborah heard the shock in his voice, but she wouldn't look up. She didn't want to see the pity or the guilt she knew would be there. Still, she made herself smile as she took another bite.

"Sorry, then. How about *your* track record?"

Mike mumbled beneath his breath. "Twice."

"I'm sorry…did I understand you to say you've been married twice?"

"Yes," Mike snapped, and poured some more pancake batter on the griddle.

"Molly's decided to join us," Evan said as he escorted Molly to the table.

"Great," Mike said.

"Have a seat," Deborah offered.

Evan looked at Molly, then shrugged. She shook her head, as if to warn him to keep quiet, but it was clearly obvious to both of them that they'd walked in on something less than friendly going on between Mike and Deborah.

"The pancakes smell wonderful," Molly said. "I feel really guilty for being such a burden to everyone. I haven't lifted a finger to cook or clean since I entered this house."

"Maybe not, but according to my son, you're a good snuggler and you kept him really warm when you two were lost. As far as I'm concerned, that nets you a free pass."

Molly blushed. "Evan, I didn't do a thing anyone else wouldn't have—"

"But anyone else wasn't here," he said. "You were, and I'll never forget it."

She frowned slightly as Deborah passed her the syrup.

"Okay, I accept your gratitude," Molly said, then took a bite. "Good pancakes," she added.

"Thank you very much," Mike said, and watched as Deborah picked up her empty plate and took it to the sink. Before he could head her off, she'd left the room.

17

The attic was cold and smelled like all enclosed airless spaces usually smelled—of dusty wood and rotting fabrics. When she was a child, the attic had been Deborah's treasure trove. When children wouldn't play with her for fear that they would be hexed, she had to occupy herself and pretend she didn't care. Playing up here had been like traveling to another dimension. Over the years, the contents had accumulated until there were countless generations of "stuff."

Johnny had climbed the stairs at her heels, then pushed in front of her on arrival. Now he was standing openmouthed and in awe, and she could almost remember what that feeling was like.

"So, Johnny…what do you think?"

"Maybe we could find a buried treasure!"

She grinned. "When I was your age, that's what I always thought, too. So let's do a little looking around and see if we can't find something you can give your dad and Daddy Mike for Christmas."

"And Molly," Johnny reminded her.

"And Molly...I didn't mean to leave her out. She's one of the best, isn't she?"

Johnny looked up at Deborah, his eyes swimming in sudden tears.

"My Gran and Granddad Pollard died. I don't need to give them a present."

"I know," Deborah said, then knelt down and gave him a hug. "I'm really sorry about that, you know."

Johnny nodded again, then sighed, as if he had the weight of the world on his little shoulders.

"When the plane broke, they didn't wake up."

"I know," Deborah said, then stood up and took him by the hand. "Let's pretend we're at a mall and you're looking for presents, okay?"

Johnny's expression lightened. Pretend was something to which he could relate.

"Yeah, but when I find something to buy, how will I pay you?"

"Hmm, well, here's the deal. This mall doesn't take money. You find what you want, and then you can pay for it by feeding Puppy for me. How's that sound?"

"Cool!" Johnny said.

Deborah grinned. "So where do you want to start?"

He paused for a moment, then pointed toward a pair of wooden trunks.

"There. Maybe there's a treasure in those."

Deborah's grin widened as she saw where he was pointing. "One man's trash is another man's treasure."

"Huh?"

"Never mind, little man. Let's go treasure hunting, okay?"

"Okay."

As they started across the attic floor, she noticed that his hands were bare and his coat was unbuttoned.

"Are you warm enough?"

"Yes. Can we look in this one first?"

"You bet," she said, lifting the lid, then propping it open.

"Hmm, looks like just old clothes in here. Let's look in the other one."

"Yes, the other one will be better," Johnny stated.

And it was.

Sunlight coming through the single dusty window caught and held in the dust motes hanging in the air. Johnny's eyes were wide with expectation as Deborah fiddled with the latch. Finally it came loose and she pushed the lid upward, then propped it against the wall.

"Oh, Johnny, look!" Deborah said as she took out a small wooden box.

"What is it?" Johnny asked.

Deborah opened the lid, revealing the ivory-handled hunting knife inside.

"It was my grandfather's hunting knife," Deborah said.

"It has a picture on the handle," Johnny said.

"Yes, it's a grizzly bear...see?"

"Ooh, cool," Johnny said. "Daddy would like that."

She grinned. "Want to give this to him for Christmas?"

His eyes widened in delight. "Yes!"

Deborah put the lid back on the box, then set it aside.

"Okay, now something for Daddy Mike and something for Molly."

"What's that?" Johnny asked, pointing to a silk-wrapped object in the corner of the trunk.

"I don't know…let's see," Deborah said, and carefully lifted it out, but as soon as she held it, she knew what it was. "Oh…I remember this."

"It's a merry-go-round," Johnny said.

"And it's a music box, too," she added.

"How does it work?" Johnny asked.

She wound the small key on the bottom of the piece, then set it down on the floor. Almost immediately, the carousel began to turn, and the little horses began to go up and down.

"It's playing a song," Johnny said, and poked a finger at every horse as the carousel turned until it had made a full circle. "I like this one best," he said, pointing to a black horse with a flowing mane and tail.

"Yes, that's a good one," Deborah said. "Hear the music?"

"Uh-huh. Does it have a name?"

Deborah got lost in the rapt attention on Johnny's face and forgot what he'd asked. His eyes were such a clear blue, and his eyelashes so long and dark. There were seven freckles on the bridge of his nose and another one above his upper lip. The bruises from the crash were still evident, but fading, and the cuts and scratches he'd suffered were healing, as well. He'd seen more ugliness in his brief life than most people ever saw in a lifetime, yet the innocence was still there.

"Thank God," she whispered, unaware she'd spoken aloud.

"The name of the song is 'Thank God'?" Johnny asked.

"Um…what? Oh…no, the song doesn't have a name. It's just music like you'd hear in a circus."

The carousel was beginning to slow down, as was the tune. Johnny traced the shape of the black horse with his forefinger, then patted the horse's head.

"He likes apples, I think," Johnny said.

"I'll bet he does," Deborah said, then leaned down and whispered in his ear, "You think Molly would like something like this?"

"What do you think?" Johnny whispered back.

"I think she would."

He nodded solemnly, then took the carousel and set it beside the box with the knife.

"Now something for Daddy Mike," Johnny said.

"Right."

They dug through the chest, but nothing appealed to either one of them. Not to be discouraged, they abandoned the chest for a stack of boxes in the corner. Almost an hour later, they were still looking and Deborah was getting cold, so she knew Johnny would be, too.

"I think we'd better call it a day, honey. We've gone through just about everything here and nothing seems right. Let's go down and get warm, and we'll try looking again later."

"What's under this?" Johnny asked.

Deborah turned around and saw the old quilt that had been thrown over some objects that were leaning against the wall.

"I don't know," she said. "Let's see."

She pulled off the quilt and then tossed it aside. Dust poofed up in the air as it hit the floor.

"Pictures!" Johnny cried. "Look at the pictures!"

Deborah went down to her knees and began pulling them out, one by one.

"They're not pictures, they're paintings," she said. "Feel the surface. Those rough patches are brush marks. Someone painted these."

"Like my paint-by-number pictures?" Johnny asked.

Deborah nodded. "Sort of." Then she smiled. "I remember this one. My mother had it hanging in her bedroom. I never missed it when she took it down. Isn't that strange?"

Johnny was leaning against her back and peering over her shoulder. "Hey! That's you! Someone painted your picture." Then he frowned. "Only your dress is all funny."

"That's not me. It's a painting of my grandmother when she was a young woman."

Johnny frowned. "But she has your face."

Deborah laughed. "Actually, she was here first, so I guess you'd say that I have hers."

Johnny sat down beside her, then leaned back on his elbows, looking from Deborah to the painting and back again, trying to figure out how that theory worked. As he did, he absently looked up and realized there was something lying across the rafters.

"Hey!" he said. "There's something up there!"

Deborah stood, then tilted her head back, squinting past the dust and glare. At first she couldn't make it out, but then, when she did, she knew they'd finally found the perfect gift for Mike.

"It's a sword!" Johnny cried as she took it down.

"Not exactly," Deborah said. "It's actually called a saber, and it was once used by a soldier in my family during a war that happened a long time ago."

"My daddy fought in a war," Johnny said. "And so did Daddy Mike, and Granddad and Grandpop."

Deborah listened to the pride in the little boy's voice and couldn't help but hope this little O'Ryan never had to go to war.

"You have a family to be proud of," she said. "Do you think Daddy Mike would like this?"

"Yeah," he said. "He already has some swords hanging on a wall in his den back home. He said someday, when I grow up, the swords will be mine."

"That's great," Deborah said. "So, are we choosing this for his present?"

"Yes, please," Johnny said.

Deborah didn't hesitate in giving away a family relic left over from the Civil War. She was the only member of her family who was still living, and saving it only to be sold in some estate sale after she was gone hardly made sense. It gave her a good feeling to know that someone like Mike would have it—a man who would know the sacrifices the soldier who'd owned it first had made.

"It's sharp, so be really, really careful with it," she said.

Johnny's eyes were big as he dragged the long saber across the floor, then laid it beside the knife and carousel music box.

"Okay," she said as she dusted off her hands. "We'll leave these by the door while we go down and warm up. Maybe we'll have some hot chocolate, okay? I'll get the Christmas paper out of the hall closet, and we'll wrap them up and put them under the tree for tomorrow morning."

Johnny nodded, but he was already through shopping and thinking about the hot chocolate she'd promised. On his way down the attic stairs, it occurred to him that his shopping wasn't quite done.

"I didn't get you anything," he said.

Deborah smiled. "My present is all of you. This is the first year in a long time that I haven't had to spend Christmas by myself."

"But you won't get to open a present."

"Yes, I will. My neighbor, Farley Comstock, always brings something. He just hasn't been able to get here because of the bad roads and weather. It doesn't matter when I get it. He'll bring it when he can."

"All right," Johnny said, but he wasn't completely convinced. He decided he would mention it to Daddy Mike later. He would know what to do.

Johnny came down from the attic full of giggles and whispers. It did Evan good to see him acting so normal.

Molly was well on her way to complete recovery and, except for some lingering soreness and fading bruises, announced she was fine.

Deborah had taken a large ham from the freezer a couple of days ago and put in the refrigerator to thaw. She would get up early tomorrow morning and put it in the oven. Even as she was making the hot chocolate she'd promised Johnny, her mind was already planning tomorrow's meal. It was all she could do not to giggle at the excitement she felt. She was humbled to realize how a disaster had turned into one of the most special times of her life.

"That smells good," Mike said as he came up behind her and gave her a hug.

She leaned against him, soaking up the comfort that came with the hug.

"I made plenty," she said. "Want a cup?"

"Absolutely," he said, then buried his face in her hair. "Your hair is beautiful…just like you."

Deborah's heart soared. *Lord, I could so love this man. Help me not to get hurt.* Still, she could no more turn away from him than she could stop breathing.

"Are you flirting with me?"

Mike grinned. "If I say yes, how far will it get me?"

She turned the heat off under the hot chocolate and wrapped her arms around Mike's neck.

"As far as you want to go," she said, then cupped his face and kissed him.

So tenderly—so gently—so lovingly.

Feelings Mike hadn't dealt with in years hit him gut-first and swamped him under. He didn't know how all this was going to turn out, but he knew for certain that he didn't want to lose her.

Then they heard footsteps coming down the hall and reluctantly parted. By the time Evan came into the room, Mike was sipping hot chocolate and digging in a cookie jar, while Deborah was pulling mugs down from the cabinet.

"Hey," she said. "You're just in time for some hot chocolate."

"I'm going outside to get some firewood first."

"I'll help," Mike said as he stuffed the last bite of a cookie in his mouth.

Just as they started out the back door, the phone rang. It was such a startling sound that for a moment, no one moved.

"It's working!" Deborah said as she ran to answer. "Hello?"

"Hey, it's me," James said. "Just calling to let you know all is well."

"Oh! Wonderful!" she cried, then waved at Evan and Mike. "Come here, come here. It's James."

"Thank God," Evan said as Mike took the phone.

"Dad! Did you make it okay? What time did you get there? Is everything all right?"

James grinned. As always, Mike wanted answers yesterday.

"I'm fine now. Ran into a little trouble on the way down."

Mike frowned. "Like what?"

"Ran into Darren Wilson. He got a shot off before I knew what was happening."

"He shot you?"

"Yeah…in the side. Hardly more than a flesh wound. When I came to, I walked the rest of the way down. Everything is in place now. All the proper authorities have been notified, and as soon as weather permits, we'll be up to get all of you off that damned mountain."

Mike suddenly felt sick to his stomach. His dad had been shot, lain unconscious in the snow, and it was obviously only by the grace of God, that he'd come to and gotten himself to help.

"You need to rest and take care of yourself," Mike said.

James snorted lightly. "I slept good last night. I hear you guys got another dose of weather…sleet this time."

"Yeah, but we're all okay."

"Good. Thorn is fine. Worried about all of you. Pay attention to what's out there, son. It appears Wilson is dead-set on getting rid of his witnesses."

"What did the authorities do when you told them about the murder?"

"Ran into a little doubt until the autopsy results. That. lit all kinds of fires. I talked to a man named Burl Tackett early this morning. He's with the state police. Anyway, he pulled strings and got the autopsy results yesterday, then put the wheels in motion."

"That's great news," Mike said. "Molly and Johnny should soon be safe."

"Not until we find Wilson," James said.

* * *

Daylight was a blessed event. After sliding off the mountain, the night Darren had just spent was something he never wanted to repeat.

He had a gash in his head that hurt like hell and was wide enough to accommodate his forefinger. It needed stitches, but that wasn't going to happen. At least the bleeding had stopped.

He'd checked and rechecked his rifle so many times that he could probably break it down and put it back together in his sleep. He had four shots left, and now that it was light and he could see to maneuver, he thought about the task ahead. He knew what would happen if he failed. He couldn't go to prison. He wouldn't last a year in a place like that.

Still, the concern was moot until he got himself out of this mess, and the first thing he had to do was get a little bit closer to the house.

The presents were wrapped. Lunch had come and gone. The mood in the house was relaxed and easy.

Mike was in the backyard knocking snow and ice off Deborah's woodpile, and loading the wheelbarrow with a fresh supply of logs for the fire.

Molly was sitting at the table, keeping Johnny company as he matched the dots on a set of dominoes.

Evan had stepped into the pantry to get a couple of cans of vegetables to add to another soup in progress.

Deborah was on the back porch skimming cream from the milk crock, while Puppy lay at her feet. She was trying to remember where she'd stored her mother's large meat platter for tomorrow's baked ham when a sharp pain pierced her right shoulder.

"Ow!" she cried, and quickly set the cream pitcher down. She'd been holding it at an awkward angle and had obviously put her muscles in a bind.

When the pain persisted, she finished skimming the cream and went inside, thinking maybe an analgesic rub would help.

"The heat sure feels good," Deborah said as she set the bucket and strainer in the sink to wash.

Johnny angled two dominoes together and then grinned. "I matched double sixes," he announced.

"You sure did," Molly said. "Can you find the double fours?"

Johnny began shuffling through the pieces, mentally counting dots as he did.

Deborah grinned. "Want to help me make pies later?"

"Yeah!" he cried, and started putting up the dominoes.

"Not just yet," she said. "In a while."

"Okay."

"We're having baked ham and all kinds of good stuff for dinner tomorrow," she said. "How does that sound?"

He looked up with a grin. "Yum."

"Yum it is," she said.

There was a flurry of scratching at the back door, which launched Johnny out of his chair.

"It's Puppy!" he cried. "I have to feed her 'cause I'm paying you back, remember?"

"Paying her back for what?" Molly asked.

"Can't tell," he said with a mischievous grin.

"Ooh, secrets," Molly said.

Johnny glanced at Deborah, who winked. He blinked both eyes back at her in an effort to wink back. She stifled a laugh.

"Do you know where Puppy's food is?" she asked.

"Yes," he said, and bolted out the back door.

"He doesn't have his coat," Molly said.

"It won't take but a few seconds to scoop some dry food into Puppy's bowl. He should be all right."

Molly nodded and went back to peeling, while Deborah started taking off her coat and boots. She was in the act of kicking off the first boot when they heard the dog begin barking in a state of frenzy.

"What on earth?" Molly said, and started toward the back door, but it was Deborah who was already running.

The moment she'd heard the dog, she'd had the vision. Even as she was running, she feared she would be too late.

"Get the gun! Get the gun!" she screamed at Molly as the kitchen door banged against the wall.

Molly froze, then turned and ran out of the kitchen, heading for Deborah's bedroom and the closet where the rifle was kept.

She didn't know why she was running. Maybe it was another cougar, maybe not, but she knew panic, and it had been thick in Deborah's voice.

Mike turned from the woodpile as Deborah's dog came flying through the screen door, hitting it so hard that it flew back against the outer wall. The fur on Puppy's back was standing up like the mane of a lion as she bounced out through the snow. Before Mike could react, Johnny came out the door, right behind the dog, calling for her to come back. He was minus a coat and spilling a scoop of dry dog food as he ran.

"Johnny! Hey, Johnny!" he called, but Puppy was barking so fiercely the boy didn't hear.

Then he saw Deborah come racing out behind them. The expression on her face made his blood run cold. She leaped off the stoop and landed in the snow in an all-out run. When he heard her screaming Johnny's name, he began to run after them, all the while searching the area for a reason to fear.

Darren Wilson had been waiting in the woods since before sunup. He'd seen a woman go to the barn with a bucket, watched as one of the men came out to get wood, and had been thinking about waiting until they all went to sleep, then torching the house.

Noon had come and gone, and he thought about the food they were eating, and the warmth and comfort they surely must be enjoying. His misery grew.

It was midafternoon when the back door suddenly opened, and to his surprise, a dog bolted out, with the kid right behind it. It wasn't until the dog began running toward him, barking in a frenzy, that he realized he'd made an error. He hadn't seen a dog on the premises and just assumed there wasn't one. But the moment it had come out of the house, he realized that he'd been

standing upwind, which meant there was every possibility the dog had caught his scent.

He stepped back into the trees, hoping he'd been
wrong, but when the dog continued running in his direction, he knew he'd been made. His mind went into
overdrive as he shouldered the rifle and took aim. He
could get the dog and the kid with two easy shots and
throw everybody in the house into a panic. If he was
lucky, the others would run out, and then he could pick
off the second witness and be gone before they knew
what had hit them.

Even though the dog's barking was making him
nervous, he stood his ground. The dog was getting
closer, and closer, but so was the kid. His entire focus
was on what he could see through the telescopic sight.

First the dog, he thought, and pulled the trigger as it
came into view. The shot sounded loud against his ears,
but he grinned when he heard the dog yelp. Seconds
later it went down. He was waiting for the boy to come
into his line of fire when he realized a third person had
entered the scene and was screaming for the kid to get
down. With only moments to make a decision, he
shifted the rifle slightly, centered the crosshairs on the
middle of the kid's chest and fired, just as the little boy
turned.

When the first shot rang out, Mike thought he would
die from the fear. He saw Puppy drop and Johnny pause,
and he knew that would make Johnny a perfect target.
Deborah was still running and screaming when he saw

Johnny turn around and start toward her. The fear on the child's face made his veins run with pure horror. Even as Mike ran, he knew he would be too late.

Deborah's throat felt constricted, as if her cries of warning could not be heard. Her legs felt weighted so that, despite how hard she tried, she wasn't gaining ground. She saw Puppy drop at the same time she heard the shot, and she tried not to focus on the blood that splattered all over the snow.

It was the boy who was in danger. She'd seen it the moment Puppy had begun to bark. She didn't know that the pain in her shoulder had been a foreshadowing of what was about to happen to herself until it was too late.

Within a second of her dog going down, she launched herself toward Johnny. There was a brief sensation of flying as she leaped, then she caught the boy on the run. He went down less than a millisecond before the bullet slammed into her body. She had a vague memory of a sharp, burning pain, then nothing.

She didn't hear Mike's cry of dismay, or see Molly come running out of the house and toss Mike the rifle as he ran past.

Evan had come out of the kitchen just as the dog had gone down. At that point, his entire focus centered on his child. He could see what Deborah was trying to do, but when the second shot rang out, he didn't know who'd been hit. All he saw was both of them falling, then neither of them moving.

"No! No!" he screamed, and came off the porch on the run.

He passed Molly, who'd fallen to her knees in the snow and was struggling to get up, and then he passed Mike, who'd already spotted the shooter in the trees. He wouldn't look at Puppy as he dropped to his knees beside his son.

"Get them into the house!" Mike screamed as he ran past Evan.

There was blood spreading across the front of Deborah's coat as Evan turned her over. Mike saw blood on Johnny, too, as Evan picked him up. It was all Mike could do to keep running, but run he must. The killer wasn't supposed to be here, but he was, and he couldn't let him get away.

Behind him, Evan thrust Johnny into Molly's arms and screamed at her to run. Then, with one last look toward the trees to make sure the shooter was gone, he scooped Deborah up in his arms and headed to the house, right behind Molly and his son.

Darren Wilson was in a panic. This wasn't the way it was supposed to happen. What the hell kind of people didn't tend to their wounded? He hadn't expected anyone to give chase—or to be armed.

And, to make matters worse, no sooner had he turned to run than he fell flat on his face, discharging the rifle again, which left him with only one shot.

He was still sore and weak from the accident, and from lack of rest and food, but he couldn't afford to give in to the pain. If he was going to get out of this mess in one piece, he had to get away.

Panic, coupled with unadulterated fury at the situation he'd gotten himself into, lent speed to his flight. But it wasn't long before he realized his injuries were going to slow him down. Danger was in front of him. Danger was coming up fast behind him. For the first time since he'd come to after the crash, he was wishing that he'd died along with everyone else. Then he would be free of his gambling debts, Finn would still be alive, and his own troubles would already be over.

18

Evan raced up the back steps with Deborah in his arms, trying not to think of the warm blood running down his hands and arms, or the pale, lifeless feel of her body. Molly held the screen door open, while the kitchen door stood ajar. As he ran into the kitchen, he saw his son crouching beneath the table. The fear on his face was heartbreaking, but at the moment, there wasn't anything he could do.

Molly came in right behind him.

"How bad is she?" she cried.

"I don't know," Evan muttered. "Johnny! Are you hurt?"

Johnny shook his head, then hid his face against his knees.

"Damn it all to hell," Evan muttered, then laid Deborah down on the kitchen floor and began tearing at her clothes, needing to assess her wounds.

The bullet had gone in, but he couldn't find an exit wound, and she was losing too much blood.

"Compresses! I need compresses!" he yelled.

Molly began grabbing dish towels from a drawer and tossing them to Evan by the handful.

Suddenly Johnny was at Evan's side. "Is she dead like Gran and Granddad Pollard?"

"No. She's not dead, and she's not going to be," Evan muttered, then looked up at Molly. "See if the phone still works."

Molly grabbed the portable phone and tested for a dial tone. It was there, the sweetest sound she'd ever heard.

"It works! It works!" she cried.

"Call the operator. We need the sheriff, and we need an ambulance, and if the roads are impassable, we need to airlift her out of here."

Molly's hands were shaking as she made the call. Within moments, an operator had connected her with the sheriff's office in Carlisle. The moment she heard the dispatcher's voice, she started talking.

"There's been a shooting at Deborah Sanborn's home. We need an ambulance immediately."

"Oh, Lord," Frances said. "Who's been shot?"

"Deborah, and she's losing a lot of blood."

Evan looked up. "Tell them we need the law, as well."

Molly nodded quickly. "Darren Wilson is on the run down the mountain, and Mike O'Ryan is chasing after him. We need the sheriff, too."

"Oh Lord, oh Lord," Frances repeated. "Don't hang up. I'm going to put out the call, but don't hang up." Frances spun her chair from the phone to the dispatch radio. "Sheriff Hacker! Come in! Come in!"

Wally Hacker was coming out of the bathroom of

Sonny's Stop and Go when he heard the panic in his dispatcher's voice. He ran toward the car as fast as he could.

"This is Hacker...come back."

"Wally...Darren Wilson shot Deborah Sanborn at her home. Mike O'Ryan is chasing him. They're requesting assistance. I'm going to call Mediflight. They say she's losing blood fast."

"Get Mediflight on the way, then contact all my deputies and send them up after me. I'm already on my way."

"Ten-four, Sheriff. Over and out."

Frances quickly dispatched Mediflight, giving them all the information she had, then turned back to Molly, who'd heard it all.

"Medical assistance is on the way. Mediflight will be landing in the clearing behind her house. The sheriff and his deputies are on their way, as well."

"Thank you," Molly said, then disconnected.

Evan grabbed another handful of dish towels and pressed them against Deborah's wound.

"Deborah! Deborah! It's Evan...can you hear me?"

There was no answer, no movement, and precious little in the way of breathing, to indicate that Deborah Sanborn was still with them.

"Damn it," Evan muttered, and pressed harder on the wound, desperate to stop the blood flow.

Johnny had crawled back under the table, lain down on his side and curled up into a ball. His gaze was fixed, his eyes shimmering with unshed tears, as he stared at the pool of blood in which Deborah was lying.

Evan didn't dare take time to go to his son, to hold him and assure him that he was safe. Hell, he didn't even know if that was true. He had no idea what was happening to his dad. He needed help, and the moment he thought it, he knew who to call.

"Molly, get the phone again," he said.

She grabbed the portable, then squatted down beside him.

"Dial this number," he said, watching as she punched in the sequence he'd given her. "When they answer, put the phone to my ear."

She nodded in understanding, listening intently as she waited for someone to answer.

James was just walking into the motel room when the phone began to ring. Thorn was stretched out on the bed asleep, and James ran to answer as Thorn was waking up.

"Hello," he said.

"Granddad, it's me, Evan. We've got big trouble. Darren Wilson shot Deborah. She's bleeding badly. We're waiting for her to be airlifted out. Dad is somewhere on the mountain, running down Wilson with Deborah's old .22 rifle. I don't know what's happening, or if they're all right. We contacted the sheriff, and he and his deputies are on their way to help Dad, but I need help. Johnny is a mess, and Molly's not strong enough physically to deal with everything."

"God in heaven," James muttered, and motioned

quickly for his father to get up. "Don't worry, boy. I don't know how just yet, but you can count on us. We'll be there, if I have to grow some damn wings and fly."

Just hearing his grandfather's voice gave Evan the peace of mind he needed.

"Thanks, Granddad. Do what you can—but hurry."

The phone went dead.

James stared at the receiver, in disbelief in the wake of what he'd just heard, then replaced it on the cradle.

"Dad, get dressed. Deborah's been shot, and Mike's on the mountain going after Wilson. And I think Johnny's witnessed one trauma too many. We've got to find a way to get to them."

"I think I know how," Thorn said, and grabbed his boots.

Mike was running as fast as he could through the snow, slipping on the icy spots and grabbing at trees to keep from falling. Wilson had about a hundred-yard lead on him, although he still caught brief glimpses of the man through the trees as they ran.

He'd had one chance for a shot when they'd gone through a clearing. It wasn't much, but it was enough, and he took the opportunity. The bullet hit a tree right beside Wilson's head, sending bark and snow flying. Darren Wilson had thrown up his arms in a defensive gesture, then ducked into a thicker copse of trees. After that, Mike was following by tracks and sound as much as by sight.

He wanted to stop and go back, to pick Deborah up in his arms and make sure she and Johnny were all right. He'd seen the blood all over her coat, and the pale, lifeless color of her skin. But if he quit, that meant the bastard who'd shot them would get away.

He was barely aware of the cold air burning his lungs or the numbness of his feet. All he wanted was the back of that man's head in the crosshairs of his rifle, and an end to the danger to his family.

The deep cuts and scratches that Darren endured during the crash and his subsequent falls were hampering his escape. His right ankle throbbed with every stride, and his vision was blurred. The pain in his body was so intense that it made him nauseated. Every tree he dodged, every limb that hit him in the face, every bush he had to go through, became the enemy.

At first he was far enough ahead of the man giving chase that it gave him a sense of false confidence. It wasn't until a bullet hit a tree past which he was running, sending splinters of wood and a limb full of snow flying in every direction, that he panicked. He felt a sting on his cheek, but he couldn't stop to check it out—not even when he felt something warm running down his face into the collar of his coat.

Damn it to hell, didn't that man ever quit?

He dodged behind a trio of pines, then used the thicket of underbrush to keep himself out of rifle range. His heart was pounding, as was his head. Every impact of foot to ground was agonizing, but nothing compared to the danger behind him. Gut-wrenching fear lent speed to his crippled stride.

"Goddamn you!" he screamed, although there was no one to hear his cry.

He ran headlong through thickets, although he could no longer feel his left foot. It had gone numb, either from the cold or from the fact that he'd torn ligaments and muscles when he'd fallen into that ravine last night. It threw him off balance just enough that when he skidded around an outcropping of rock, he went down to his knees.

"Oh, shit," he cried as he scrambled to his feet. But in that moment of shock, he saw salvation only yards away.

A truck was pulled up next to the woods! And off to the right, he could see a man swinging an ax, cutting wood. The closer he got, the more certain he became that the woodcutter was the same man who had that crazy wife and all those kids.

At that point, Darren wouldn't look back. He wouldn't let himself see how close O'Ryan had come. He couldn't—not when escape was in sight.

Mike was less than fifty yards away and gaining. Wilson was struggling, and the closer Mike got, the more apparent that became. Once he'd gotten a glimpse of Wilson's face and had been shocked by the mass of cuts and bruises.

All of a sudden Mike saw a change in the shooter's stride. Something had changed—but what? Then he saw it.

There was an old truck…and a man cutting wood.

God, oh God, he couldn't let Wilson escape. If that bastard got to the truck first, he wouldn't be able to catch up with him. That left Mike with only one option.

He broke stride and stopped, sending snow flying as he braced himself, then raised his rifle to his shoulder. Within seconds, he had the shooter in his sights.

At first only one shoulder and the left side of the man's head were within view, then the back of his head and the coat he was wearing, then a better-than-fair view of the upper half of his body

At that point Mike fired, twice and in rapid succession. He didn't know for sure that he'd hit him until the man fell face forward across the hood of the truck, but he knew the shot was righteous when the body slid off the truck and into the snow.

I'm dying... I'm dying. Oh, God...oh, Jesus...it wasn't supposed to end this way.

The snow was cold, but he felt colder. The sunlight was dimming, and he could hear his pursuer coming through the trees. He tried to reach for his gun, but his arms wouldn't work. He tried to curse, but the words wouldn't come, because breath had become a rare commodity.

He coughed. Blood spilled from his mouth onto his chin. He could feel someone grab him by the shoulders. He flopped like a rag doll onto his back. He didn't want to look. He didn't want to see the expression on the man's face—but there was nothing else to see.

"Help," Wilson mumbled.

Mike was so angry he was shaking.

"You tried to kill my grandson. You shot a woman who means everything to me. You want help? Yeah, sure…why not, you sorry bastard. I'll help you, all right…all the way to hell."

He moved the barrel of the rifle to the point on Darren's chest where the bullet had exited, then pushed.

Darren Wilson would have sworn there was no air left in his lungs to say a prayer, let alone power the scream that broke the silence on the mountain.

Mike pulled the trigger.

Wilson's body bucked, then went still.

Mike looked up to find the owner of the truck staring at him in wide-eyed fear.

"He's dead," Mike said. "He can't hurt anyone ever again."

"Say…what do you reckon I should do?" Farley asked.

"Call the sheriff if you want. I don't care."

Then he turned around and started running back up the mountain, the way he'd come.

The ride up the mountain was exhilarating. If it hadn't been for the seriousness of the reason, Thorn would be loving this. A good portion of the population of the United States considered anyone over the age of eighty to be old as dirt and completely useless. He could have given them a lesson in capability.

"Watch the bump!" James yelled.

Thorn nodded as he swerved the snowmobile around

the drift and then accelerated past it, leaving rooster tails of snow flying out behind him.

James considered it genius on the part of the old man to have thought of these machines. Thorn had told him as they'd been packing to leave that he'd known about them only because he'd been left behind. Because he'd been too old to take the mountain on foot when they'd begun their search, he'd stayed behind at the motel and seen a group of teenage boys on snowmobiles playing chicken in a Kmart parking lot.

It hadn't taken long to find the boys. Money changed hands, and less than half an hour after the phone call, James and Thorn were on their way up the mountain.

The ride was far easier than they'd imagined, even when they reached the elevation where the roads had turned icy. They were following tracks made by the sheriff and his deputies, flying along at a pretty stiff clip, when Thorn suddenly saw a truck and three county cruisers parked off the road and up in the trees.

He pointed.

James nodded to indicate that he'd seen them, too.

They slowed and headed for the cars. James saw the sheriff first and brought his snowmobile to an immediate halt. Thorn quickly followed suit.

"You boys on your way up to Deborah's?" Wally Hacker asked.

"Yes," James answered. He could see a body on the far side of the truck.

"According to Farley here, Mike got to Wilson before

we did. When you see him, tell him to come down to my office. We need to talk."

"He's not in trouble, is he?" Thorn asked.

"Not if what we heard was true. I just need the info to close up the report."

"We'll pass the word on," James said. Then they got back on their snowmobiles and rode away.

It was slower going up the mountain than it had been going down, and added to that were the cold and exhaustion Mike was now feeling. He had pushed himself past every threshold he'd had in him and was paying for it now. His muscles were cramping, and there was a burning pain in his side from the wild run that he'd made. Still, he wouldn't let up. He needed to get to Deborah, and he had to make sure that Johnny was all right. He was moving as fast as his body would let him, and he used every survival skill he'd learned in the military to push physical discomfort from his conscious mind. And it was because he was so focused on ignoring the pain that he didn't hear the snowmobiles until they were almost upon him.

Mike was in the middle of a large curve in the road when he became aware of engines behind him. He turned abruptly, only to see two men on snowmobiles bearing down on him. His grip tightened on the rifle as he stepped backward to give the riders more road room and was all the way in the ditch when he realized who they were.

Relief came so unexpectedly that he didn't have time to hide his emotions. When James stopped, got off and started toward him, moving in long, anxious strides, Mike's vision blurred.

"Good to see you, son. Are you all right?" James asked as he thumped Mike roughly on the back.

"Yeah," Mike said.

"We came across the sheriff and his deputies. They'd found a body. Sheriff said when you got a chance to stop by the office and fill him in so he can close the report."

"Yeah, all right."

"Was that Wilson?" James asked.

"Yeah."

James's frowned deepened. "We heard he shot Deborah. Is that so?"

"I don't know anything for sure except that he killed the dog and was aiming for Johnny when Deborah grabbed him."

"For God's sake!"

Mike grabbed his father by the sleeve of his coat. "You've obviously talked to Evan or you wouldn't be here."

James nodded.

Mike opened his mouth, then hesitated. He was almost afraid to ask for fear of the answer. Finally, he had to know.

"Deborah…is she—"

James quickly put a hand on his shoulder. "She's alive…or at least she was when we talked to Evan. But she was losing a lot of blood and he'd requested an airlift."

"Jesus," Mike said softly. "Can I ride on the back of one of those things?" he asked, pointing to the snowmobiles.

"You sure can," Thorn said. "Hop on. Mine's bigger. It'll pull double better."

James got back on his own machine.

"Hold on!" Thorn yelled.

Mike slid his arms around his grandfather's belly and did as he'd been told, praying for Deborah's well-being as they skimmed across the snow.

Less than a half mile had passed when they saw a shadow on the snow, cast from something overhead. They looked up, only to see the silhouette of a chopper passing above them. At that point, Mike's heart sank. That would be the airlift for Deborah, and he wasn't there to go with her. He needed to see her, to touch her—to know that she was going to be all right.

"Can you go any faster?" he yelled.

Thorn shook his head.

Mike had no other option but to let the incident play out and pray that the medics made it in time.

Deborah came to in the middle of the kitchen floor. Evan was leaning over her, and Molly was sitting on the floor, her back against the cabinets, with Johnny cradled in her lap. Deborah had a vague memory of running in the snow and then a sharp, piercing pain. After that, nothing.

"Evan…"

Startled by the sound of her voice, Evan jerked, then rocked back on his heels.

"Deborah? Thank God… How do you feel?"

"Hurts," she muttered, and reached toward the source of the pain.

Evan grabbed her hand and pushed it back. "Don't touch it, honey. You've been shot," he said. "Lie still."

"Shot?" It was such a foreign thought that for a moment she couldn't make her mind focus. Then she began to remember. The vision. She'd seen Johnny fall, seen the snow turn red from blood. The shooter must have missed Johnny and hit her.

"Johnny?"

"Thanks to you, he's physically okay. I don't know about the rest."

Tears spilled from the corners of Deborah's eyes. "So sorry," she whispered.

"Jesus, honey, don't apologize about a damn thing. Once again, I owe you for the life of my son. Now, hang in here with me. I don't want to have to face Dad and tell him I let you die."

At that point Deborah realized Mike was nowhere in sight. "Mike…where…?"

"He went after the shooter. It was Darren Wilson."

"Oh, God…"

"No," Evan said. "He'll be fine."

"Go help—"

"I'm not going anywhere until your ride arrives."

"What—"

"You're being airlifted to a hospital, honey. Just lie still and relax until they get here."

Pain and an overpowering weakness were pulling her

under. She didn't know if this was how it felt to die, but if that was what was happening, she needed Mike to know something.

She reached for Evan's arm, her fingers curling around his wrist tighter than he would have believed possible.

"What is it, honey?" he asked.

"Mike...tell Mike I—"

"You tell him yourself when you see him," Evan said.

Deborah shuddered as a wave of pain rolled through her body. "Mike..." she mumbled, then, blessedly, passed out.

Evan's heart skipped a beat as he quickly put a hand to her neck, checking for a pulse. To his relief, it was still there.

"Damn, damn, damn," he muttered, more to himself than to Molly. "Where is that chopper?"

"It will come," Molly said, and cuddled Johnny closer.

Evan looked long and hard at his son, trying to imagine what was going through his mind. His father had come home from a war looking like he'd been put back together like a patchwork quilt. He'd seen his grandparents die, seen a man murdered, and now this.

"Johnny?"

Johnny heard his daddy, but he wouldn't look up.

"Hey, little man, Daddy loves you," Evan said softly.

There was a brief moment of silence, then a tiny voice. "I love you, too, Daddy."

"We're gonna get through this…okay?"

Another hesitation, then another brief answer. "Okay."

Evan's gaze shifted from Johnny to the woman who held him. "Molly…"

"I'm here," she said.

"I don't know what I would have done without you," Evan said.

"Same here," Molly said.

A long silent look passed between them. A look filled with curiosity, passion and promises.

"I'm not exactly Prince Charming," he said.

"Who ever said I was looking for a prince?" she replied.

"Okay, then."

Before they could say anything else, the sound of an approaching helicopter cut through the conversation.

"They're here!" Molly cried.

Evan jumped up. "I'll be right back," he said, then gave Deborah one last glance and hurried outside.

19

The EMTs had applied pressure bandages to Deborah's wound and established an IV before strapping her to a stretcher. They were just about to carry her out to the waiting chopper when they all heard the sounds of approaching engines. Evan ran to the window and looked out.

"Reinforcements have arrived," he said, and ran out onto the porch. "In here! In here!" he yelled.

James saw Evan on the front porch and steered toward him, coming to a stop at the bottom of the steps. Thorn and Mike were right behind.

Evan was more than a little surprised to see his great-grandfather easily dismount from the snowmobile as if he'd been riding a horse.

"Grandpop?"

"We're here, boy. How are you doing?" Thorn asked.

"We've been better," he said. "They're just about to take Deborah."

Mike jumped off the snowmobile and bounded up the steps, then paused beside Evan.

"Johnny?"

Evan shook his head. "He's pretty out of it, Dad. I don't know what's going to happen."

Mike felt sick. Such a little boy to have suffered in such a dramatic way.

"Deborah?" he asked.

"I think they've stabilized her. Hurry. She's been asking for you. They're in the kitchen."

Mike gave his son a pat on the shoulder, then hurried into the house. He could hear voices coming from the kitchen, and none of them were Deborah's. He ran into the kitchen just as the EMTs were lifting the stretcher.

"Wait!" he cried as he ran forward. Her clothing was bloody and in shreds from having been cut away to tend her wound. Her skin was pale—too pale—and there was blood on her lower lip. He couldn't help remembering that sweet mouth on his body, and winced. "Deborah, sweetheart. It's me. Mike. Can you hear me?"

Deborah moaned.

Mike could see her eyelids fluttering and knew she was trying to come to.

"I'm here, baby. I'm here," he said.

She sighed, then relaxed.

"Can I come with you?" Mike asked.

"It's policy to take only the—"

"Please," he said. "She doesn't have anyone else."

"Yes, all right," one of them said.

"Dad!"

Mike turned. Evan walked into the kitchen with his son in his arms.

Mike ran to them, hugged them both, then whispered into Johnny's ear.

"Daddy Mike loves you, boy. I'm going to go with Deborah so she won't have to go in the chopper by herself, okay?"

"Puppy is dead," Johnny said.

"I'm so sorry," Mike said.

"Is Deborah going to die, too?"

"No," Mike said, but he could tell by the look on the little boy's face that he didn't believe him.

The EMTs were halfway to the chopper with Deborah when Mike came running. He caught up with them, then helped them carry her the rest of the way.

Within a few moments, they had her inside. Mike squeezed himself into a small space on the floor beside her, then reached out and took her hand as the chopper rose. While he watched her face for signs of distress, they took off across the sky like a dragonfly moving above the surface of a frozen pond.

Alphonso Riberra learned of Wilson's demise in the time-honored tradition of people everywhere: on the news.

In his business, trust was a rare commodity and one he shared with few. Darren Wilson had not been among that number. He was nothing but a little man with a big ego who owed Riberra money. People in his business knew Wilson owed him. Ordinarily, he would have had to get rid of Wilson himself when the man didn't pay or else lose the respect of his peers. But he'd lucked out.

Wilson was dead, and Riberra's hands were still clean. He was out the money, but it was only a drop in the bucket to what he made each week. As far as he was concerned, it was over.

Farris owed a phone call to Burl Tackett. Once they'd ID'd Wilson's body at the truck, he got out his cell phone.

Tackett was at home, watching his kids opening their presents, when his phone rang. He glanced at caller ID, then frowned and went into the hall to answer.

"This is Tackett."

"Agent Farris here."

Tackett leaned against the wall in the vestibule of his home.

"Did you catch him?"

"Mike O'Ryan caught him. He's dead."

"Good enough," Tackett said. "Thanks for calling."

"No problem," Farris said, then added, "Merry Christmas."

"Merry Christmas to you, too."

James was sitting in the living room with Johnny on his lap. When he heard his cell phone ring, he motioned for Evan to come get the boy. The last thing he wanted Johnny to hear about was more trouble.

"Mr. O'Ryan, this is Agent Tackett."

"Yeah...I can barely hear you," James said.

Tackett raised his voice. "I need to ask you a couple of questions."

"Yes?"

"Have you heard from your son, Mike?"

"Yes. We're all together and back up at the Sanborn house, although Mike is with Deborah on their way to the hospital," James said.

"Good enough," Burl Tackett said. "We'll all be in touch later for statements. Until then, have a merry Christmas."

"Thanks," James said. "You, too."

Deborah came to long enough to learn what was happening, but it was Mike's voice and seeing his face that calmed her fears.

"Mike?"

He leaned down until her lips were right against his ear so he was able to hear her over the noise of the rotors.

"I was afraid," she said.

Mike rose up and nodded, so that she would know he'd understood, then he put a finger across her lips to indicate no talking.

She shivered, then closed her eyes.

Mike cupped her cheek, then ran the tip of his forefinger across the surface of her lower lip. She frowned, as if it hurt.

He leaned over, then brushed her lips with the gentlest of kisses.

She reached for his hand, and when their fingers connected, they curled together. Mike sat beside her, counting the minutes until they would reach the hospital and praying she wouldn't die. As he watched, tears suddenly rolled out from under her eyelids and then down the sides of her face. The sight broke his heart.

He leaned down until his lips were right against her ear, then he spoke.

"Deborah…can you hear me?"

She opened her eyes.

He took it as a yes. "Don't leave me."

Her fingers tightened around his. He could see her lips moving but couldn't hear what she was saying over the noise. He leaned down again, then put his ear to her mouth.

He thought he heard the word "love," but he couldn't be sure. Maybe it was just what he wanted to hear.

Mike woke up around daylight. His first thought was of Deborah as he looked toward the hospital bed where she was sleeping. She'd come out of surgery with flying colors. Nothing permanently damaged, and once she'd been transfused with donor blood, her strength had begun to return.

For Mike, it had been a small source of pride that they shared the same blood type, and that his blood had been part of what saved her. It seemed only fitting, considering what she'd given to him and to the entire O'Ryan family. Because of her, they had survived tragedy several times over.

He glanced at the heart monitor, taking comfort from the continuous beeping, then got up from the chair and stretched. Morning was only a short time away as he moved to her bedside, watching her sleep.

As he stood there, another tear rolled down her

face. Knowing she was in pain cut him to the quick. Instinctively, he reached for her hand, taking care not to disturb the IV needle and wires to which she was connected.

Her skin was soft and blessedly warm.

"Merry Christmas, darling," he said softly. "This is a hell of a place to be on Christmas morning, but it doesn't matter where we are, as long as I'm with you."

Deborah flinched, then exhaled softly.

Mike waited, taking comfort from the steady beat of her heart.

Deborah had been hiding. At least that was what she imagined she'd been doing when she tried to open her eyes. She had vague memories of blood on the snow, of a sharp, burning pain, and then being carried somewhere warm.

She did remember Evan crying and Johnny hiding under her kitchen table, but she couldn't remember why. She thought she remembered being on a carnival ride with Mike, but that didn't make sense.

She did know there had been a bright light and a cold room, and someone telling her she was going to be all right. She thought someone had told her to count backward from one hundred, but remembered nothing after that.

Now she was coming out of hiding. Soon all would be revealed, including the reason for the antiseptic smell and the constant pain in her shoulder.

She took a slow breath, testing the motion, and

winced when it hurt. She exhaled even slower, and when she did, it came out as a moan. Within seconds, she felt a hand on her arm.

"Sweetheart, it's me. Mike."

Mike. It was Mike. She wanted to open her eyes in the most urgent way, but they didn't want to cooperate. He would tell her what was wrong. He would make the pain go away. She felt her mouth opening, heard herself speaking, and couldn't understand why it sounded like a scream.

Mike saw her nostrils flare; then the tip of her tongue came out from between her lips and slid from one corner of her mouth to the next.

Her mouth was dry. That had to be it. He grabbed the water glass next to her bed, took out the straw and let the moisture on the outside dribble along the length of her lips—enough to lubricate, but not enough for her to try to swallow, for fear she might choke.

She opened her mouth to the water like a baby bird opening its beak to be fed. He could tell she was trying to speak, but the only thing that came out was a sharp cry. He shoved the straw back in the glass and quickly took her hand.

"Deborah, you're safe. Don't be scared, baby. Don't be scared. I'm right here with you, and I'm not going anywhere."

He saw her shudder, then try to swallow. He rang for a nurse. Within a few moments, a voice came over the intercom.

"How can I help you?"

"I think Deborah is waking up and in pain."

"We'll be right there," the voice said, and less than a minute later, a no-nonsense woman he knew to be named Elinor came flying into the room.

"So she's waking up, is she?" Elinor said.

Deborah heard the voice and moaned. Why did everyone speak as if she wasn't in the room? She was lying right here. She could answer for herself.

"She hurts," Mike said. "Can't you give her something for the pain?"

"She's getting it through her IV," Elinor said. "Let me take her vitals and we'll see what's up."

Deborah felt the blood pressure cuff on her arm. While she was trying to make herself heard, she promptly faded back into that place where she'd been hiding. It wasn't until the pressure and the nurse were gone that she came out of hiding again.

Only this time she looked because she needed to see Mike O'Ryan's face.

"Hey…there's my pretty blue eyes," Mike said softly, as he watched Deborah's eyes slowly opening. "Merry Christmas, darling."

Deborah sighed. "Mike."

He could no more have stopped the grin on his face than he could have stopped breathing.

"Yeah, it's me." He leaned over and kissed the side of her cheek, then her forehead, before straightening up. "You gave us quite a scare, my love."

Deborah's heart stuttered.

Mike heard the little blip on the machine.

"Am I...?" she whispered.

"Are you what?" Mike asked.

Deborah licked her lips again, trying to lubricate them enough to form the words.

"Your love," she finally said.

Tears quickly blurred Mike's vision. "Yes, baby...very much my love."

Her eyelids fluttered, then shut, but there was a slight smile on her lips.

Mike patted her hand, then kissed her again.

"Sleep good, little soldier, and get yourself well," he said. "I can't wait to take you home."

There had been a lot to do once the chopper was gone. James and Thorn had taken it upon themselves to do cleanup so Evan could tend to his son. Before Evan knew it, they had all the blood mopped up from the floor and all the bloody towels in the washing machine.

Then they'd gone outside, recovered Puppy's body from the snow-covered yard and wrapped it in an old bedspread they'd found under a table on the back porch. At first they'd been uncertain as to whether they would be able to dig a grave deep enough to bury her, because the ground was frozen. But then Thorn had tested the ground inside a small three-sided lean-to and found that not only was it dry, but it was also loose enough to dig.

When Molly found out what was about to happen, it was she who argued Johnny's case.

"It will be better for him if he's there. It's part of the grieving process, and he won't get better if he isn't allowed to mourn. He's already seen the worst in man. And if that isn't enough, Deborah's dog dies right at his feet. When I brought him into the house, Puppy's blood was all over his pant legs, for God's sake. The least you owe him is the chance to say goodbye. He hasn't been able to do that for his grandparents. He wasn't part of the process then, and it's never going to seem real to him that they're gone. Please, Evan. Trust me on this. Take him to the grave. Let him help put Puppy in the ground. Let him help shovel the dirt. Let him put up a marker, or something pretty on the grave. It won't be easy for him, but it will be good for him. And let him cry. Lord knows he deserves it."

Evan had listened to Molly's fervor with the heart of a father. He'd wanted to spare Johnny any more pain, but he knew she was right. Johnny couldn't heal until he'd had a chance to grieve.

So he'd gone to his son and told him the dilemma. That they were going to bury Puppy but were unsure as to what Puppy loved most, so they didn't know what to put with her.

Johnny's lethargy had shifted instantly. Tears were still running down his face, but the tone of his voice was almost animated.

"I know, Daddy! I know! Puppy's chew toy is by the fireplace. She needs that."

"Good idea, son," Evan said, and mouthed a thank-you to Molly, who nodded in return.

Within minutes they all left the house, walking single file through the snow to the shed where Puppy's body was lying.

The background color of the old spread was ecru. The pattern consisted of all shapes and sizes of leaves, in different shades of blue.

"That's pretty, Daddy," Johnny commented when he saw the bedspread they'd wrapped around the dog's body.

The men looked at the old spread with new eyes. Molly remained silent as she stood with Johnny, letting him make all the first moves.

"You're right, Johnny boy. That is a pretty blanket," Thorn said.

"Yeah, and it will keep the dirt off her, right?" James added.

Johnny nodded as he studied the scene. The hole was about four feet deep. The pile of dirt beside the hole was dark, rich earth from countless years of cows in residence.

"So how do you think we should do this, son?" Evan asked. "Should we put Puppy in first and then her toy, or should the toy go first and then Puppy?"

"Oh, put Puppy in first," Johnny announced. "She wouldn't want to lie on her toy."

Evan looked away. He couldn't bear seeing his son's heartbreak. This was almost as difficult for him as the day he'd buried Johnny's mother. Then, Johnny had been too young to know what was going on. Now, in a symbolic way, Johnny was burying everyone he'd seen die, including his grandparents, Senator Patrick Finn and Deborah's dog. God bless Molly. She had been so right.

"Then Puppy it is," James said.

He and Thorn bent over, each taking a corner of the spread, and carefully laid Puppy's body down in the hole.

"Now Puppy's toy is next," Evan said.

Johnny handed it to Evan. "Here, Daddy. You give it to her. I can't reach."

Obviously the toy was not to be tossed in on top of the dog. So Evan got down on his knees and laid the toy on top of the spread.

Molly stepped forward.

"Usually at a funeral the preacher says some nice words about the person who's going to heaven, but there's not a preacher here today. So maybe we should each just say what we think about Puppy instead. Evan, you go first."

Evan bit the inside of his lip to keep from coming undone and couldn't bring himself to look at his son. In that moment he knew that this funeral was going to be as healing for him as it was for Johnny.

He'd left part of himself in a foreign land, and even though they'd shipped him home in more or less one piece, he'd still felt as if the man he'd been had died there. The man who'd come home had to become someone else. The only stable thing in his life was his son. Every step of this odd little service was, for him, like coming out of the dark. He looked at his grandfather and great-grandfather. They were watching his son's face, and he could do no less.

He walked to the pile of dirt, picked up a handful, then walked back to the edge of the grave.

"Puppy was a good and faithful dog. She considered it her job to protect. She died protecting Johnny because she loved him. I'm thankful for Puppy."

Molly stepped up next with her handful of dirt.

"Puppy was a very pretty dog. She had the warmest brown eyes and a lick ready for any friend. She kept us all company at her place by the fire."

She scattered her handful of dirt over the spread as devoutly as if it had been a person of great importance.

James and Thorn followed suit, talking about Puppy's great hunting abilities and thanking her for saving Johnny's life. Then finally it was Johnny's turn.

He had his handful of dirt. And he'd been standing silently at the edge of the grave for several minutes without talking. Evan was afraid that it had all become too much for him, but Molly's expression had urged him to wait. Finally, when Johnny spoke, Evan was glad he'd waited.

"Puppy, I didn't get to play with you for very long. But sometimes you can have a best friend for just a day. Ever since I came here, you were my best friend."

There wasn't a dry eye among them as they watched the little boy turn his hand upside down, then open his fingers. The tiny handful of dirt scattered as it fell.

Without speaking, James and Thorn picked up shovels and began shoveling dirt back into the hole, covering up the body as they went. No one moved, no one spoke, until the hole was filled and the dirt on top had been carefully mounded and smoothed.

"That's that," James said softly.

"Amen," Thorn echoed.

Johnny looked up at his father.

Evan picked him up, then gave him a hug as he buried his face in the curve of Johnny's neck.

"Don't cry, Daddy," Johnny said. "Puppy's gone to heaven now."

"You're right, son. And I'll bet she's chasing rabbits in the sunshine right about now, don't you?"

Johnny almost smiled as he nodded.

They walked back to the house, but with lighter hearts than when they'd walked to the shed. With each passing hour, Evan had come to realize how much he cared for Molly and how much he'd come to depend on her. Now that the trouble and turmoil were over, and passage between Deborah's home and Carlisle was finally possible again, he knew they would be leaving. Trouble was, he didn't want to leave Molly to go one way and them another. But he couldn't imagine a woman like her wanting to be saddled with a traumatized child and a man who'd come home in pieces.

Evan walked into the living room, and found Molly and Johnny sitting on the sofa near the fireplace. She had wrapped his son in an old patchwork quilt from off her bed and was holding him in her lap. At first he thought she was talking, then he realized she was singing to him.

Emotion welled up inside him so fast that it took him unaware. One moment he could see her, and the next he couldn't see anything at all for the tears. He could hear James and Thorn back in the kitchen, talking as they prepared a meal for everyone to eat.

Just for a moment, it felt like home.

He walked across the room and sat down beside them, only then realizing that Johnny was asleep.

Molly looked at him, then sighed. She'd known from the moment she'd seen his face that he would be a hard man to leave behind.

"I don't want to lose you," Evan said.

Molly smiled through tears of her own. "You don't have to," she said.

Evan's heartbeat accelerated.

"What do I have to do to keep you with me?"

She reached for his hand, curling her fingers through his and then giving them a slight squeeze.

"Just don't let me go."

Epilogue

For the media, Senator Darren Wilson's death on Christmas Eve and the news that he'd committed murder almost overshadowed the arrival of Santa. There wasn't one member of Patrick Finn's family who felt obligated to grieve, and the same was true for the O'Ryans.

Alphonso Riberra had lifted his wineglass to the friends with whom he was playing cards and made a small toast.

"Hey, guys…to the big spenders."

"Hear! Hear!" the men echoed, then downed their wine.

At which point Riberra laid down his cards amid a chorus of groans and raked in the pot.

Farley Comstock had been taking care of Deborah's chores while she was gone and was happy to get his old rifle back, but he'd been a bit bothered that a bad man had been using it. To remove what he considered "bad vibes" from the rifle, he'd taken it apart on his kitchen floor and set to cleaning it from one end to the other.

Once he was satisfied that all traces of Darren Wilson had been wiped from the gun, he called it his Christmas present to himself, and put it back over the kitchen door, where it had been hanging for years.

The new baby that Ruthie had given birth to was wailing as he went outside to bring in more wood. He just grinned at the sound. Another little Comstock was in the world and making herself heard.

A week after the shooting, Mike brought Deborah home. After the hustle and bustle of the hospital, and the number of people who'd been in the house with her before, it was too quiet and too empty. Puppy's absence was palpable. She couldn't get rid of the image of the old dog's shattered body bleeding out in the snow. If it hadn't been for Mike, she would have been so depressed, she wouldn't have known how to cope.

As it was, the holiday decorations that were still up looked tattered and sad, like someone who'd been too late for the party. The presents she and Johnny had chosen were still tucked under the tree, as was the one that Farley had finally brought over for her.

Even though she was a bit wobbly, she still insisted on walking through every room in her house. It was her odd way of homecoming, as if she felt obligated to explain and apologize for having been gone so long.

Mike could also feel her trying to distance herself from him. If he hadn't been so sure that she loved him, it would have made him nervous. He followed her into her bedroom, then sat down on the bed as she prowled through her closet. When she came out, she'd changed her clothes for a loose-fitting flannel nightgown.

"Honey, are you hungry? Would you like to take a nap? Just tell me what you want and it's yours."

Deborah looked at him as if seeing him for the first time. He was so absolutely gorgeous in her eyes, and he'd proved himself quite a warrior. She'd heard only bits and pieces of what had happened after she was shot, but when he'd held her later, she'd known the truth. Through his touch, she'd seen the chase, felt the fear and seen the end of Darren Wilson.

"You know what I really want? I want you," she said.

Mike arched an eyebrow. "I don't think you're up to—"

"But right now I'll settle for a hug," she said.

He grinned. "I can do that."

He held her close, afraid to squeeze for fear of hurting her healing shoulder.

Deborah laid her head against his chest and closed her eyes. The rock-steady rhythm of his heartbeat beneath her ear was as comforting as the flannel nightgown she was wearing.

"Where are we going with us?" she asked.

He took the ribbon out of her hair and let it fall, then nuzzled the side of her neck, scattering butterfly kisses along her chin, then centering on her mouth.

At that point he dug in his pocket and pulled out a small velvet box.

"I was going to wait to do this, but I don't know why. This seems as good a time as any."

Deborah saw the box, and her heart skipped a beat.

"Oh, Mike," she said, and then pressed her fingers against her lips to keep from crying.

He set her on the side of the bed, then got down on one knee.

"I could talk all day about why this seems right, but the bottom line is so simple. I love you, Deborah. More than I've ever loved a woman in my life. Will you marry me?"

"I never thought I would hear those words," she said.

"I'm still waiting for an answer," he reminded her.

"Yes, yes, a thousand times yes. I will marry you."

Mike slid the ring on her finger, got up from the floor, then scooted onto the bed beside her.

"Sealed with a kiss," he said softly, as he tasted the tears on her lips.

Deborah wrapped her good arm around his neck and kissed him back.

"So did I answer your question?" he asked as he smoothed the hair away from her forehead.

"Yes," Deborah said, then turned her mouth against the palm of his hand and traced his lifeline with the tip of her tongue.

Now it was Mike who was groaning.

She turned the ring toward the light and shivered with excitement. This was such a good day. Still, she eyed her bed longingly. Mike saw the look and understood. He turned around, pulled back the covers and pointed.

"Climb in, honey. I'll check out the kitchen and see what there is to eat."

"Mike. Wait," she said, as she crawled into the bed. He sat back down. "Yeah?"

"There's something we've never talked about."

Mike grinned. "I hope it doesn't have anything to do with having babies."

Deborah chuckled. "No. I'm fine with that omission."

"Thank God," Mike said. "I'd hate to have a child younger than my grandson."

This time Deborah laughed out loud. "Well, it's your own fault for being such a young father."

He shrugged. "It sort of runs in the family, although I wouldn't do it any different. Evan's the best thing that ever happened to me…until you."

"Thank you. However, I'm talking about Darren Wilson. You had to shoot him. Does it bother you?"

All expression disappeared from Mike's face. He started to argue, then remembered who he would be arguing with.

"I don't know how we'll ever have a fight if you always know what I'm thinking ahead of time. As for being bothered by killing a snake…no. Now, I'm going to check on the food situation. You rest, okay?"

"Okay."

He leaned down to give her a quick goodbye kiss, then was kissing the ring on her finger, when they heard someone knocking on the front door.

"Who in the world could that be?" Deborah said.

"Who even knows we're home?"

"Go see," Deborah said.

Mike grinned and winked as he hurried out of the room, but his smile widened even more when he saw who was at the door.

"Dad! Granddad! Where on earth did you guys come from?" Then he saw a second car pulling up in the yard, and he laughed. "All of you?"

"Is there any other way to celebrate Christmas?" James asked.

Mike clapped his hands together, then ran out onto the porch as the others got out of the car.

"Hey, Johnny boy. It's sure good to see you," he cried, and caught Johnny on the run as he jumped into Mike's arms.

"Hey, Daddy Mike, Molly is our girlfriend!" Johnny said.

Mike turned and grinned at Evan and Molly, who were coming up the steps carrying presents.

"Is that true?" he asked.

"Yep," Evan said.

Mike's smile widened. "Smartest thing you two men ever did."

"Thanks," Evan said. "We think so, too."

Mike leaned down and kissed Molly on the cheek. "Hello, girlfriend."

She grinned. "Thanks. As it happens, I'm pretty happy, too."

"Come on, everybody," Mike said. "Let's go see Deborah. She's going to be thrilled to see you."

They moved en masse down the hallway, laughing and talking as they went. Deborah had heard the commotion, and she came out of her room to meet them, smiling and waving as they swarmed her.

"You're here! You're here! You're all here!" she cried.

"Merry Christmas, Deborah," James said. "And this is the only O'Ryan you have yet to meet. Dad…this is Deborah. Deborah, my dad, Thornton."

"Call me Thorn," he said, and kissed Deborah lightly on the cheek.

"Thank you," she said.

"Yeah, and check out her ring. You'll be calling her 'daughter' pretty soon," Mike said.

The announcement brought another round of excited comments from everyone, including Johnny.

"Does that mean you'll be my Grammy?" Johnny asked.

Deborah laughed and ruffled the top of his head. "Yes, it does."

"Cool," he said, then tugged on Evan's coat. "Now, Dad? Can we give it to her now?"

"Let's all go sit down first," Evan said.

"You up for all this, honey?" Mike asked.

"I wouldn't miss it for the world," Deborah said as she followed the group into the living room.

When she saw the presents, she grinned.

She watched as Evan exclaimed over the hunting knife Johnny had picked out for him, and then smiled as Molly was immediately entranced by her music box carousel. Then she saw Johnny drag the long, oddly wrapped present out from behind the tree and give it to Mike.

Mike arched an eyebrow, then looked at her.

She just smiled back.

When he saw the saber, he was beside himself with excitement. He thanked Johnny over and over, but he knew it was Deborah he really had to thank.

"Is this for real?" he asked.

"Just like me," she said, and laughed.

"Good Lord. It's Civil War, isn't it?"

"Yes. About four greats' worth of a grandaddy put it in the rafters of this house when he came home from the war, and it's been up there ever since. Johnny thought you might like it."

"But wouldn't someone in your family—"

"I don't have any family, remember?"

"Not true," Mike said softly. "You have us now, remember?"

Deborah smiled through tears. "How could I forget?"

"Now it's your turn!" Johnny cried, and began handing her presents right and left.

She opened them all, exclaiming happily in all the right places, but it wasn't until Evan and Johnny went out and then came back inside with her special gift that she found herself speechless.

"Oh," she said, and then put her fingers to her lips to keep from crying. "Oh, my. Oh, Mike."

"Don't look at me," Mike said. "I didn't have anything to do with this."

"I hope this is okay," Evan said. "It was Johnny's idea. We didn't have the heart to tell him no."

"It's the best gift ever," Deborah said, and held out her arms as Johnny set a black Labrador puppy in her lap.

The puppy took one look at Deborah and licked her cheek. Everyone laughed as Deborah hugged the puppy to her chest and kissed her back.

Johnny was beaming as he tickled the puppy under her chin. The little pup reciprocated by licking Johnny's face, too.

"Does she have a name?" Deborah asked, as Johnny scooted onto the seat beside her.

"I named her Candy, 'cause she ate the candy canes off our Christmas tree."

Deborah nodded, then picked up the puppy and held her so they were eye to eye.

"Hello, Candy. I'm Deborah. Welcome home."

New York Times
bestselling author

HEATHER GRAHAM

On a weekend vacation, Beth Anderson is unnerved when a stroll on the beach reveals what appears to be a human skull. As a stranger approaches, Beth panics and covers the evidence. But when she later returns to the beach, the skull is gone.

Determined to find solid evidence to bring to the police, Beth digs deeper into the mystery—and everywhere she goes, Keith Henson, the stranger from the beach, seems to appear. Then a body washes ashore, and Beth begins to think she needs more help than she bargained for....

THE ISLAND

MIRA®

New York Times bestselling author

CARLA NEGGERS

The largest uncut diamond in the world, the Minstrel's Rough is little more than legend. Brought into the Pepperkamp Family in 1548, it has been handed down to one keeper in each generation. Juliana Fall has inherited its splendor from her uncle—and, unwittingly, its legacy of danger.

There are others who seek the Minstrel's Rough: a U.S. senator, a Nazi collaborator and a Vietnam war-hero-turned-journalist, among them. Now Juliana has only two choices: uncover the past before they do...or cut and run.

"No one does romantic suspense better!"
—*New York Times* bestselling author
Janet Evanovich

*Available the first week of March 2007,
wherever paperbacks are sold!*

REQUEST YOUR FREE BOOKS!

2 FREE NOVELS
FROM THE ROMANCE/SUSPENSE
COLLECTION PLUS 2 FREE GIFTS!

BOB07

DINAH MCCALL

32161 BLOODLINES	___ $7.50 U.S.	___ $8.99 CAN.
66808 STORM WARNING	___ $6.50 U.S.	___ $7.99 CAN.
66675 THE PERFECT LIE	___ $6.99 U.S.	___ $8.50 CAN.
66584 THE RETURN	___ $6.50 U.S.	___ $7.99 CAN.
66894 WHITE MOUNTAIN	___ $6.50 U.S.	___ $7.99 CAN.

(limited quantities available)

TOTAL AMOUNT	$ _____
POSTAGE & HANDLING	$ _____
($1.00 FOR 1 BOOK, 50¢ for each additional)	
APPLICABLE TAXES*	$ _____
TOTAL PAYABLE	$ _____

(check or money order—please do not send cash)

To order, complete this form and send it, along with a check or money order for the total above, payable to MIRA Books, to: **In the U.S.:** 3010 Walden Avenue, P.O. Box 9077, Buffalo, NY 14269-9077; **In Canada:** P.O. Box 636, Fort Erie, Ontario, L2A 5X3.

Name: _____
Address: _____ City: _____
State/Prov.: _____ Zip/Postal Code: _____
Account Number (if applicable): _____

075 CSAS

*New York residents remit applicable sales taxes.
*Canadian residents remit applicable GST and provincial taxes.

MIRA®

www.MIRABooks.com

MDM0307BL